WIDE
RIVER
WIDE
LAND

WIDE RIVER WIDE LAND

William Barnaby Faherty

Piraeus Publishers

To My Mother and Father

Published simultaneously in Canada
Printed in the United States of America
Library of Congress Catalog Card Number: 75-37091
ISBN: 0-913656-15-1

Contents

Historical Setting

All the historical events in this book are factual, among them the founding of Saint Louis, the events of the Revolutionary War in the West, Pierre Vial's journey from Santa Fe to Saint Louis and back, the Louisiana Purchase, the expedition of Pike to the headwaters of the Mississippi, and the battle of New Orleans. Among the historical characters are Pierre Laclede, Chief Pontiac, George Rogers Clark, and Zebulon Pike. The author presents the events and individuals as contemporary records reveal them. Only in the cases of Father Sebastian Meurin, Commandant Noyen de Villiers, and Senator Eligius Fromentin did he go beyond historical data in supplying physical and psychological charateristics. Father Pierre Gibault is portrayed as historical documents show him except for some conjectures about his views on certain political issues apart from the American occupation of Illinois.

The fictitious characters are: all the O'Romes, the Thomures, the Laurents, the Brunets and their relatives by blood or marriage (except James MacKay, who actually existed); the Missouri Indians named in the book; and three other individuals, Amnon, Camille, and Jeremy.

I

Laclede Plans a City

I can't remember when I first came to love the Mississippi that flowed free down the middle of the rich land. That feeling was always there. It began at full force, like a spring surging out of the rocky Ozarks. Later, I simply became more deeply conscious of an ever-present belief.

On one memorable day, while I stood on a bluff one mile below the village of Ste. Genevieve looking out over the vast circling expanse of the wilderness, my heart filled with awe at its wonder. As far as my eyes could see, unbroken forests stretched on both sides of the river, their late fall leaves a combination of reds, golds, and faded greens. Down the middle rolled the mighty river, a half-a-mile in width. I felt the call of its beauty and power that has never left me. I was fourteen years old at the time. The day was November 3, 1763.

My uncle Nick Soumande, mother's younger brother, and I, Hugh Roe O'Rome, had climbed this height for its spectacular view down-river. We were anxious to see the fur traders coming upstream from New Orleans, under the command of a Frenchman named Pierre Laclede. With a commission from the King, he was going to set up a fur trading post on the Mississippi, near the mouth of the Missouri, fifty miles above Ste. Genevieve.

Rumor had it that Laclede would also bring astounding news. King Louis XV had signed a treaty giving the east bank of the river to the English. I could not understand this at all. We lived near Fort Chartres on the east bank, a strong citadel no English army had ever approached and could not have taken had they done so. How could men thousands of miles away split our country when the wide river united it? I could not believe the rumor to be true.

Uncle Nick first spotted the low-built *batteau*, moving along the east bank. A stout mast stood in the center of the vessel, with one man guiding it. Twenty *voyageurs* walked along the bank pulling the barge with a long rope. As the muddy green waters slipped past the barge, the taut rope and the straining arms of the bent figures showed the deceptive power of the current.

"There they are!" Uncle Nick said, and scrambled to the top of the rocky ledge for a better view. I followed him to the higher point.

The boatmen on the east bank stopped. They tied the barge to a cottonwood, put the *cordelle* — the long rope — on small *pirogues* lowered from the barge, and started across. When they reached the west bank, the *cordellers* pulled the *batteau* across the current, while several men with axes moved ahead cutting a path. Then the boatmen struggled upstream and began to chant a river song. Nick and I climbed down the bluff.

One of the men shouted a greeting. "*Ai! Mon Ami!* How far Ste. Genevieve is?"

"You're almost there," Nick responded. "Two miles more."

The men shouted gleefully.

"*Sacre bleu*, she is tough work," one boatman said as they all took a short rest. He mopped his brow with the edge of his elkskin sleeve.

No matter what their ages might be, the unshaven, perspiring *cordellers* carried the ravages of a hard life on their faces. Some had slung their wide leather belts across their shoulders to prevent the ropes from cutting into their skin. They wore gloves of muskrat skin, with the fur on the inside.

"King Louis, did he really give the east bank to the English?" I shouted.

"Yes, he did," one of the *cordellers* answered. "*Stupide*. On the west side we'll have to build Laclede's post."

I had known in my heart that the man in Ste. Genevieve spoke the truth that morning when he said that British territory would extend from the Atlantic to the Mississippi. Somehow or other news seemed to come up the river faster than the men who presumably brought it. Yet, I had hoped that on this one occasion the story might be wrong.

Gray clouds swept in from the northwest. As the wind blew colder, I pulled the hood of my woolen *capote* over my head. The fringes of my buckskin leggings flapped against my legs. It was time to move on ahead of the *batteau*.

"We'll tell Ste. Genevieve you're coming," Nick said.

We shoved our canoe into the swift waters and moved up the west bank. The *cordellers* were soon far behind.

When we brought news of Laclede's approach, excitement swept the village. Along with most of the several hundred townsfolk, we waited at the riverbank in anticipation of the arrival.

As the *batteau* moved toward the town, I noticed Laclede, the leader of the expedition. He moved with an air of command. Surrounded by his disheveled, grim-faced *engages*, or hired hands, and the thickset *habitants*, or farmers of the village, he presented a remarkable contrast. His frame was lithe and wiry. His face was thin, his complexion clear, his features like cut stone. The frontier depended upon raw strength and endurance. Yet it met its match in this moderately built man with the look of a falcon in his eye.

Even his clothes set him apart from the buckskin-clad voyageurs who pressed around him. A coat of dark brown wool sloped away to the back in two narrow coattails. He carried a silver-handled pistol at his belt. Only his black boots, soiled from the long journey, suggested that he had been on the river since August.

"Tomorrow," Laclede shouted with an edge of steel in his voice, "we move on up the river to Fort Chartres."

I expected some complaint from the *cordellers;* but Laclede's men shrugged their shoulders, one or two in disgust, the rest in seeming unconcern.

"Let's go," Nick jabbed an elbow into my arm. "The Commandant at the Fort will want to hear the news of Laclede's coming."

I followed my uncle. At the edge of the river, Nick stepped into the canoe. I pushed the craft away from the bank and took my place in the bow. We rowed faster in the swift water. Off in the gray distance loomed the stone wall of Fort Chartres, the unchallenged center of a mighty empire that was falling without a fight. The fort was like a city in itself, one hundred yards square, with walls twenty feet high, and protruding bastions at each corner to fend off attackers trying to scale the sides. The soldiers said they had ample supplies of powder, and lead from the mines fifty miles west was always plentiful. I myself had seen the cannon. Our farms were rich with grain. So I believed the soldiers when they said that all the habitants of the region could come into the fort for protection, and it could hold out against any force sent against it. I had worried only when I heard the soldiers say: "No heart, the Commandant." We paddled silently, angling across the current.

Nick broke the stillness of the journey: "Laclede begins a new world. Commandant De Villiers buries an old one. He has already called in the garrisons from the outlying posts to Fort Chartres. Rumors say he will depart for New Orleans."

For the first time in my life, I realized in a pointed way what I had felt so often. Life was not complicated for Uncle Nick. He knew what I had to learn — that life meant a succession of changes. I spent too much time thinking how easily it might have been different — had the King been more interested in the Illinois Country, or had the English not beaten our troops under General Montcalm at Quebec, or had mother and two of my sisters not died during a terrible winter three years before. Since that time my father had been up north, fighting alongside Chief Pontiac and the numerous tribes he had united to fight the British. They had been besieging the fort at Detroit since early May, according to rumors.

My two younger sisters and I lived with our grandparents on their farm in Prairie du Rocher, not far from Fort Chartres. I spent most of my time with my uncle who took his position as *parrain*, or godfather, extra seriously since my father had gone off to battle. Even though he was twelve years older than I, Uncle Nick, short of stature like *Grandpere* Soumande, hardly reached my shoulders. But he had a deep chest, arms like oak, and short thick legs. No matter how he traveled — by foot, on horseback, or in a canoe — he always drove straight ahead with determination. He made up his mind, not precipitantly like my father, or hesitantly like me, but calmly and unchangingly. He stood as sure as a black walnut tree in a windstorm.

Nick had taught me to hunt, to work in the fields, to swim in the river, to find blackberries, to trap muskrat, to know when the sumacs would turn, to judge if the waters would flood the bottomlands, to tell an ash from a butternut even after the leaves had fallen. In fact, Nick had taught me everything I knew except to read and write.

The old missionary in our village, the Jesuit *Pere* Meurin, had done that. He had taught me much French history too. I had shared the old priest's hopes for France in America. I had always believed that *le bon Dieu* intended the wide river to hold together a peaceful land. Now that the British would control the east bank, where we had our home, I thought the end of the world would come.

Not Uncle Nick, however! Politics and empires simply did not enter his mind. He and my Irish-born father had fought bravely in the battle on the Monongahela, when the French and Indians of the Northwest under Charles Langlade of Green Bay, the son of a French *seigneur* and the daughter of an Ottawa chief, had almost wiped out Braddock's command. Nick could, however, accept the coming of the British without comment.

Not so my father! He looked at things simply, too, but in an entirely different way; all in reds and whites: red and bloody and bad, like the British uniforms and the *croix batarde*, as he called the British flag; or white and lovely and good, like the flag of France with its golden lilies.

Nick accepted facts. He bounced back to see the advantages in any changed situation. He saw his goal but could take various paths to meet it. He never looked back with regrets or "if onlys." "Latch on to the future, *mon filleul*," he would say, "with hope in your heart."

I liked the way he now addressed me as his godson. Before it had simply been: "My nephew." But what he advised was not easy to do. Just as the box elder clung to the bank even though the river had cut away much of the ground beneath it, so in my heart I longed for the clustered villages of Ste. Anne and St. Phillippe near Fort Chartres, and my own Prairie du Rocher under the shadow of the limestone bluff three miles away; and for the Soumandes, the Thomures, the Laurents, quiet people for the most part, who just wanted to be left alone. My roots were as deep as those of the shagbark hickory in the dark loam of the prairie. I knew the people. I loved them. In a way I was more like them than Uncle Nick who was entirely French himself.

But then the words of my father, Brendan O'Rome, stirred my memory: "The British — Cromwell — destruction — hunger — death." Not only the words of my father but the look on his face when he spoke of those events had imprinted on my mind a horror for the British.

Nick guided the canoe into the bank with energetic strokes, rousing me from my day-dreaming. I jumped out, and we heaved the canoe up the embankment.

"The Mississippi Valley above the Ohio is a huge funnel," Pierre Laclede began one morning several weeks later. He spread a crinkly map on the table in the Council Room at Fort Chartres. Several of his voyageurs and a dozen young men of the region, including Nick and myself, gathered around. Several older habitants of the Illinois prairie smoked their pipes. But the aroma of tobacco could not blot out the heavy odor of men who had been four months on the river.

"The Missouri comes in from the northwest," Laclede said. "Above it from the left smaller streams like the Des Moines and the Cedar. From the right, the Illinois, the Rock, then the Wisconsin." He placed his right forefinger just below the mouth of the Missouri. "Somewhere in this vicinity — our post. Where the funnel narrows. We can ship our furs down the channel to the gulf."

His voice was high-pitched. His gestures were as staccato as his sentences. He wore different clothes than he had worn upon his arrival, but he had the same trim look. "On the west bank, so we are on French territory. Near the mouth of the Missouri, but below it. Not on a bluff. Not on the bottomland either. With easy access to the river, but safe from floods. Not just a little narrow creek valley, some tributary that might overflow its banks and flood us out in time of high water. A place where the land rises gradually in terraces. Not too far from the river, but still high and dry when the Mississippi is at flood tide."

"*Bon! Bon! Bon!*" said Artime Thomure, a robust cousin on my mother's side. He had already signed up with Laclede. Uncle Nick would work part-time for the first year.

"Some of you men know this up-river country better than I do," Laclede went on. "I want you to come along on our scouting trip — to size up every spot. We'll look them over carefully. Maybe you will have a suggestion. Maybe I. We'll find the place we want." He paused a moment and then asked: "Any questions?"

"When do we get going?" Nick said.

Laclede looked at the square-built, hawk-nosed Nick. With a smile, he put out his hand. "You're my type of man. We leave tomorrow." He looked at me. "How old are you, *garcon*?"

"Fourteen," I said.

He shrugged. "If thirteen-year-old Auguste Chouteau can go with us, I suppose you can too."

"Thank you, monsieur," I said, and was grateful that Auguste was along. I had seen the boy on the barge when Laclede came up the river and had spoken to him on several occasions.

We traveled in six *pirogues*. Even though it was early December, the weather was good in that year 1763. We paddled up the west side of the Mississippi, checking the land. High bluffs lined the bank.

Laclede halted eighteen miles above Fort Chartres at a lead mining camp called Herculaneum. "This place has some advantages," Laclede said.

"Do you think it's near enough to the mouth of the Missouri?" Nick questioned.

"No!" Laclede shot back. "We must get closer." His voice was grim. "But we must check every possibility."

When we returned to our canoe, Nick said, "We'll stop when we get to the mouth of the Meramec. But he won't find what he wants there either. I know where he'll find the spot."

"Directly across from Cahokia?" I asked.

"Yes, on the terraces," Nick answered. And then in another vein, he went on, "The problem in dealing with a *patron* is not to get him to see what is best. The whole thing is getting him to think that *he* found it. We won't tell Laclede where the place is. We'll let him find it himself."

As Nick had predicted, we stopped at the mouth of the Meramec. The land proved too low, the adjoining bluffs too high. We pushed on. Laclede had a trained eye. He would recognize the right place immediately.

We passed the mouth of the *Riviére des Péres*, the River of the Fathers. I recalled hearing that the first Jesuit mission had been set up there around the time of *Grandpere* Soumande's birth in Canada.

Just above this stream the bluff rose high again. Then it leveled off. The river arched eastward. Back from this arc, terraces rose gradually. Nick winked at me. "This will be the place," he said. "Nothing above or below equals it."

Laclede stepped out of his *pirogue*. He hurried up the bank. The rest of us followed. Laclede smiled in satisfaction. The December afternoon seemed as bright as the first day of spring. Nothing would change his mind now.

"What do you think of it, men?" Laclede said. But there was no question in his voice.

"Good! Good! Good!" shouted Artime. "It's as pretty as a picture of the Channel from the French coast."

"So?" Laclede said with a smirk. "I've never seen the Channel from either coast."

"Neither has Artime," Nick broke in. "But when he was a boy, his parents had such a picture on the wall of their home in Canada. It was too cumbersome to bring down by canoe. It's the memory of all things that are 'good! good! good!' to Artime."

"That is right," Artime answered.

"We agree then," Laclede said, "that this is as pretty as a picture of the Channel from the French coast. But we'll travel on up to the mouth of the Missouri just to make sure."

"That's a wise suggestion," Nick said to Laclede. Then he whispered to me with a chuckle, "I can tell by the look in his eye that this is the spot."

"I think you're right," I grinned.

We returned to our canoes and pushed up the river the last few miles to the great confluence. The hills dropped back to the west. The bottomland at the junction of the rivers was broad on both sides of the Mississippi. I took my first long look at the muddy Missouri. I did not like it as well as I did our own Mississippi.

Then we floated back down to the spot we had chosen. Laclede notched a few trees, then sped downstream to Fort Chartres. When we landed, Laclede walked up to Commandant Noyen de Villiers. No one could forget the look in his eyes as he said: "I have found the place. Someday it will be one of the finest cities on the whole continent. . . ."

"Will Daddy be home for Christmas?" the older of my two little sisters asked early in December when I returned home.

"I hope so, Eileen," I responded.

"Where *is* Daddy?" Bernadette, the ten-year-old, asked.

"He's up near Detroit," I said, "fighting the British." I realized how hopeless it would be to try to explain to Bernadette what Pontiac's War was all about, or why our father should be in the battles. "You pray that he gets home." I wondered if he were alive. We had heard nothing from him and little about him since he went north to fight two years before — after the terrible winter when my mother and two other sisters had died, Dorothy older than I, and the baby who had just arrived.

We had heard rumors of victory after victory for Pontiac in the first year of the war, that the Indians continued against the British after the French gave up. Uncle Nick had talked to voyaguers who were in Pontiac's villages that fall. One of them had spoken to my father. According to the few rumors, the second summer had not gone so well. Travelers from the north grew less as the months went on. We could only wait and pray.

After the little girls had gone to sleep at night, *Grandmere* Soumande sewed new dresses for their Christmas. Uncle Nick and I talked with *Grandpere*. He seemed certain that my father would return that winter. I hoped so. As the day got closer and the winds grew colder, however, I began to lose hope.

Christmas Eve was soon upon us. We spent the afternoon decorating the house. Eileen and Bernadette helped *Grandmere* with the cooking. At least, she let them believe they were helping. The adults ate only a slight evening meal, both to keep the fast and to be ready for the big feast to come. It would be an empty Christmas for me without my father and midnight Mass.

After the meal, Uncle Nick walked out on the front porch. Suddenly, he shouted: "Brendan."

"Papa is home!" I yelled, and ran to the porch. My father gave Uncle Nick a hug that might have strangled a less strong man.

I threw my arms around him. "It's so good to see you, Papa."

"It's good to be home, my son."

The little girls ran to his arms. Tears filled his eyes. "All of you have been growing up so fast. *Grandpere, Grandmere*, and Uncle Nick have taken good care of you."

"How did things go with you, Brendan?" Uncle Nick asked.

"The war did not go as well as last year. Someone betrayed Pontiac and warned the defenders of Detroit. Had we taken that village, we would have driven the British back to Canada. Oh! I have so many stories to tell, and I want to hear all about each of you. But maybe I had better get ready for midnight Mass.

"There will be no midnight Mass, Brendan, only prayers," *Grandpere* said. "The King recalled the Jesuit missionaries. Father Meurin went down to New Orleans. He said he would be back. We hope so."

My father had to shave and bathe for church; stories had to wait. Eileen got his village clothes out of the cedar-lined chest. At about a quarter to twelve, we walked down to the village street toward the little church. The sky was clear. The air was not too cold. Above us the stars glimmered in an ebony sky as they had stood over Bethlehem seventeen hundred years before. We passed house after house under the protection of oaks, pecans, and hickories and the limestone bluffs behind them. Each house was a compact, one-story dwelling, just like the next. The two-pitched roofs extended at the same slope over wide verandas. Families came out and greeted us.

The men gathered around my father shaking his hand, welcoming him back, asking about Pontiac and the progress of the war. I realized even more strongly their awe of his spirit. They were farmers; he was a warrior. Only he and Nick of all of them had fought on the Monongahela. He alone had joined Pontiac. If France would regain its empire, it would be men like my father who would win it back.

Someone began the *Chansons de Noel*, and we resumed our pace toward the old log church. When we entered, the trained voices of the choir took up the beautiful melodies as if their voices filled the Cathedral of Notre Dame in Paris instead of the log *eglise de St. Joseph* at Prairie du Rocher in the Illinois county. An altar boy rang the midnight bell. Christmas had come again.

The *sacristain* of the church took the pulpit and read the story of *le premier Noel* as Saint Luke had told it. The choir sang several more hymns. The *sacristain* led the congregation in prayer.

After services, we did not long delay outside the church as on ordinary holy days. Instead, all the relatives — the O'Romes, the Laurents, the Thomures — hurried to the home of *Grandpere* Soumande to take part in the *reveillon*, the Christmas breakfast. *Grandmere* Soumande and the two girls had spent so much time preparing it. It was a family reunion — a special one for the O'Romes with our father home — a thanksgiving feast, and a time, too, for the exchange of gifts.

After all had eaten, Grandma gave the new dresses to Eileen and Bernadette.

Then Uncle Nick brought a musket into the room, its metal polished, its wooden stock shining. He turned to my father. "Remember your British friend on the Monongahela? I brought his musket and saddle bag along as souvenirs."

"I remember him well," my father said. "Surly fellow."

I recalled how often my father had spoken of the arrogant leader of Braddock's troops who had led his men into the ambush.

"Do you think Hugh Roe is old enough to have it, Brendan?"

My father looked at me, with a quizzical look on his face. Would he say yes — or no? I wondered.

He broke into a smile. "I guess you've made a man out of him, Nick," he said. "Yes, I guess you have."

I wanted to hug them both and the gun, too. But I settled on the gun. I turned it in my hand. I aimed it at the ceiling. I beamed: "It's grand! Thank you, my father. Thank you, Uncle Nick."

"Now one more gift — and this is a working gift for the young man." Nick said this to the entire assemblage. Then turning directly to my father, he went on:

"Father Meurin used to tell Hugh Roe that he should continue his English even when you're away, Brendan, but when you're away he has no one who talks English. There is only one book in English that I know of in the whole Illinois country."

"I've never seen one," my father said.

Turning to me, Nick said, "Here it is. Your Christmas present."

I put my musket in the corner, unbuckled the saddle bag and pulled out a large book. It had a leather cover. I opened it. The name "William Shakespeare" and the words "Complete Works" were on the first page.

I looked at Nick, then at my father. "Thank your uncle for that gift, too." my father said.

"O yes!" I said, deeply embarrassed. "Thank you, Uncle Nick."

"Read a bit of it for your father," Nick said. "And show him you still know the language."

I opened the book. The front page bore the title *The First Part of King Henry VI.* I read it hesitatingly: "Hung be the heavens with black, yield day to night! Comets importing change of times and states, brandish your crystal tresses in the sky, and with them scourge the bad revolting stars that have consented unto Henry's death." I paused and looked up.

"Good! Good! Good!" said Artime Thomure. "I don't know what it means. But it sounds like a nice language. The British must be fine people. Now that we are going to be neighbors, I'll bet we'll get along well."

I knew how the habitants enjoyed baiting my father, but I wondered if Artime had gone too far that time.

"They're going to be our neighbors?" my father asked, leaning forward in his chair.

"Yes, Brendan, hadn't you heard?" Uncle Remy Laurent, the husband of my mother's oldest sister, said with studied calm.

My father bristled. His expression grew as formidable as the limestone bluffs above the river. His frame menaced the entire group. "I have been telling you for ten years that the British would come. Soon they'll be here, burning our homes, detroying our fields, killing our stock."

"But Brendan," Uncle Remy said, "the British have not mistreated our brothers in Canada."

"That's right, Remy. For the moment, they need the *Canadiens.* When they no longer need them, it's the end. I know England, Remy, as none of you know her. My father knew her. My grandfather knew her. Above all, my great-grandfather knew her."

The peaceful men of the prairie had heard the anger of my father before. Now, coming like the Mississippi at floodtide, his words freed the pent-up wrath of a long summer of defeat.

"Those grim-faced men came from England, riding black horses. They marched up to Drogheda near my grandfather's home, arrogant, unstoppable, because they so completely outnumbered the defenders. To avoid useless bloodshed, the commander of the garrison asked Cromwell for honorable terms. Instead, the English smashed his skull, streamed through the city with pike and firebrand, and killed every man, woman, and child in an orgy of blood-lust rarely seen since the sweet Christ lived on earth."

A shiver passed through the listeners. *Grandmere* Soumande and the ladies in the kitchen stopped their work. My father's normally soft baritone was strident now.

"The few men who escaped lived in frightful memory of that

night of nights. Oliver Cromwell turned our green land into a black desert. He leveled our homes. He wasted our fields. He burned and slew and crushed. Then he took ten thousand children away from their parents, from their homes, from their country. He put them on boats and sent them down to the islands in the Caribbean — such a crime would have made another nation go down in everlasting infamy! Finally, he decreed that we change our names. He had us take the names of English cities or foreign countries. My great-grandfather survived to take the name of a city. Not a fog-filled English city. A city he loved, one where our hearts would always be pointed. He took the name of Rome."

My father clenched his fists. "We stand as a sign of contradiction for England. We should all have died. We should have gone down as the people of Drogheda went down. But we lived! And as long as we live, we are on England's conscience." My father's voice was almost a shout. Little Bernadette cuddled up to me, quivering.

"Someday, after Britain has won the world and then finally lost it," my father went on, "she will have nothing to preoccupy her. Then she will face herself. She will have to get down on her knees and say she is sorry. She will have to admit that we, the people she despised, kept our faith, the one thing necessary." He ended abruptly, his fury spent.

The men sat in silence and conspicuously puffed their pipes. The women in the kitchen gradually began to resume their work. Little Bernadette walked over to our father who was now sitting quietly. He reached down and lifted her high over his head, as easily as a child would lift a baby swallow back into its nest. A smile melted his craggy brows. Suddenly the tension was gone.

"With a few more nice weeks like this," someone in the rear ventured, "we'll be through winter easily."

"With the excellent moisture we've had recently," Remy Laurent said, "we should have good crops next year."

"Laclede will begin his post sooner than we expected," Nick whispered to me.

It was up to *Grandpere* Soumande to say the last word. "Life will change for us, my sons, in one way or another. Being under the king of a different country is not a happy thought for Christmas. But each of us must think what is best to do. May *le bon Dieu* bless us always."

The relatives said goodnight and went to their homes.

I lay awake a long time, thinking of what my father had said. Even though I had never met an Englishman, I felt a strong dislike for the British. After all, one might expect that of an O'Rome. And my French relatives had fought England for three generations. What right did the English have to the Illinois country? It was our home. Why should they take it and divide the wide land along the wide river?

Gray wool clouds moved across the January sky from the northwest, with intermittent patches of blue between them. The whole day had a strange uncertainty, neither promising fair weather nor foreboding ill. Commandant de Villiers had called a council of officers, village leaders, and Laclede's fur traders to discuss their future plans. My father had determined to attend as soon as he heard the Commandant's proclamation. Nick said nothing until the morning of the meeting.

"Let's go out to the Fort for the council," Nick said. "If we walk, I can find out if you still know your trees."

"Fine," I said. "We'll walk. If we start now, we'll be there in plenty of time."

I put on my heavy moccasins and threw my *capote* over my shoulders.

"Let's take the easy trees first. What's that one?" Nick asked. He pointed to a thin tree whose bark seemed to be peeling off like shingles.

"Shagbark hickory," I said. Pointing to the hillside, "The one with the light brown bark that peels off as it gets higher is the sycamore." We walked toward the edge of town.

"The tree in front of Laurents' house?" Nick asked.

"The easiest of all," I answered. "The only tree that has no trunk higher than twelve feet. It spreads its branches wide like a fountain — the elm."

Even on a day when men discussed the future of an empire, Uncle Nick still talked of trees. Maybe he was right when he said that the hackberry would be standing long after Fort Chartres dropped into the Mississippi. Maybe planting a tree was more important than building a fort. Maybe if a man had his tap roots as deep as a hickory in the black loam of the bottomland, *croix batardes* and Bourbon Lilies could not disturb him.

By this time, I could see men from all over the middle valley converging on the fort. My father and the others from Prairie du Rocher rode up behind us. The Ste. Anne villagers already had entered the magnificent main gate. Joseph Labusciere led the men from St. Philippe as they rode two abreast. Jeremy Maligne, the miller of St. Philippe, rode alone a few yards behind. All but Jeremy planned to leave St. Philippe for Laclede's new post. As we approached the gate, I could feel the growing excitment. We rode by the officers' quarters and the soldiers' barracks on our left. Cannon bristled from the walls.

The chief men gathered around the split-oak table in the *grand salle* of Fort Chartres. The room was a bit damp in the January thaw but not quite cold enough for burning logs in the fireplace. The lanterns, too, were unlit since the windows allowed in some light.

At the head of the table stood an empty chair, waiting for the Commandant. An officer sat on each side. Laclede and several of his men sat on the right side of the table away from the door; on the near side sat my father, along with Remy Laurent, Joseph Labusciere, who had served as notary for successive commandants, and other village elders. Nick and I joined the crowd lining the walls.

The Commandant strode into the assembly, a tall impressive man. His black curly hair grew in over-abundance. His nose, narrow at the top, widened as it went down his face, so that it almost stretched half-way across his cheeks. His beard pointed outward. In profile, his head looked like the map of Ireland, according to my father. Father Meurin had insisted that it was a head out of the fifteenth century. It looked exactly like the picture in his history book of an Italian count of that century.

The men stood until the Commandant took his place. De Villiers motioned them to be seated. He asked Labusciere to keep a record of the meeting and began with exaggerated formality: "Men of France. Forced by circumstances beyond his control, our beloved King has given up the east bank of the Mississippi. All of us know that it will be some time yet before England will be able to send troops here. I know that you do not wish to live under the flag of the enemy of our country. I have called in the garrisons from the smaller stockades. Captain Louis Saint Ange de Bellerive will come from Vincennes to take charge of Fort Chartres until the British arrive. My plan is to leave the area and go to Louisiana. We will find new homes there and live in peace. The British will not chase us from our homes, separate families, and scatter us all over the continent as they did our brothers, the Acadians."

De Villiers paused. He let his hearers mull over his proposal for a few minutes. Then, smiling at Pierre Laclede, he said, "Our guest Monsieur Laclede, also has a proposal. We are glad to hear from him."

"Thank you, Commandant de Villiers," Laclede began. "It is a privilege to speak to the people here. I am Pierre Laclede, representative and junior partner of Maxent, Laclede and Company. Our firm has received a grant to trade with the tribes along the Missouri for a period of eight years. We plan to set up a post at some place between here and the Missouri River."

Laclede smiled at the men around the table. His formality contrasted strongly with the rough way he had spoken to the voyaguers and habitants several weeks before. But it seemed appropriate for the occasion. He went on: "It would have been a privilege to establish our trading post in this flourishing area. That is impossible now. Since France has given the east bank of the Mississippi to the English, we have chosen a location on the west bank across from Cahokia. Some of you men helped me make that choice. The site is perfect. The land is fertile, though not as rich, of course, as this bottomland. What could be?" He smiled. "We invite all to come with us — either as traders or as farmers."

"Thank you, Monsieur Laclede," de Villiers said. He turned to one of the habitants of Ste. Anne. He knew this man would move to Louisiana.

"With your Excellency's gracious permission," the habitant began, "I have only one thing to say. My family and I, as well as many of my relatives, will depart with you for Louisiana. We have already decided."

Buoyed up by this suggestion, de Villiers turned to Remy Laurent, the next man at the table.

"This is our home," Remy Laurent began slowly. "We have lived in Prairie du Rocher a long time. So long, some of us cannot remember France or even Canada. We have dwelt on these peaceful prairies. We have obeyed our God. We have followed our King. Now we are to be moved around as if we were cattle. I speak for many when I say this: I will stay. My family will stay. Let the river rise. Let the English come. This is our home."

I wanted to cheer. Many did so. I looked at my father, wondering if he would react in anger, as he had done on Christmas morning.

Joseph Labusciere, the notary spoke. He was dark and straight-featured, but lacked the outdoor look of the other habitants. "I speak for all the people of St. Philippe, except one," he said. "We plan to go with Laclede to the new post he will set up. It is not our intention to live under British rule." His note of finality was sharp.

"Tromperie," whispered Jeremy Maligne. "The only reason these people are going with Laclede is to avoid paying the debts they owe me at the mill."

Nick looked at the tight-lipped young man next to him. "Jeremy, why don't you forget the mill and go with the rest?"

"They can't do this to me," Jeremy said. "I'll get what's due."

Nick whispered to me, "France is losing an empire. What is more important: Jeremy is losing a mill!"

At last, my father raised his hand.

"Monsieur O'Rome," de Villiers motioned to him to speak.

"There is another way we could look at this matter," my father began slowly. "We have fought well in this war. Through no fault of our own, we have lost. The English cannot come up the Mississippi. New Orleans controls the access. They cannot come down the waterways from Canada. Chief Pontiac will prevent that. They must come from the east. The closest English post is almost one thousand miles away at the headwaters of the Ohio. Should they come out this far, we have the power to drive them back. The Court at Versailles is a long way off. What thought can it have for us?"

My father leaned forward and, with the look of a lion, gazed intently at one man after another around the table. "Why don't we stand on our own feet and be men? Without any fanfare, why don't we just set up our own rule? The soldiers will be happy to settle here, marry and make their homes. This will be our land, and we'll rule it ourselves. Men will come from Canada to join us."

"Let's be realistic, Brendan," the calm voice of Remy Laurent spoke for the habitants of the prairie. "You mentioned that

England's closest fort is hundreds of miles away. But you yourself have always said that they will come here sooner than we expect. Is that not right?"

"Yes, Remy, I have often said that." My father seemed baffled for a moment by this unexpected counter.

"Perhaps you have heard the word from Canada," Remy went on. "The English have not proscribed our holy religion. They have not upset the lives of our brothers there. I suggest that we wait and see."

"Do you have to wait and see what the devil will do?" my father shot back, on the attack once again. "If you do not know what he will do, remember this: I know. I was born in a country that feels the terror of the British rule. I have fought them all my life. I will never stop fighting them until they are gone — or I am dead." His rage flared. He ended with a shout: "Let's stand up and be men! Let's fight for our homes."

"Good! Good! Good!" said Artime Thomure.

"Count our votes with O'Rome," several men standing near blurted out.

"Me too," I shouted proudly from the far end of the room and raised my clenched fist in the air.

There was a sudden silence. De Villiers stared at me. I looked back at him a moment, blushed and sat down.

"Gentlemen," the Commandant interrupted, barely curbing his annoyance. "Britain has control of the seas. That is why she was able to beat us. We could match her in the field. Even though New France has only fifty thousand people, and the *Bostonnais* number over a million, we beat them in battle after battle."

De Villiers paused and nodded benignly toward my father and toward Nick standing beside me. "On the Monongahela, where Monsieur O'Rome and Monsieur Soumande fought so gallantly, at Oswego, and at Fort Ticonderoga. You were there, too, I believe, Monsieur O'Rome."

"Yes, I was there," my fathered answered. "Wherever the Black Watch fought, I fought them. But I don't want them coming here."

"Nor do I, Monsieur O'Rome," De Villiers said. "In the end it was not the British Army but English seapower that turned the current against us and forced our King to make peace."

I could see that my father raged inwardly, but he kept quiet.

De Villiers went on, confident now that he had made his point. "Frankly, I like the idea of setting up our own commonwealth here. But if we cut ourselves off from France, we will have no supplies, no presents for our allies, the up-river tribes. True, we have lead mines in the hills across the river. That's why we built Fort Chartres here. But what else?"

"Food to feed all England and France," Nick whispered. "Waterways to travel on. Cotton and furs for clothing."

I recalled the words of *Granpere* Soumande. In the spring of 1748 alone ten large *batteaux* had carried 800,000 pounds of grain grown in the Illinois Country down to Louisiana.

De Villiers' words interrupted my thoughts. "Monsieur O'Rome," he said, "I admire your courage. But I think we must choose the more practical solution. Before the British come, we will have to move out.

"Monsieur Laclede, I wish you well in your enterprise. Those who want to go with you, may do so.

"Monsieur Laurent, you villagers will have to trust in God and hope for the best. If any of you should reconsider, you are welcome to go south with us."

I smiled. Uncle Remy never changed his mind, Nick always said.

De Villiers had convinced no one. Each seemed more determined than before to do what he had already planned.

My father had more to say. He spoke without bitterness, wrath or anger now. "Men of France, I respect the prudence of Commandant de Villiers, the strength of Remy Laurent, and the challenge of Pierre Laclede. I have been fighting England so long, I cannot stop. Pontiac no longer hopes for victory. He can, at least, delay the British advance for a few years more. That will give you ample time to settle your affairs. I will stand with him."

After de Villiers closed the meeting, I walked home with my father and Nick. I held my head high and waited for my father to speak. "France's days are over, Nick," he finally said. "But England's wont last much longer either. You remember the Monongahela. You saw how bitter the English colonials, the "Long Knives," as we call them, were at the British. The Long Knives knew how to fight in the wilderness; the Redcoats did not."

"Colonel Washington had to regroup the shattered remnants after Braddock fell," Nick said.

"Since that time," my father went on, "I have seen the growing hostility. If we capture a Long Knife, he blames all his troubles on the British. Now that France has surrendered, this bitterness will grow to hatred and to war."

My father then turned intently to me. "You listen to your Uncle Nick, son. He's a wise man. He doesn't say too much, as your father does. Go with Laclede as soon as you can. He will do what he says he will do." He put his huge hand on my shoulder. He stopped, turned and looked straight at me. "It's twilight for the Lillies of France. Also for the *croix batarde*. Keep your eye on the far future. You may not understand now what I am saying; eventually you will. Someday, this will again be one wide land along the wide river. The Long Knives alone can bring that about. I may not live to see that day. You will. Remember, son, welcome that day. That's the way *le bon Dieu* wants it."

It was too much for a fourteen-year-old boy to grasp, as my father had said. But I remembered his words.

The January thaw continued throughout the month. Some of the oldtimers predicted that when December and January sang sweetly, February and March would howl like hungry wolves.

Laclede presumed otherwise. He believed that he was a favorite son of *le bon Dieu*. There would be no severe weather that winter. On February tenth, he gathered his men at the river. They loaded tools and provisions and some goods for barter.

"Land at the place where we marked the trees," Laclede ordered. "Clear the site. Build a large shed for the provisions and the tools and some small cabins to lodge the men. I will join you before long."

With the *cordelle* over their shoulders, twenty men started along the bank. It would take them four days to pull the boat from Fort Chartres to the site, forty miles up the curving stream on the west bank. Nick, Artime, and I would start two days later and make the journey on horseback. Artime had agreed to work full time at the new post. Nick and I had signed up for part-time work until our family could decide whether or not to move across the river. My father would ride north to fight the British when spring came. Until then he would stay with the two little girls at home.

We rode down the bluffs into Cahokia in the late afternoon of February 14th, just as the barge reached the site on the far side of the river. We stayed with friends in Cahokia that night and ferried across the river the next morning. Laclede's men soon began the tool shed. They felled trees for the cabins. They worked fast to provide shelter against the cold nights. Laclede rode up the east bank of the river and crossed from Cahokia by pirogue. As he jumped from the boat, the men shouted: "Laclede! *Bienvenu*, Monsieur Laclede!"

"This place," a voyageur suggested, "let's call it Laclede."

"Laclede it shall be," the rest agreed.

"*Merci, mes amis*," Laclede said. "But I must say no to that. The patron saint of our King Louis XV is Saint Louis IX. In his honor we shall call our post Saint Louis." All joined in a cheer.

Laclede moved rapidly to lay out the plans of the village. He walked about three hundred feet back from the river, drew a line, and said, "*The Rue Principale*. On the west side of this street, I want my home and office." He looked up and smiled proudly. "The business headquarters of Maxent, Laclede and Company." He gave directions for digging the cellar and for the assembling of the materials to build the house. "The block for the church will be beyond it. The village will stretch along the river for many squares; but will be only three blocks deep."

All of us caught Laclede's *elan*. We worked steadily during the day, cutting and trimming oaks and walnuts, hauling limestone from the bluffs, turning an open terrace into a place to live. We still slept in tents but knew that soon we would have log shelters. As the mild weather continued, the buildings along the *Rue Principale* began to take shape, and we could see a village in the making.

After about seven weeks, planting time approached, and Nick and I had to return to Prairie du Rocher.

"Do you think *Grandpere* will move?" I asked on our way back.

"I'd like him to go to Saint Louis, my god-son, but I do not think he will move at all. If he does, it will be only across to Ste. Genevieve."

"Will you talk to him about it, Uncle Nick?"

"No, I think not. Talking will do no good. He'll make his own decision."

My father sat on the porch the night before he planned to leave. *Grandpere* sat with him. The rest of us had already gone to bed, but I could not sleep. At first I heard little of what they said. But at last my father's voice became intense, and the words carried more clearly.

"*Grandpere*," he said, "have you heard about Britain's latest crime, *le grande derangement*? They burned the homes of the peaceful Acadians. They separated families, and scattered them along the Atlantic coast."

My father paused a few moments, then abruptly stated: "*Grandpere*, you must move the family across the river. I have looked at land on the *Grand Champ*. Ste. Genevieve is the place. *Grandmere* and the children will be happy to go. You've got to get them out before the British come."

"My son," I heard my *grandpere* say, and it sounded as if he were talking to a boy of twelve. "I know how you feel about the British. I understand that. But this is my household. I never interfered with your household even though I thought you were doing foolish things. You have to take the responsibility for that. I will run my affairs as I see fit, and take the responsibility before God and man for that."

I pictured in my mind the amazing contrast: my tall strong father with his menacing frame; my wiry little *grandpere* with the patriarchal air and oak-like immobility. "If you want to take the children across the river, you take them," *grandpere* said. "But you set up a household and be responsbile for them. If you want to go and fight — as I think you should, and have always said you should — then leave them to me."

Grandpere paused a moment. "I could say harsh words, my son. You could say harsh words. It is better now that we keep quiet. The matter is closed."

The next morning my father asked me to ride with him the first few miles on his long journey back to the Ottawa village. "It may be our last chance to talk," he said, "at least for some time." He bade goodbye to *Grandpere* and *Grandmere* and shook hands with Uncle Nick. He hugged the little girls a long time. I walked to the barn to saddle the horses; we rode south along the bluffs toward the church.

When we reached the graveyard beside it, he dismounted and without a word, walked to the grave of my mother and two sisters. He knelt down. I knelt beside him and prayed with tears in my eyes.

He rose, blessed himself deliberately, and remounted.

We rode up the long *coulee* that clawed its way into the hills. My father had not said three continuous sentences to me in my whole life. But now the words burst out like water from the hills after a spring downpour. "All the long years I fought the British, hate filled my heart," he began. "Last week I finally was able to confess to the bedridden Franciscan father at Kaskaskia that I was putting bitterness out of my life. Had I died on the Monongahela, or at any time since, I would have gone with rancor in my heart. But I came back and brought death to your wonderful mother, my dear wife, the little baby I never saw, and your sister Dorothy, whose dead body you stumbled over in the deep snow that terrible November morning."

I shuddered to recall the memory and realized that he was taking us toward the place of those dread memories.

His words rushed on. "I killed them by building the house out there on the height of land. It was my stubborn pride and my unwillingness to admit my mistake when Dorothy died. On the day Father Meurin baptized you, your mother said that other women's husbands sometimes drank too much but her husband's weakness was hating the British. That was true until I let your sister Dorothy die. Then I couldn't face myself. My drinking brought death to Anne and the little one. May God forgive me.

"But I know they are in heaven praying for me. When a man drank too much — it wasn't I — and betrayed Pontiac's plans, so that we could not take Detroit, I realized even more that drink can bring unending evil. I have never touched another drop."

"My father, I know that you have always done what you thought best for us."

"Yes, my son. What *I* thought best. I should have listened to your dear mother once in a while."

By this time we had reached the top of the bluff. We reined in our horses and looked in silence at the old house that held such awful memories. Even abandoned and run-down it looked no more horrible to me than it had when I lived there. It had no inside ladder or stairway leading from the first to the second story where my sisters and I had our rooms. And no porch, so that we had to go out into the rain or sleet or cold to go from the first floor to our rooms.

My father had built an enclosed stairwell, open at the front, but closed on both sides, on the inner side of the east wall. When one looked at the house, he saw the door to the first floor alongside the west wall, and the open stairs to the second floor inside the east wall. I had seen some houses with a stairway to the second floor attached to the outside wall of the house. But none was like this. My sisters had called it "the dragon house." It did look like a dragon with the left side of its mouth open.

The only year we lived in that house, my older sister Dorothy had taken ill early in the fall. My father had worked on the house with so much enthusiasm he could not adjust to our dislike of it. He did not seem aware of Dorothy's continued illness.

Winter came early that year. In late November, I had gone into town for my lessons with Father Meurin. Snow began to fall, and he sent me home by mid-afternoon. Even then, I barely made it back through the deep drifts.

It seemed to me that these events had happened just a day or two before. My mother's depression had hung like a dark cloud ever since we had moved to that monster house. We were so far from the neighbors among whom she had always lived. My father had thought only of having land of his own, entirely our's, with no common fields, as in town. Dorothy lay ill upstairs. When Eileen, Bernadette, and I had to go outside into the sleeting November night to get to our rooms on the second floor, mother had said: "This is the end!"

So it turned out to be. That night Dorothy had wandered in delirium from her room next to mine. I recalled the horror of stumbling over her body in the deep snow the following morning. She had frozen to death during the night. Depression so gripped my father after that, that he no longer seemed aware of how weak my mother had become. When my baby sister came, two months later, she and my mother both died. Uncle Nick then took the two little girls and me to *Grandmere's*. That had been three years before.

My father dismounted, and I stood beside him, looking at the run-down house with tears in my eyes. He put his arm on my shoulder, and I felt the amazing strength of the rippling muscles. His huge frame shuddered. "I'm sorry, my son."

"My father," was all I could say.

At last he remounted, and I followed him to the crest of the bluff.

He broke the long silence. "I fight now to hold the British back for just a bit more, to give you time to move across the river." Then he looked at the broad expanse of land, lush with growth along the Mississippi. "Someday, after I am gone, it will be a free land along this wide river. Do all you can to hurry that day."

"My father, I will do what you say."

"If I do not return this year," he said, "remember, I went away, ready at last, to meet the good God."

He spurred his horse north along the ridge. He did not turn and wave until he was almost out of sight. Tears filled my eyes.

The British troops had not yet arrived to take over Fort Chartres. Instead, as de Villiers had promised, Captain Louis St. Ange de Bellerive had come from Vincennes with a contingent of thirty men. I had often heard my father speak of this man. He had served for forty years in the French army. He was known for fair dealing among his countrymen and the Indians. He had a powerful influence among the tribes, and especially a strong attachment to Pontiac, chief of the Ottawa. Since I wanted to serve as interpreter when the transfer came, I walked to the fort. "I would like to see Captain St. Ange," I said to the sentry.

"*Avancez!*" he answered. I walked into the main gate and up to St. Ange's headquarters.

"Come in," St. Ange said.

"I am Hugh Roe O'Rome. I think you knew my father."

"We fought together in many battles. He is a brave man." St. Ange looked like one who controlled a canoe with a calm paddle, a man it would be easy to like.

"Thank you, *mon capitain*. When the British come, I would like to serve as interpreter."

"O'Rome, I have heard you are the only one in this country who speaks English."

"This is true. Since there is no one to talk to in English, I don't get much practice when my father is gone. But I read and understand most of what I read."

"That's good. We don't expect the British for awhile yet. They'll come someday. So don't get too far away — at least in the summer months."

I promised to be at hand.

As I looked at the lithe Canadien, I thought: If only this man had come five years before. He might have been able to build the empire my father dreamed about.

After St. Ange came, a big exodus occurred. Noyen de Villiers moved down the Mississippi with a fleet of twenty-one boats and eighty habitants, most of them people who had lived in the immediate vicinity of the fort. The villagers of St. Philippe abandoned their farms and moved to Saint Louis. Only Jeremy Maligne, the miller, stayed. Nick moved back and forth between Prairie du Rocher and Laclede's village as the needs of the farm demanded. I rode to Saint Louis with him for a few weeks at the end of summer.

After several cold days at the turn of September, October came in, warm and relaxing. Sumac fires burned along the terrace about two hundred yards back from the river. The hickories yellowed in the warm sun. Ash leaves took the color of ripening pears. Clear days followed in happy succession.

On October tenth Laclede remarked: "It's a real summer day."

"It looks like an *Indian* summer day to me," Nick said nodding to the north. The workmen digging the basement for Laclede's new house looked up. A large group of friendly Indians walked across the newly cleared area. Their bright costumes matched the October foliage.

"Good! Good! Good!" said Artime Thomure. "They're Missouri Indians. Friendly fellows from up the Missouri River."

"We'll be trading with them soon," Laclede said. He walked toward the group. "Welcome, my friends."

The Indians returned the Frenchman's greeting.

Laclede ordered some of his men to bring food from the storehouse. "We'll give them something to eat and send them on their way," Laclede said.

"He may think so," Artime whispered to me. "My guess is that they'll stay."

Artime proved correct. The Indians set up their camp all over the cleared area.

I counted over ninety men in the motley group. Most wore buckskin clothing, with little beadwork or other decoration. Counting the women and children, I estimated that the tribe numbered about two hundred and fifty in all. "That's going to take a lot of food," I said. Then turning to Nick, I laughed, "Now we'll see how good a leader Laclede really is."

After the Indians had lolled around the post for a full day, Laclede called the head men together the following morning, "Today, my friends," he said, "the Missouri people will help dig the cellar of the warehouse."

"So it will be," the chief responded. "We begin right now."

The chief gathered the braves. He harangued them a few minutes. They nodded their heads in agreement. Then he ordered the squaws into the diggings. The women brought wicker baskets and carried the dirt from the excavation. The braves lounged under the trees.

At first a few Frenchmen laughed. The rest shrugged their shoulders and went on with their work.

"This will not do," Uncle Nick said. "The men don't mind that the squaws are helping. But they don't like to see all those muscles lounging under the trees."

"Step up the pace," Laclede said. "That will annoy the squaws, and they will quit."

They did not quit at the end of the first day. Nor the second.

Before the end of a week, the French *engages* threatened to quit. "If the Indians don't work," they said, "then neither will we!"

Laclede called the tribesmen together. "You may go back to your villages now, my friends, We have finished the work, thanks to your help. We will come to your villages in the spring."

When the braves hesitated, he went on, "If you don't go, I will call the troops from Fort Chartres, and they will take you back to your homes."

The Chief agreed. "The Missouri see that the work is finished. We will see our French friends again. You come to our villages. We will have many fine furs."

"That is good, my friends," Laclede answered.

As the Indians moved away, Uncle Nick remarked, "Laclede passed the second test."

The Indians were not the last problem, however. Word came a few days after the departure of the Missouri tribe that King Louis had ceded the entire Louisiana territory to Spain. Laclede had received his license to trade from the French ruler. Would the Spanish King reconfirm his trading privileges, we wondered.

"What will Laclede do now?" I asked.

"He will go right on with his plans," Nick said. "A fellow like de Villiers might quit. Did you hear that he left the Ste. Anne families in Louisiana and fled to France? Some of them have come back to the Illinois country. Laclede is stronger. He brought his men up the river. He invited us to settle in his village. He will see it through."

I expected such confidence from Uncle Nick. But with Spain in the picture, I wondered if the wide land would ever be one again.

Nick and I went to the old homestead for Christmas. New Year's Eve came. All through the afternoon, the whole family talked of *La Guiannee*, the celebration that would begin in the evening and welcome the New Year. The little girls watched from the window and looked down the street. Soon they could see a parade of people dressed in varied costumes.

"Here they come, *Grandpere*," Bernadette shouted. We gathered at the front window to watch. At the head of the marchers, the leader beat time with a cane.

"He looks like a goldfinch," Eileen shouted in joy. I noticed, as the light poured from the window, that he wore a costume with yellow, feather-shaped pieces of cloth sewed to it. These flapped as he bounced along. It took ingenuity to design that masquerade.

Behind him came the fiddler, dressed in clothes I thought a man in Paris might wear.

"These two have been leading the parade as long as I can remember," *Grandpere* said. "They always manage to come dressed in interesting costumes that we have not seen before."

A crowd followed. One man wore the uniform of a soldier. Next came a lady in a long gown. It looked like a wedding dress turned pink. Some wore masks. Others did not. In the rear walked the uncostumed spectators, enjoying the fun, joining in the songs, and hoping for a drink of wine.

As they reached the door, their leader started a song. His voice had more confidence than tone.

When the first verse was finished, the chorus repeated it. Then he began the second verse, asking for "a pork backbone to make a fricassee." The chorus reechoed his words. By that time, more spectators had gathered in the background. The third verse asked to see the eldest daughter of the house.

"That's me!" Eileen shouted. "That's me!"

I suddenly recognized that my little sister was getting tall. She was already eleven years old.

Grandpere Soumande threw open the door. Singers and spectators alike trooped in, until the large front room was filled. They formed a circle around the wall and continued to sing.

Grandmere Soumande passed around little glasses. Nick brought out several bottles of wine. He measured out a drink for each.

The strongest man in the crowd went around with Nick. "Don't pour too much," he said.

"Okay, *mon petit,*" Nick answered. When the crowd looked at the guard's 210-pound frame, they agreed that he was the man to see that nobody had more than his share.

"That's enough for this fellow," the huge man said. "I have to watch him. Last year he already had much to drink by the time we reached the third house. Before midnight, he couldn't sing a note — on key, that is."

They all laughed. The man handed back his unused glass with a disappointed look.

I joined in as the crowd sang the songs over again. We followed with several songs of Canada, and one or two *grandpere* remembered from his boyhood. Gladness filled my heart as our neighbors walked out and went on to the next house.

For a few days, we could enjoy the happy New Year. But our joy was brief. Within a week, sorrow struck, keen, sharp, deep, draining us all. Word came down the waterways that my father had died in battle.

Shortly after, Father Meurin came back from New Orleans to take up residence at Ste. Genevieve. He planned a memorial Mass for mid-January in our church in Prairie du Rocher. Relatives gathered

from all over the lower valley. Those from Ste. Genevieve ferried
Father Meurin across the river. The day turned cold and the wind
stung and burned, bitter as our sorrow.

As the old priest drove his *caleche* to our home, *grandpere* said,
"Thanks for coming to visit us, *mon pere.*"

"It is good to be back among friends, you understand, even
though the occasion that brings us together is not a happy one."

Grandpere showed the priest to the place of honor in the front
room. "We heard that you were the only Jesuit allowed to come
back," someone said, trying for a moment to turn the conversation
from our deep loss.

"That's right, you understand. Orders had come from Versailles
to return to France, but I appealed before the Council in New
Orleans. I pestered them until they said I could go back. So here I
am. They want me to stay in Spanish territory on the west bank of
the river. I am setting up headquarters at Ste. Genevieve. But you,
my people, live on both sides of the river."

Grandpere and the relatives from all over the *Grand Champ* sat
quietly. Father Meurin paused. He knew that he had to say a few
words of consolation. He began tentatively: "Brendan O'Rome — an
amazing man. He seemed so indestructible — as if no storm or bullet
could bring him down. I still remember the first time I saw him. It
was a Sunday. He sat in the last pew of the church and seemed far
more interested in our dear Anne than in the sermon I had so
carefully prepared."

The entire assembly relaxed a bit; the old priest smiled, and went
on. "I don't prepare so carefully any more. You all know what I am
going to say.

"I thought this voyageur would move on as so many others did,
but he loved Anne too much. I had misgivings about the match, you
understand. But it's not for me to tell a man whom he should marry
— or a woman either. I can only put them off a few months, or a
year if they are too young. I remember the day I pronounced them
man and wife. Brendan towered above Anne. His dark eyes glowed.
His hair glistened like a grackle's wing. You remember Anne's golden
hair, her heart-shaped face, and tender flower-like beauty. May *le
bon Dieu* bring them both to heaven."

The priest paused a moment, wondering if perhaps he was talking
too much. None of us said a word. I looked around the room. Each

man sat rapt. The priest turned to me, and said, "I remember the day you were baptized, Hugh Roe. I walked out of the rectory after signing the baptismal record. It was a bright warm Sunday in early March. The first warm day after a long cold spell. We did not know at the time whether spring had come, or if the day was simply a mistake in late winter."

"In those days," *Grandpere* Soumande broke in, "we had a picnic every time we had a chance. I remember the day well. The women sat in the sun along the south wall of the church. The men smoked under the bare branches of the pecans and that lone shagbark hickory. As it got warmer that afternoon, we took off our mackinaws and joked about the colors of the wool shirts we had gotten for Christmas."

"When *le pere* walked out of the church," Nick said, "I asked him if there ever was a saint by the name of Hugh."

"You men always enjoyed baiting Brendan," Father Meurin said, "so I purposely did not tell about the great French saint, Hugh the Abbot of Cluny. I remember exactly what I answered. 'Yes,' I said. 'There's a saint by the name of Hugh. An Englishman. Saint Hugh of Lincoln. He was a bishop there.' "

Nick broke in: "Then I said to Brendan: 'So you wanted to name my godson after an Englishman!' What a storm that brought on us all! Just like Christmas when Artime thought the English language sounded nice, and the British would make good neighbors."

"I wasn't present on that Christmas, you understand," the priest said. "But one outburst was like another. On your baptismal day, Hugh Roe, your father told us that you were named after a great Irishman. Hugh Roe O'Neill, I believe his name was. A brave man who fought the British. Now it seemed to me at the time that this did not set him apart from ten thousand other Irishmen. But it seemed to satisfy your father."

Uncle Remy joined in: "That was the first day that Brendan warned us the British would come and take our lands. We all thought he was talking about phantoms. But time has proven him right."

"France had many chances over here," the priest said. "But she never overcame a few problems."

Now the conversational tone disappeared. His face grew serious. His tone a bit higher. The furrows in his brow deepened. He leaned forward and beat his fist on the arm of his chair.

"For one, France is simply too nice a place. No one wants to leave. So we have few people in this fertile valley. Of the few we have, most are habitants, like yourselves, who want to be left alone to till these rich acres, forgotten by the rest of the world. The rest are *coureurs de bois*, hunters, trappers — men always on the go, as Brendan was. They are empire *travelers*, not empire builders."

The priest paused. His face grew more intense. He spoke more fluently now. "England is an island. She depends on her navy and looks to the world beyond Europe. France is on the mainland. She depends on her army and points to the heart of the continent. The small provinces of Alsace and Lorraine mean more to her than whole continents beyond the seas. England has a more flexible government too. When she needs a change she gets one. We were winning the last war, until William Pitt became England's prime minister. He changed the entire picture from disaster to plans for victory."

Then he spoke with deep regret in his voice, "If in the days of the last king, Louis XIV, *Le Grand Monarque*, France had spent one-tenth the energy and resources here that she wasted in winning parcels of land along the Rhine, we would have an empire that all the might of Britain could not dislodge."

At that instant, *Grandmere* came in to announce that it was time to eat. *Grandpere* led Father Meurin to the place of honor. The rest of the men gathered around the large table. They ate in silence. After the meal was over, the priest asked: "Could Hugh ride back with me to the church?"

"Most certainly, *mon pere,*" *Grandpere* said.

As we got into the *caleche*, Father Meurin said, "You have seen deep sorrow, my son. First your sister, Dorothy, then your mother and the new baby, now your father. They were all my friends. I know that when your father left the last time he took upon himself the blame for your mother's and sisters' deaths. Remember, there is no question here of blame. As I will say in the sermon tomorrow, while your father did unwise things, he never did malicious deeds. He was as strongheaded as a bull elk. No one can deny that. When he got an idea he was going to do something for others — for his family or whomever it might be — he never asked what they wanted. He did what *he* wanted to do for them and then would be hurt when they did not show enthusiasm. Like when he built that unbelievable house out on the remote height of land."

As the priest spoke, I recalled that terrible winter five years before. The house had been unbelievable, as Father Meurin said. I wondered again if there were another like it in the entire world.

My musings ended abruptly when Father Meurin's horse stopped at the stable beside the church. I felt drained, and I shivered in the bitter cold.

"Your father was a near-great man," Father Meurin said, getting out of the cart. "He saw grand visions; he sought them intensely; that he was not able to carry them out was often the fault of circumstances. His failures were not inconsistencies, but excesses of his strength."

"Thank you, *mon pere*," I answered, even though I did not understand at the time the full import of what he said. "I hope you say something like this tomorrow for my *grandpere.*"

The next morning more people gathered at the church in the bitter cold than on the mildest Easter day anyone could remember. Father Meurin spoke plainly: "This man was our friend. We admired him. That's why we have come to pay respects to him and to his family. He differed from the rest of us. He was like the tree that grows along the north wall of this church. Planted so close, it could not spread its branches in all directions like the rugged hickories out in the square. It grew up rich on one side, but cramped on the other.

"Brendan O'Rome grew up in the shadow of the Anglo-Saxon. He grew strong. He grew mighty. But his growth was a half-way-round growth. Hatred played a great part in his life. That was understandable. His hatred made him forget many small things. Only in his last year we knew hate had gone out of his heart. Now he is with God.

"He may have done unwise things in his life, but never deliberately evil things. We commend his soul to God's mercy. We offer our sympathy to his children and relatives. We pray and dedicate ourselves to the task he set for himself: that someday this be one peaceful and free land along the wide river. Amen."

As we walked out of the church, *Grandpere* said: "Beautiful words, my son. And true. I loved your father deeply and admired him even more. We had our disagreements — many of them. At last he is at peace."

"Will all of us find peace only in heaven?" I asked.

"*Full* peace only hereafter," *Grandpere* said, "but partial peace here below—enough to make us appreciate it, and not get discouraged, but not enough to make us so satisfied we forget to look forward to eternal peace. We must work for peace on earth. Not all of us in the same way as your father. There are different ways to gain it. All of us must strive for it."

I walked over the frozen earth to the graves of my mother and sisters. Little stone tablets marked them. Alongside lay a wooden tablet, marking not the grave, but the memory of my father.

"Dear Lord," Father Meurin prayed, "give him eternal rest."

I prayed that the good God would give me strength to work for the earthly peace he sought in vain.

Shortly after the memorial Mass, Uncle Nick and I went north, along the road on the east side of the river. I'll never forget the view of Saint Louis that day. A brisk west wind had cleared the sky. The air was like a cup a spring water. Even the Mississippi had a bright blue cast. As we ferried across the river, we could see the village stretching for almost a mile, while it went back from the stream only three blocks. The roofs of the houses on the terraced land seemed to form a giant stairs up from the bank of the Mississippi.

We walked up from the landing, strolled through the *Place d'Armes*, the public square, and crossed the *Rue Principale*. The streets were laid out at right angles. The blocks were rectangles about 240 feet by 300 feet. The longer side extended north and south. It was something my Uncle Nick would notice, but not I, had he not mentioned it. Each block had four lots of the same size. Many owners had begun to enclose their plot with stakes driven into the earth. I recognized an old practice the people brought with them from Illinois.

Directly west of the *Place d'Armes*, we saw the finished headquarters of Maxent, Laclede and Company. It was the only stone house in the village, and the largest, stretching about sixty feet in width north and south and slightly over twenty feet in depth. It faced the river. It had a high basement and a *galerie* all around.

"The other houses are mostly of upright logs," Nick said. "They called them *poteaux en terre*. More people will build of stone as time goes on. It's easy to get limestone from the bluffs. The supply will never run out."

As we passed Laclede's house, voyaguers carried pelts into the ground floor. "The basement serves as the warehouse," Nick said. "The family lives upstairs. Laclede plans to build a home in the next block north later on. We'll stop here a moment, then go over to see our old neighbor, Joseph Labusciere."

We left our gear at the warehouse and walked across the empty block to the west. "Here's where we'll build the church," Nick said. "That street is called *Rue d'Eglise*, the Street of the Church, and the next is *Rue des Granges*, the Street of the Barns." He pointed out a row of thatched-roofed barns that stretched along the road.

We turned south on *Rue d'Eglise*. I noticed that most of the houses were built of upright logs. All had large *galeries*, verandas that stretched along the entire front of the house and allowed a lot of outside living on rainy spring or fall days. Some had verandas on two or three sides. Laclede's headquarters alone, I noticed, had a *galerie* entirely around the house.

In Prairie du Rocher the pitch of the roof was the same over the dwelling and the porch. A few houses in Saint Louis followed this pattern, but more had a steep pitch over the dwelling and an almost horizontal roof over the front and rear porches.

As we walked down the street, Uncle Nick could not see over the *palisades*, but I was tall enough to see the neat back yards. All had outside ovens; behind some houses stood a little hut with an entire kitchen for summertime use. Some habitants had already put in young fruit trees on one side of the yard and a garden on the other. All had an enclosed henhouse and some a small stable for milk cows. Each house had its own well.

"If I build a house here," I said, "It will be out where I can see the distant hills, watch the sun rise over the river, and hear the mockingbirds — but still close enough to see my neighbors."

By this time we reached the house of Joseph Labusciere. Our old neighbor from St. Philippe had come out on the porch to greet us. "*Bon jour*, Nick. *Bon jour*, Hugh."

"*Bon jour*, Joseph," we said in unison.

We entered a large central room that extended across to the rear door that looked out toward the Mississippi.

"We have two rooms on the north side and two on the south that open on to *la salle*, as you can see," Labusciere said. "In the stone house we plan an attic and a basement. For the present we have to be satisfied with one level."

I noticed that the carpenters had used fine walnut in some of the woodwork. The floor was oak.

"We brought our furniture, our doors, and our windows over from the other side of the river," Labusciere said.

"You've done a fine job, Joseph," Nick responded.

"Thank you, Nick," Joseph answered. "By the way, are you here permanently?"

"No, Joseph. I'll work for Laclede at the warehouse a few months each year until things clear up on the other side. Hugh is staying only a few days. He's to be interpreter for St. Ange when the British come. Eventually we both hope to move up and join Laclede's company."

"We're still granting land titles, Nick. So don't wait too long. Most of the land near the river is taken already."

"Since you mentioned it, Joseph, how about that section on the bluff near Sugar Loaf mound? It's far from the village, but that's the place I'd like."

"It's all yours, Nick, for the asking."

"Why don't you put me down for that area!"

"Fine, Nick. Then you see Laclede and get his approval. I'll put your name on the list right now."

"Thank you, Joseph," Nick said. We shook hands and left.

We walked uphill to *Rue des Granges*. We crossed the dirt street and stopped at the fence on the west end of the village. "With the creek running down through it," Nick said, "the woodland makes a fine pasture — black jack oaks and elms down by the stream, and white and red oaks on the hillside."

"Laclede chose well for the common fields, too," I said. To the north of the pasture land, strips one acre wide stretched forty acres in depth westward. Here each townsman had his plot of tilled ground. We walked along the cultivated strips.

"I guess this ends your tour of the village," Nick said. "Let's go back to the stone house and see if Laclede is home."

We stepped ahead briskly now, angling across the church square.

All was bustle at the ground-level warehouse. Voyageurs had already brought in pelts from up the Missouri.

"When everyone hustles," Nick said, "it is a sign Laclede is at home. That man's all energy. His energy catches."

"*Bon jour*, Nick," one of the voyaguers said.

"*Bon jour, mon ami.*"

I recognized most of the *engages*, the hired men, who had come up the river with Laclede, and the Illinois men who had moved across the river. Several faces were unfamiliar.

"A few new people show up every month," Nick said. "Some from Canada. These are from Prairie du Chien up north."

Uncle Nick stopped to talk to several former residents of St. Philippe. I walked over to check my equipment.

"That your gear, *garcon*?" a harsh voice said to me.

I looked up. A barrel-chested young fellow with a flattened nose stood before me. He was perhaps four or five years older than I. His thick eyebrows grew together, accentuating the sullen look of his eyes. I had never before disliked anyone in my life, but I was instinctively wary of this man.

"Yes, it is," I said.

"Well it's in my place! Get it out of there." He pushed me out of his way, turned, and kicked my gear into the corner.

Some primal instinct of survival told me to stand for my right. This fellow spoke as if people constantly cowed before him. Down deep I felt that if I gave in now, he would try to browbeat me often in the future.

I stooped to rearrange my possessions.

He spun me around and swung hard. I ducked away and the blow that would have stunned merely glanced off my head. He lunged again with a wild swing. I side-stepped and jabbed his side with my right fist as he went by.

I feared him, but I knew I had to stand my ground. The muscles in his bull neck bulged. His arms were thick. Physically I could not match him. I could only dance away from his blows and tire him. Maybe I could outlast him. I saw that he carried a knife sheathed to his belt. The hub-bub in the room subsided.

The air was rank with the odor of pelts. My mouth was dry. I had trouble uttering the first words. "My uncle Nick Soumande told me to put my gear in that place," I said deliberately, loud enough for everyone to hear. A deadly stillness gripped the room.

Suddenly an equally deadly voice broke the silence. "If you dare touch my nephew again, I will strangle you as readily as I would cut up a polecat. And I would not feel it necessary to tell the priest at Eastertime, because that is what I think you are."

"Take it easy, Amnon," a voice broke in. "Nick Soumande was with Langlade on the Monongahela."

Ammon's sullen eyes showed surprise — and fear. I knew the word "Monongahela" held magic for the voyageurs. I knew, too, the intensity of my uncle's anger on the rare occasions one aroused him.

Amnon stood uncertain for a moment, then backed toward the door. He looked at me. "I'll see you again, *garcon*," he said.

"I'm sure you will," I answered. I felt I had met an antagonist, and I hoped that he was not as *formidable* as he tried to appear. There would be times when Uncle Nick was not around, and I might have to face Amnon alone.

Laclede walked into the room. "*Allo*, Nick," he said.

"*Bon jour*, Monsieur Laclede. Do you have a free moment?"

"Free?" he asked with a sweeping gesture of both hands and a sardonic smile. "In his new book, *Contrat Social*, Jean Jacques Rousseau says no man is free once he moves out of the forest. I've been reading him the last few evenings when my work is done. Come upstairs and see my library."

Nick and I followed Laclede up to the wide *galerie* and into the front parlor. Laclede motioned us to chairs and sat down behind a desk.

I noticed a large case of books. Two of them bore the name Rousseau: *Contrat Social* and *La Nouvelle Heloise*.

"What can I do for you, Nick?" Laclede asked.

"I'd like to put in a claim for a strip of land on the bluff just beyond Sugar Loaf mound."

"No one has claimed that area," Laclede said, "but it is far from the village."

"That's true," Nick said. "My nephew has to be able to see Illinois all the time so he doesn't get homesick."

"I get homesick once in a while, too," Laclede said. "When I was a boy I could see the peaks of the Pyrennes from the hills above my home at Bearn in southern France. In New Orleans the land was so flat I couldn't see a mile. At least from my office here I can see the Illinois bluffs. What's that distance? Four miles?"

"Three or four," Nick said.

"My original plan," Laclede admitted with a shrug, "was simply to open a trading post. The hope of building a village immediately became possible only when France gave the east bank to England and you people were willing to move with me." He abruptly returned to the present. "I'd prefer that you would take a section of land nearer town. But if you want to be near the Sugar Loaf mound, the land's yours."

Laclede took a map out of the drawer of his desk. "See, here is the line of bluff. Here's the Sugar Loaf mound. Your section." He wrote the name "Nicholas Soumande" in the empty space and replaced the map.

"Thank you, Monsieur," Nick said.

Laclede rose and smiled. "Adieu, Messieurs."

We walked onto the wide *galerie*. "Uncle Nick," I said, "Laclede doesn't waste time, does he?"

"Always to the point, my nephew. Always in a hurry. But never brusque."

After I returned to Prairie du Rocher from Saint Louis, my *grandmere* insisted that I go to Ste. Genevieve once a week for my lessons under *Pere* Meurin. Three boys from the village came every morning during the week and one more occasionally.

Latin was our main subject. Hard work clean through! The old Jesuit made a game of our reading the Latin; and that part was easier than when we tried to put French into Latin. He had one book, Caesar's *Gallic Wars*, or rather part of one, where Caesar beat the Belgians.

"If you know Latin," *Pere* Meurin said, "other languages will come easily."

I always wondered about that. It seemed to me that those who learned Latin easily, learned other languages easily. Those who found Latin hard found other languages hard — even if they knew Latin.

One of the boys learned languages readily. Another liked arithmetic. History was my line. When *Pere* Meurin finished the Latin lessons, he talked French history. Talked, yes. He really didn't teach us history. He never asked a question to see if we remembered what he said. He simply talked and talked, especially about the reign of Louis XIV. It seemed so long ago. The other boys were not interested, but the Jesuit never seemed aware of that. He talked for about an hour, then suddenly seemed to come out of a trance. "I'm sorry, boys," he would say and send us home.

But he did teach me what made a well-run country, and why a strong land like France had done so little in the Illinois country.

On the afternoon of October 9, 1765, I heard an unearthly howl coming up from the river bank next to Fort Chartres.

"Bagpipes," Nick said in disgust. "Just what your father and I heard on the Monongahela. Dreadful noise."

A courier from St. Ange asked me to come to the fort immediately.

"Which way did the British come?" Nick asked him.

"Down the Ohio from Fort Pitt," the courier responded. "They tried to come in from the gulf, but couldn't get by New Orleans. They hoped to send troops down from Detroit, but Pontiac and the Ottawa choked the waterways. Now they're here."

Nick and I mounted and rode fast to the fort.

The British marched up from the river. A detachment of one hundred men came around the north wall of the fort towards the central gate.

Only one hundred, I thought. *My father was right. We could have held them off forever.* When I saw the red faces and the surly looks, I knew how my father and Uncle Nick must have felt on the Monongahela. The Scottish soldiers threw their knees high to make their plaid kilts swing, as if it were necessary for soldiers who wore skirts to appear so much more fierce, lest people would laugh at them. There was something so unreal for men to fight anywhere, much less in the wilderness, in skirts. Yet the arrogance of these men evoked an instinctive dislike. One would either fight them to death — or flee. *Thank God my father is not here*, I concluded.

I stood beside St. Ange. Nick was behind him, a little to my left. I tried to assay Uncle Nick's reaction. I saw his expression out of the corner of my eye, but it told me nothing.

The Captain of the Black Watch Regiment, Commissioner of His British Majesty, King George III, presented his credentials.

He was tall, light-complexioned, handsome, and utterly disdainful. The arrogance of the entire regiment seemed to be galvanized in this one man. There was no trace of respect for a gallant but defeated enemy.

I looked at St. Ange as he accepted the papers gracefully. On his face was neither cringing fear nor the arrogant disdain of his adversary. New France had gone down. Because of men like St. Ange, it had gone down with honor.

I received the British officer's credentials. I read them aloud, translating each sentence carefully, and handed them back to St. Ange. While he kept his poise, I choked and a tear came to my eye. I bit my underlip to hide my heartbreak.

The haughty British Captain outlined the terms, and I translated them. The French soldiers would be allowed to depart in peace. The inhabitants of the surrounding area would receive kind treatment. I did not believe what he said. Even the word "kind" from the officer's tongue sounded to me like a death sentence. This was the worst moment of my life since I had found my sister dead in the snow. Now I knew why my father hated the British so. This was the first Britisher I had ever seen. Yet through my father's hatred, the British had always been a living reality. This one certainly lived up to the image my father had painted.

The two officers signed the papers. I wrote my name as interpreter, and Nick and another man as witnesses.

The flag with the Lilies of France came down. The *croix batarde* rose high on the unchallenged wall of Chartres. French soldiers marched out of the great fortress for the last time. My eyes filled with tears.

By orders from New Orleans, St. Ange went to Saint Louis with the title, "Commandant of the District of Western Illinois." Nick, and I, and several others, including Jeremy Maligne, moved up the river with him. We agreed to work two years with Laclede, but

Jeremy had other plans. It was good to get away from the British rule. Every look at the British flag above Fort Chartres had made me feel sad.

"Keep your eye on the future," Nick said. "Don't waste energy worrying about what might have been." It was to take me a long time to learn to do as he advised.

St. Ange would be Governor, Judge, and Military Commander until the Spanish officials came to Saint Louis. We believed that they would come soon.

St. Ange's rule proved to be light-handed. The old warrior commanded the soldiers and kept public order. He left most of the civil duties to an aide, and to the notary, Joseph Labusciere. Jeremy Maligne, still irked that Labusciere led all his neighbors away from the Maligne mill at St. Philippe, began to keep a self-appointed eye on the notary, that he did his work carefully. Pierre Laclede now devoted his full time to building up a fur trading enterprise.

As I watched St. Ange guide the new village, I thought: if only such a man had been in charge of Fort Chartres a few years earlier, he might have sought independence in Illinois as the people of Louisiana were then trying to do. Here was a man who might have succeeded — a brave soldier, a wise commander, trusted alike by his own countrymen and by Pontiac and the Indians.

How sad it was that a man who might have been the builder of an empire, a Champlain or a Bienville, had been destined to lay the French regime to rest on the east side of the river and now on the west. I wondered if men would remember St. Ange as the man who presided at the funeral of the French Empire, or as the hero who set up the first organized government in the city named for a saintly king.

When the first flotilla came up from Ste. Genevieve the following May, we had a chance to see our old pastor, Father Meurin, once again. Those who had been in Saint Louis since its start saw him now for the first time since he left Illinois for New Orleans two and a half years before. When word came that he had arrived, Nick and I started for the riverbank. A crowd had already gathered. Almost all the Saint

Louis people had been his parishioners once, either at Kaskaskia or Prairie du Rocher or St. Philippe. As he got out of the canoe, we knelt down to get his blessing.

"*Notre pere*," someone shouted. "We're glad you came back to us."

"We heard that you told the Superior Council to go to — to go wherever priests tell people like that to go," Artime said.

Father Meurin laughed. "I didn't tell them to go anywhere, you understand. I simply told them that *I* wasn't going anywhere. They got their orders from the King; I got mine from God — indirectly in both cases."

"Good! Good! Good!" Artime said.

"Years ago I volunteered for the Illinois missions, you understand. My superiors sent me here. They did not change their orders. The King of France ordered me out. I did not take vows to him, but to God."

Someone behind me whispered: "It wasn't the King who wanted the Jesuits to go away. I heard it was the King's girl friend. They wanted him to send her away."

"Well, the Pompadour couldn't budge old man Meurin," another voice said.

"Good for him," the first man came back.

The chunky little priest with his impish face and thinning hair had never looked like a hero. Heroes should be tall, handsome, commanding. But Father Meurin had stood up to the Superior Council that determined policy for Louisiana. He had come back into the wilderness alone. No longer young and vigorous, he had only twilight ahead of him. He put God's will as he saw it above the word of the King.

As yet we had no church in Saint Louis. Father Meurin offered Mass in a tent. It was the first time many had gone to Mass in over a year. The old priest baptized Louis Rides and the older DesChamps' little girls, Catherine Bissonet, and a Pawnee boy whose father was French. Uncle Nick offered to be godfather to the French-Indian boy, but Father Meurin had already accepted the offer of another man.

Uncle Nick turned to me, "I wanted an Indian godson, so you would have an Indian brother-in-God and would never forget all of us are brothers."

I pondered the words of my uncle but would not fully fathom them until years went by and many changes had come. I stood close to Father Meurin as he wrote the names of the newly baptized and their godparents in the records. He concluded with the words: "In the country of Illinois, in Saint Louis, in a tent for want of a church, on the ninth day of May, 1766."

In the afternoon, Nick and I ferried our old friend across the river to Cahokia, where he had left his *caleche.* Halfway across the river, he turned to me and said: "Introibo ad altare Dei."

"Ad Deum qui laetificat juventutem meam," I answered.

"I see you still know your Latin prayers for Mass. But what do the words mean?"

"I will go to the altar of God; to God who gives joy to my youth."

"Good, my boy," he said. "When were you at Mass the last time?"

"At the funeral Mass for my father."

"That's a long time. Not good at all."

Father Meurin turned to Nick. "There's work here for ten men, you understand. I think Bishop Briand will soon send help down from Canada. Maybe all of you can get to church more often then. Have you ever thought that you might do more for the Church, Nick?"

II

Mighty River, Endless Plains

When Laclede chose Artime to lead a big summer trading expedition, Nick and I signed up. Now that I was seventeen I did not have trouble convincing the patron that I could handle my share of work. To our dismay, Amnon, the belligerent fellow in the incident at Laclede's warehouse, signed up, too.

"Don't challenge him," Nick said. "But don't let him walk over you either. Just stay out of his way — if you can."

We were not taking the *batteau* that Laclede's original *engages* had brought up the river. Instead we were travelling in four pirogues. These long narrow boats fashioned from cypress or cedar logs could move more easily upstream but readily tipped over and sent men and valuable merchandise into the gulping waters. The bigger pirogues could carry as many as thirty men and up to 100,000 pounds of merchandise. Eight men each propelled our four medium-sized vessels with a ton of trade goods.

When we pushed off from the bank, I felt immediately the exhilaration of the wide waters. When we turned up the Missouri, however, I felt less sure of myself. I loved the Mississippi, but the Missouri baffled me. It reared and reversed itself and roared at its banks, like a dun-colored stallion trying to break out of a corral.

"I would never swim in this river," I grumbled.

"Only a wild man would," Nick said. "The Missouri doesn't challenge me. It's too changeable. You conquer it today. It bounces back new and unbeaten tomorrow."

This was the first time I ever heard Uncle Nick admit caution in anything he did. He never seemed to have to fight fear. It simply never entered his mind that he might not be a match for anyone or anything he tackled. He did not hesitate to do anything he had to do, but he never tried foolish things.

Nick wore a beard now. It cut down the sharpness of his protruding jaw but strengthened the look of his entire face. Even though only thirty, he moved like a veteran among the voyaguers.

By four in the afternoon of the first day, I wished I had never left home. My arms ached, and my legs were cramped. I realized we would have no comfortable bed to sleep on at night. When we made camp in the evening, the marshy river bottom steamed with a breathless, sultry heat. Clouds of mosquitoes rose from a slough, whining about my head. I breathed, coughed, and spat mosquitoes.

Even after I piled leaves under a deerskin to sleep on, I was uncomfortable. The overworked muscles in my arms twitched. I tossed most of the night, plagued by heat, mosquitoes, and fatigued muscles. I fell into a deep sleep just before dawn. All too soon the camp was astir. We cooked breakfast and started upstream again. We had to stay close to the wooded shore — and the mosquitoes — or fight the full force of the current.

The second day proved even harder than the first. I could not admit it to Uncle Nick, but I wished I was at home in Prairie du Rocher. When Artime selected a camp for the night — this time on a sandbar away from the mosquitoes — Nick angled the pirogue into the bank. "A good fellow, Cousin Artime," he said. "Easy to deal with in ordinary circumstances, but tough enough when troubles come. Lucky we are to have him in charge."

"Do you think he can handle Amnon?" I asked.

"Only in time we'll know that, my godson. As they seem on the surface, Artime accepts people. He trusts them. Fair he is. But Amnon — a parasite, an ivy vine that uses a friendly tree for a trellis and then grows up to strangle it. As I trust a wolf, I would trust him at a safe distance." He paused. "Two days after he tried to bully you, he started a fight with someone his own age. As soon as he knew he had met his match, he pulled his knife and slashed the man. Treacherous, yes. But more."

Nick stopped. His expression changed. A compound of sheer disgust and begrudging respect came into his voice. "The only braggart I ever met who can do almost as well as he brags he will do. Most dangerous is this kind."

Then, as an after thought, he countered his own words. "Artime?

Too jovial, some think. Because he always says 'Good! Good! Good!' many take him for a fool. Wrong, they are. Let's hope he and Amnon never meet head-on." Nick said no more, leaving me to mull over his words.

The next morning, as we pushed on beyond the mouth of the Osage, the river turned sharply northward. About forty miles farther on, it turned westward again. The heavy woods of the lower Missouri gradually disappeared. The oaks and hickories were gone; only cottonwoods, willows, elms, and a few soft maples filled the river bottom.

Suddenly to the right, ahead of us, we saw a huge section of the north bank crash into the river. We stopped paddling a moment to watch a huge elm shake in the still air. It began to fall slowly, then faster. It tore the air with a rush of wind, and came down into the water. It bounced a few times, then held firm. Anchored by its roots to the broken shore, it dammed the stream for thirty yards out. Driftwood piled against it, checking the rush of the water.

"I'm glad we chose the south side this morning," Nick said as we resumed paddling. "The current may lunge back this way. The main channel used to go behind that island." He pointed to a stretch of sand and a stagnant slough separating an island from the south bank.

Day followed steady day with little change from one to another. Finally, when we camped one night on the left bank of the river, a feeling of expectancy was in the air.

"Tomorrow," said Artime, "we should rendevous with the Missouri Indians."

"Kansas squaws are nice," said a sallow-faced man. "Omaha squaws are even better. But for me, give me a Missouri girl anytime."

"You talk too much," Nick said, irritated. "No woman would look at you even if there were only boys and old men in the world."

The man looked up, but when he saw Nick's strong wrists and thick chest, he slunk back like a coyote before a mountain lion.

Amnon broke in. "Only a chief's daughter for me. That's the way to do well in the fur trade."

Had this idea come from anybody else, I would have dismissed it. I heard many men boast that they could take women at will, but they never got within arm's length of their claims. This man, I knew, was different. I felt I should defend every girl in the world from his approach.

Amnon went on: "You marry a chief's daughter and you get the best trades."

"Once there was honor among traders," I broke in, my voice quivering. "When a *coureur de bois* married an Indian girl, she was his wife everywhere. He accepted the children as his own. Either he lived with the Indians as a member of the tribe, or he brought his wife and his children to live in the French villages."

Nick took up when I stopped. "Today people act like scum. They use the Indian woman for their convenience. They scatter children all over the Indian encampments. Then, after they have had their day, and made their money, they go back and take a wife in the French village. What did they have in mind? Did they want the squaw in the first place or didn't they want her?"

He paused and then went on in a deadly tone. "They cannot do these evil things without hurt to others, hurt to the woman, hurt to the children. Someday it will sweep back on them. You mark my word." Those who knew Nick listened to him with more attention than they gave to Father Meurin's sermons.

To everyone's dismay, Amnon made the mistake of breaking into a laugh, and the even more terrible blunder of saying: "Hey Nick, I bet you have a squaw in some Indian village. What about it?"

As swiftly and effortlessly as a panther leaping at a huddling sheep, Nick grabbed Amnon by his cotton shirt and pinned him against an oak. "Look me straight in the eye and tell me whether I ever abused a woman."

I had never seen my uncle so outraged in his life. I could not blame him for reacting to what Amnon had said, but had not expected Nick to snap back so fiercely.

Just then someone shouted, "Kill *le bâtarde*, Nick. It would be good riddance."

Amnon cringed and looked down. Nick threw him to the ground.

"My nephew is right," he said, challenging the crowd. "Each one of you who feels he can play it fast and loose, play it fast and loose. But someday, remember, your evil deeds will catch up with you."

Suddenly, far off across the prairie we heard the cry of the coyote. A shudder shook me, and the hair on my head tingled.

The next day we reached the first village of the Missouri. Chief Silent Elk presented an imposing figure as he strode down to the river bank to greet us.

"*How kola*," he said, raising his hand in peace.

"*Bon, Bon, Bon*" said Artime with a smile and a wave of the hand.

"Bun! Bun! Bun!" the chief responded, in an effort to imitate Artime's French. He went on in the Missouri tongue, and Artime translated. "Chief Silent Elk welcomes his white brothers who have come in peace to trade. They will find the Missouri a friendly and hospitable people. He hopes these, his new white brothers, will not be like some who have come from beyond the Mississippi, who had given the Missouri cheap goods for the fine deerskins they brought to them."

I noticed the chief's grander gestures never quite seemed to fit what Artime said he was saying.

Silent Elk resumed with even more resounding gestures and proud manner. At the end, Artime said again: "The chief said much the same thing as before, only more so. The Missouri have always wanted to live in friendship with everyone, especially their kind French brothers. So, the great chief of the Missouri, Silent Elk, welcomes us with many words. He hopes that we will not be like the other white men who have taken advantage of the goodness and kindness of the Missouri people and did not treat them fairly."

When the chief repeated a third time for Artime to translate, the jovial Frenchman said, "Old Babbling Brook said the same thing over again. But I'll have to take up a few minutes in further speech-making while he gets his breath. Did you ever hear the story of the voyageur who came to the warehouse just after a new barge-load of pelts arrived? 'I feel like old King Solomon,' he said, 'when he came home to his hundred wives and three hundred porcupines. I know what I have to do, but I don't know where to begin.'"

We burst out laughing. The Indians looked at us in surprise. Then at Silent Elk. The equally surprised chief turned a quizzical gaze at Artime.

Artime rose to the occasion. He beamed at Silent Elk. Then bowed to him. We voyaguers cheered. The chief smiled and, as his braves grunted in approval, led us into the encampment.

Nick and I walked by about sixty lodges in a little *coulee* that indented the bluffs an eighth of a mile from the river bank. A freshet of water flowed beside the village, coming from a spring at the far end of the *coulee*. Braves stood around, eyeing us cautiously. The squaws kept busy in their tasks. Some of the younger girls looked up and giggled. Mangy dogs walked to and fro. Indian ponies grazed among sparse cottonwoods.

Nick and I selected a site under a maple tree on the far side of the stream, within the confines of the village, but not too close to the main lodges. We set up camp.

When the trading began during the following week, we found that old Silent Elk had spoken the truth about the peltries. They were of prime quality. Trading was brisk. The chief promised an equal number of excellent pelts on our next trip. Prospects for long-range trade looked bright.

One fact caused us to worry. The chief had twin daughters. Tall, sturdy and well-formed girls, they walked with an air of self-possession that their father only feigned. Their features were straight and attractive, their faces oval, their complexions perfect.

Artime asked, "Did you see those twin daughters of the chief?"

"How could anyone miss them?" I answered. "At first they seem so alike; but the one called Yellow Throat is soft, sweet, and womanly; the other, Hawk's Wing, moves like a man."

"Amnon has his eye out for Yellow Throat," Nick said.

"She seems to have *her* eye only for Blue Cloud," I said. "The young brave seems to be a nice fellow. But if Amnon would offer more gifts to the chief for the hand of his daughter, I am not sure what the old man would do."

"You know what that old fool would do," Artime shot back. "He would sell her to the highest bidder. All she means to Amnon is someone to sleep with when he comes through the Missouri villages and someone to pave the way so he could get more advantages when he no longer works for Laclede."

"What will happen if Amnon makes the highest bid?" I asked.

"It may mean trouble for all of us," Artime said. "If Blue Cloud loses Yellow Throat, he will cause trouble. But he can do nothing

while we are in the village. The custom of hospitality forbids that."
Artime looked grimmer than I ever remembered seeing him. "I'm
afraid that Blue Cloud and some friends will waylay us after we
leave. Amnon's the kind of fellow who may come out all right
himself. But others will get hurt."

As the weeks went on and trading continued briskly — Laclede
had sent only first-class merchandise to barter with the Indians — it
became more evident every day that Amnon had his mind set on the
Indian princess.

I could not get the problem. — or rather the girl — out of my
mind.

"You are not thinking of Yellow Throat yourself, my nephew?"
Nick said with an impish grin.

"I am getting to like her, yes." I blushed. And then in self
defense I blurted out, "Who would not like her?" I stopped. Nick
smiled reassuringly. I went on, "She does not care for me nor for
Amnon. She has Blue Cloud in mind, I'm sure. Even if she liked me,
the day is over when Indian women can live as wives in our villages.
Even Father Meurin can no longer perform the marriages between a
white man and an Indian. It is some crazy British law. If I do like this
girl, perhaps I can do something for her that may be better."

Artime came over the next day from his lodgings. Seeing his
perturbed look, we asked, "How are things?"

"Good! Good!" he answered tensely.

"That bad?" I asked.

"Yes!" Artime responded.

"If Artime ever uses only one 'good,' " Nick said, "a tornado will
strike when the Mississippi is over its banks."

"There may be trouble, *mes amis*," Artime said.

"What is it?" I asked.

"Some Indians want to talk to us," he said.

Nick and I walked with Artime to his tent. Two young braves sat
inside, fellows I had often seen with Blue Cloud.

"These two friends of Blue Cloud," Artime began, "are sure

there will be trouble if Blue Cloud does not marry Yellow Throat."

"Tell them," Nick said definitely, "that we do not want trouble. We want to live in peace with our Missouri brothers."

Artime translated. There was a sharp response.

"He wants to know what you intend to do about it," Artime said.

"Does he think Silent Elk would give his daughter to someone else in preference to Blue Cloud," Nick asked, "if that man offered larger gifts?"

When Artime translated his words, he could understand from the guttural mutterings that the answer was what he feared.

"Does Blue Cloud have gifts to give Silent Elk that outweigh the gifts another could give?" Artime asked. The answer was a flat negative.

"Uncle Nick," I said, "you gave me the finest musket in the Illinois country. Could I give it to Blue Cloud as a gift for Silent Elk?"

"When I gave you that gift, it was for you to use as you saw fit. We will still be on the river many days. A man without a gun can be in trouble. But I believe, my nephew, you would be doing a generous thing."

The Indians looked quizzically at this exchange between Nick and me. Finally, I said to Artime, "Tell them that if Blue Cloud's gifts cannot counterbalance the gifts of his rival, he can add to his gifts the finest musket Silent Elk has ever seen."

The Indians' faces brightened. They spoke rapidly. "They think that will be enough," Artime translated, "and peace will be kept between the Missouri and the white man."

The next day the two braves returned. Blue Cloud had a counter-plan. The white man with the rifle should buy the princess. The old chief would readily grant her to him. Then the night before the wedding, Blue Cloud would steal off with her.

"This is getting more complicated than I had expected," I said to Artime. Thomure translated for the Indians. They would not budge. Blue Cloud's plan was the best.

I wondered momentarily whether or not I ought ever again to offer a favor to another.

"It has to be," Nick said.

That was my only reassurance.

The day came for the bidding. The girl would have nothing to say. What presents a suitor brought the father would settle her fate — and marriage to Amnon seemed like the bottom of the river. We knew what the old chief's attitude would be. To Silent Elk, a daughter was a daughter. He had two almost alike. What difference did one or the other make? If a man wanted her, and he had the presents, that man would get her.

Amnon came forward with a variety of gifts — a woolen shirt, traps, ammunition, and a silver medallion. The chief looked at them in admiration. He rose. He told the assembly how he would like to have Amnon as his son-in-law. Amnon would be his successor as chief of the Missouri. He would be a big man in the tribe, and there would be much trade and good relations with the white man.

I waited until he finished. Then to the surprise of everyone except Nick and Artime, I arose. I looked at Amnon. I looked at the chief. I looked at Yellow Throat sitting under a cottonwood beyond the council circle. Her look of indifference annoyed me. I had gone to sleep thinking of her the night before. I thought of her now. For a moment the world beyond the village was gone, forgotten. Just two days before I had said I liked the girl and would do something for her. I had promised that I would help Blue Cloud win her. Now, I wanted her myself. Yes, I did. How could I bid in the name of someone else? How could I buy a girl I was coming to like and then give her to another man?

Then I looked at Amnon. The blunt fact called me back to reality. That face made me see not just the present, but the past and the future. I stood quietly a long time, bringing myself to do what I knew I had to do. I would win Yellow Throat for Blue Cloud.

I offered a red cotton shirt and my musket — far more valuable than anything Amnon had offered. The chief picked up the musket, stood erect, aimed it at a cottonwood leaf high above the farthest tepee. He fired. The leaf fell. He smiled. "I accept," he said.

Amnon pierced me with the look that reminded me of a lynx I had trapped years before. As I recalled that the lynx, to my surprise, had fought his way free just before I could kill him, Amnon turned back to the old chief, completely masking the emotion that gnawed at him. He spoke of the chief's other daughter. If Silent Elk did not see fit to grant him Yellow Throat, then still the Chief might accept him as a son-in-law by giving him Hawk's Wing.

Though it seemed to take him a half-an-hour to say it, Silent Elk announced that he would do that.

That night Blue Cloud took Yellow Throat and fled from the village. I didn't sleep, thinking of Yellow Throat, then of Amnon, fluctuating between frustration and anger. The night seemed endless.

The next morning we pushed our canoes downstream, leaving Amnon with his new bride. I hoped I would never see him again, ever.

"It's time we planted some trees," Nick said one day in early November. "St. Ange has approved our land grant."

We rode out of the growing village of Saint Louis and south along the river. The maples and ashes had already lost their leaves. Only the oaks still held some remnant of the glorious colors of the previous month.

As we crossed *La Pètite Riviere*, the stream that flowed through the common woodlot, we passed below the dam and the mill that the Taillon brothers had built. We climbed the south bank, and could see the lovely pond growing up behind the dam and already becoming a gathering place on the many holydays, such as *le jour de fete de St. Jean Baptiste* in June.

Travel with Nick had taught me to observe carefully; not only the trees — I could tell each at sight along the horizon — but the flow of the clouds that indicated changes in the weather, the varying growth of crops on north and south sloping fields, the marks of deer and small game.

We climbed the hill, passed Sugar Loaf mound, and found an open space on the bluff. The view across the river was breath-taking. I felt as free as a hawk that rode the wind above the river. I had no feel for the deep, closed-in woods, or the forests of homes men built next to one another. I loved the wide spaces, the river rolling below me, and the distant bluffs beyond.

Trees grew thick at the edge of the crest in front of us and in ravines to the north and south. Nick contrasted the elms, ashes, hickories, an occasional sassafras and a red bud.

"Do you know every tree in the midlands, Uncle Nick?" I asked in amazement.

"All but one," he said, as matter of factly as if he were commenting on the quality of a pelt. "There is a little tree in *Prairie des Noyers* west of here. All the rest are walnuts. The odd one's shaped like a basswood. About ten years old. The leaves are like an elm, except that they turn bright red in the early autumn, and stay that way for about six weeks."

My uncle seemed more perplexed that he did not know this one tree, than proud that he knew all the rest.

We scouted the woods nearby until we found two small sugar maples. We dug the saplings and carried them in an old deerskin. When we set the first tree in place, three boys from a little farming settlement of Louisbourg, a few miles to the south, rode by. They were headed for Saint Louis. Nick recognized the young fellows from earlier years at Kaskaskia.

"It's nice to see a person from Saint Louis planting something once in a while," one of the newcomers said.

"Our friends from 'Empty Pockets,'" Nick said. "Everybody has empty pockets down there."

"Well, you 'Scanty Bread' folks ought not complain," the farm boy retorted. "You're so busy making money in the fur trade, you're short of bread all the time."

"That's unfortunately true," Nick said. "We need you fellows."

"We'll go back to *Vide Pôche*, as you call our place," the farm boy said. "We'll plant our crops so you in *Pain Court* can have something to eat next winter. But in the meantime, while you've got a few dollars in your pockets from this fur trading business, how about a few pieces of Spanish silver for a glass of wine?"

"We'll make a deal," Nick said. "You bring us a load of fertilizer tomorrow. We'll give you the silver today. We're going to put in cedars for a wind-break."

"Fair enough. We'll have the wine today. You'll have the fertilizer for your trees tomorrow."

The first company of boatmen came down from Canada early in the spring of 1768. Nick, Artime, and I were working near Laclede's warehouse. Suddenly Artime said, "This morning the Mississippi looks prettier than a picture of the English Channel from the French coast."

I looked up from my work, and saw the reason. Nick joined the two of us as we hurried to the riverbank.

A flotilla had come down from the north. The dockhands were less loud than usual, and much less profane. As Artime, Nick, and I approached the docks, we recognized several voyageurs. Greetings were warm.

"Remember Pierre Gibault?" one of the boatmen said. "He used to trade on the upper areas of the Lakes during the summer."

"I remember the name Pierre Gibault," Artime whispered to me. "A Canadien. He worked in the area above Mackinac. That was about ten years ago. I never met him."

"He entered the seminary and has been ordained a priest in the meantime," the voyageur went on. "Bishop Briand appointed him Vicar General of the whole Illinois country. He's planning on taking up residence in Kaskaskia."

"Good! Good! Good!" Artime said.

"Welcome, Father Gibault," I said, as the priest stepped on the bank. "This is Artime Thomure, Nick Soumande, and I'm Hugh Roe O'Rome. We're all originally from Prairie du Rocher down the river a bit, near Kaskaskia."

"Good-day, gentlemen," Father Gibault said warmly. "It's good to see you." Then turning to the older lady in the large pirogue, "Mother, may I present some members of my scattered flock." As he spoke, he helped his mother from the vessel.

Pierre Gibault moved gracefully from the pirogue to the wharf. While not thick-set, like most of the voyageurs, his wiry frame indicated that his seminary years had not lessened the tone of his muscles. His face carried no inspiration, his features were plain. He did not have the air of distinction and command I had sensed immediately in Pierre Laclede. Nor did I think he had a noticeably spiritual look. Suddenly the thought struck me that Uncle Nick had a more religious cast to his countenance.

Had I not known beforehand that he was a missionary, I am not sure that I would have recognized him as the curé. Certainly he did not have the priestly mien of old Father Meurin. Maybe it was a matter of age, and such an appearance would come in time, no doubt. For the moment he could move more easily among the voyageurs than old Father Meurin had been able to do. What kind of missionary he would make we could only wait and see — and help him in his task.

In the meantime, several of the men were helping an attractive young lady out of the pirogue. Father Gibault turned to them and said, "This is my sister, Marie Louise."

"Good, good, good," Artime said. "Welcome to our beautiful village."

"She's done more to beautify this place in four minutes than we've been able to do in four years," I responded.

"There's no problem in this country that a hundred pretty girls couldn't solve," Artime said.

During the next year, Pontiac, chief of the Ottawa, came to visit his friend St. Ange. A man whose name brought fear to fortified towns on the English frontier from Maine to the Carolinas received a welcome in the unwalled French village of Saint Louis.

When Nick heard of Pontiac's arrival, he said: "He was with us at the Monongahela, but I'm not sure which one he was. He wasn't famous then."

"My father said Pontiac would have destroyed all the British posts in the Northwest in 1763," I said, "if someone had not warned the commandant at Detroit."

"Pontiac was like your father. Kill the British! Spare the French! Those were his rules."

I laughed. "An uncomplicated view. We have a harder task — to choose between good British and bad British."

"Your father thought the only good Englishman was a dead Englishman!"

Nick and I went over to St. Ange's dwelling. At first glance, Pontiac was a disappointment. He was not the tall, strong man my father had spoken about, but a toothless panther, pressed by confusing forces, retreating, beaten. A weary look was in his eye, the look of a man who had tried to end his sorrows by strong drink. He seemed happy to be among friends. When St. Ange introduced me, the old chief looked up and smiled. He said something in the Ottawa tongue. His first words made St. Ange laugh, and then he nodded in admiration.

St. Ange translated: "When I described your father, the chief said seriously: 'I know the one — the British-hater!' Then he brightened up, and went on. 'A great warrior; he never missed a shot, or touched a woman.' "

In the reaction of the group, I noticed once again the awe the French held for my father.

Pontiac spoke on. St. Ange translated. "The chief said that your father was with him a long time. He died as he lived, a brave man."

Then Pontiac spoke at length. St. Ange turned sadly to the entire group. "The chief wants to visit his friends in Cahokia. I'm trying to dissuade him. He should stay away from the English, but he intends to go."

Pontiac spoke reassuringly. St. Ange translated, "He says, 'My French friends there will take care of me!' "

St. Ange sadly shook his head, "They may not be able to do so."

St. Ange proved right. A few days later I heard the story. Pontiac and his friends in Cahokia had celebrated together. While the French could hold their wine, he could not. As he staggered around, unable to defend himself, a local Indian, bribed by a British trader, had killed him.

St. Ange sent a contingent of men across the river. The next day they brought back the body of the great chief. Nick and I stood beside the Mississippi. With full military ceremonial, St. Ange laid to rest a great hero of the French and Indian Wars.

The days grew ominous in 1770 — I was almost 21 by that time — as the rumors came that a Spanish force was moving up the river. Many of our young men moved out on the rivers so that they would not have to be at hand when the Spaniards came. General Alessandro O'Reilly had moved into New Orleans with a force of 2,000 men and dealt drastically with those French who had opposed the early Spanish leaders. In Saint Louis, the Papins and the Chauvins felt a great unease, since their relatives in New Orleans had openly defied Governor Antonio de Ulloa and suffered severely.

The next rumors claimed that Captain Pedro Piernas would become Lieutenant Governor of Upper Louisiana with headquarters in Saint Louis. He had gone up to the mouth of the Missouri the year before, then stopped at Saint Louis on the way back. He had conferred with St. Ange. The old Canadien thought Piernas took himself too seriously. So did one of the Indians who shot at the Spanish captain because he wasn't French. Fortunately for Piernas, the Indian missed.

Piernas arrived in Saint Louis on the 20th of May with a troop of soldiers. We villagers gathered in the *Place d'Armes,* wondering what lay ahead. At first I thought the Spanish official a bit haughty. Then I realized he was more scared than we were. After all, we had enough men to drown him and his small troop of Spaniards in the Mississippi; and further, all the Indians within hundreds of miles were allied with us. If we threw Piernas out, as the Louisianans had expelled Ulloa, retaliation would not be easy. O'Reilly could transport two thousand men by ships to New Orleans from Havana. To come as far as Saint Louis with any kind of effective force would prove a far more difficult task.

Piernas escorted his wife from the boat. Then I saw that he was in reality hiding behind her. He left his soldiers drawn up in line at the bank of the river. It looked as if he hoped to make his coming seem like a formal visitation, not like a military conquest.

When he saw the women and children gather in the open space, he obviously relaxed. He was almost pleasant when he read a proclamation in Spanish. He covered the administration of justice, attitudes towards the Indians — at least that's what I thought he said.

Some of the Spanish words sounded like Latin. I still remembered a little of the Latin Father Meurin had taught me.

Finally, with a sigh, Piernas reached the end of his proclamation. Gallantly, he presented his wife.

"*Mes amis,*" she said, melting the tension. In fluent French, she went on, "You have made the coming of my husband and myself a most happy event." Madame Piernas smiled. "The Lieutenant Governor knows you have been loyal subjects of Louis, *Roi de France.* He hopes you will find Louis' ally, *Rey Carlos Tercio,* an equally benign monarch."

The townspeople, hitherto silent, broke into applause.

Piernas spoke to St. Ange through an interpreter. He seemed to be making a request of St. Ange. The old Canadien declined, then countered with a request of his own. Piernas reflected a moment, then solemnly agreed. "*Si! Si! mi Capitain,*" he said.

St. Ange turned to the townspeople. "Lieutenant Governor Piernas has asked me to accept a commission as captain in the Spanish army. I declined this honor. Then I asked that he approve our existing land titles. This he has done insofar as his authority goes."

The men applauded again. Piernas dismissed the troops. The ladies gathered around Madame Piernas. Madame Chouteau, the mother of Auguste, and the only woman in the village from New Orleans, offered the hospitality of her home. Madame Piernas accepted.

Saint Louis seemed to have surmounted a second hurdle, but I knew that nothing would be permanent until once again a united land stretched along the wide river.

Not long afterward, Nick and I had to return to Prairie du Rocher for a sad event that we had long anticipated, Grandpere Soumande's funeral. Before we left, Laclede offered his condolences and had a message for Father Gibault: "Tell him to come up and dedicate the church of Saint Louis IX."

On the 24th day of June, 1770, Father Gibault arrived in Saint Louis. He blessed the first church in the city of the King — a hastily-built structure of upright logs, with a *pierrotage*, a melange of clay, straw, and gravel casually thrown between. I wondered if it would keep out the cold. Perhaps the priest wouldn't come in winter.

The villagers were happy that the six years without Mass were over. They were grateful to Lieutenant Governor Piernas for ordering the construction of the church. All the ladies of the town came. Most of the men, too, felt that six years had been a long time since they had been to church. It was a busy time for Father Gibault.

"The way he writes every detail so carefully in the parish records," I said, "it's going to take him the entire winter to describe the baptisms and marriages of the past few days."

"It gives him an excuse to stay longer," Nick said, "hear more confessions, counsel more people. He has an unusual work to do, he believes. In France, and even in Canada, the church is part of the community life, like the maple trees on the side of the street. People go on Sunday not simply because they like church, but because everybody does."

"With no church for six years," I said, "that hasn't been the case here."

"No!" Nick went on. "Here we have to be religious because we realize we ought to serve God. Father Gibault knows that. He claims that he's building an entirely new religious outlook — a religion not of routines, but of personal concern."

"If his other visits are as busy as this one," I concluded, "he may do just that."

If Father Gibault had a big day in Saint Louis in June, he had another gala day in Kaskaskia on the eleventh day of September. He celebrated the wedding Mass of his sister Marie Louise and one of his parishioners.

After the wedding I learned that the Eighteenth Royal Irish regiment had replaced the kilted devils of the Black Watch at Fort Chartres. Since Catholic chaplains in the British army were as rare as Presbyterian ministers in the Roman Curia, Catholics stationed at the fort came to Kaskaskia occasionally for Sunday Mass.

One Sunday, I walked up to one of the Irish soldiers. Feigning a haughty air on the spur of the moment, I said, "My name is Hugh."

The soldier looked back equally defiant. He said, surprisingly, "My name is Hugh."

"My name is Hugh *Roe*."

The soldier squared his jaw. "*My* name is Hugh Roe."

I stuck my jaw out a little farther and said, "My name is Hugh Roe *O'Rome*."

"My name is Hugh Roe *O'Neill*." The soldier offered his hand. "You're the first Hugh Roe I ever met who wasn't an O'Neill. What are you doing way out here?"

"First, what are *you* doing in the British service?"

"I asked before you," O'Neill said. "I should get first answer."

"All right," I said. "I was born here. My father was chased out of Ireland years ago. My mother was born near Fort Chartres. I've been living here or working on the river ever since. If my father knew one of you fellows fought with the British army, he'd shoot you on sight. He probably shot more Britishers than anybody but Pontiac himself. He fought at Fontenoy, on the Monongahela, at Ticonderoga, at Quebec, yes in every battle the French had against the English from the time he left Ireland until he died in the Pontiac War."

"I'd like to fight them myself," O'Neill said.

"Well, why did you ever join the British service?"

"It was the only way I had of getting out of Ireland," O'Neill came back. "I'll serve a little time over here, and when the opportunity comes, I'll just get lost somewhere. That's the way it is with most of these men. The British service was our one way of getting out of Ireland. We didn't have any money."

Just then Eileen came up. I said to O'Neill, "This is my sister, Eileen." O'Neill said something in English. Eileen responded in French. There was no need for me to translate. They were oblivious of my presence by that time, so I discretely backed away.

While I scarcely noticed it, my sister had grown into a tall, nimble girl of seventeen with a lovely face and long blond hair. When she made up her mind, the willowy one could become an oak.

Six months later, I ran into O'Neill again. He had obviously learned a lot of French in the meantime. "Eileen and I went up to see Father Meurin," O'Neill said. "He knew I had a fine plan. I figured some night I'd just desert and cross the river to the other side and forget about Britain and all her works and pomps. Eileen thought it was a good idea. You know it's a good idea."

"It *is* a good idea," I said.

"But Father Meurin answered: 'The test of love is time and

distance, you understand. You serve this year out, you understand, even though they move the regiment to some other place; and then when the year's over, you come back. And if you do, then we'll know you're worthy of marrying Eileen O'Rome, you understand.' "

"Do you understand?" I said with a laugh.

"Yes, I understand," O'Neill said.

A short time later, I heard that O'Neill had disappeared in the river while on duty one dark night. His Irish comrades keenly lamented his sad departure. They only winked at each other when Father Meurin suggested a memorial Mass.

The following summer O'Neill sent Eileen a message from Ste. Genevieve. He had slipped across the river to Spanish territory, gone south to enter business in New Orleans, and had come back to win Father Meurin's approval. The old missionary had the wedding Mass in Ste. Genevieve. In giving away the bride, I felt much older than twenty-one. A few of O'Neill's Irish comrades from Fort Chartres got an assignment to patrol the river that day, and — "the saints be praised!" — as they said, the current was so treacherous it carried them to the wrong side of the stream. They reached Ste. Genevieve late for the Mass but in time for other festivities. During the afternoon, my other little sister, seventeen year-old bouncy and resourceful little Bernadette told Father Meurin that she wanted to get married, too. But she came back to me and said in disappointment: "Michel Levasseur and I went to see Father Meurin. Father asked what Michel did. Michel said he helped his father and brothers on their farm but planned to be a fur trader on the river. 'You go and work on the river for a year,' Father said. 'When you come back with a little money in your pocket, if your relatives have no objections, ask me again. I'll probably say yes, you understand. The test of love is time and distance.' "

Prairie du Chien, a favorite rendezvous of the upriver tribes, stood in British territory, on the east bank of the Mississippi, just above the mouth of the Wisconsin. Nick was in charge of a September trip to the Sioux Country northwest of the village.

Eighteen voyageurs would travel in two large pirogues. Nick and I would paddle our small canoe. We would push ahead, visit the town to appraise the possibilities. The other men with the slower moving supply-laden vessels would hide in a prearranged place below the town on the west bank. If it seemed safe to proceed, we would go on up to the land of the Sioux and see how prospects looked for trade.

We pushed off from Saint Louis in the beautiful fall of the year. We clung to the east bank as far as the mouth of the Missouri, then swung out for a short distance to view the curving line that divided the brown muddy waters of the Missouri from the deep green of the Mississippi. It was surprising how different the wide river was above the mouth of the Missouri. The ashes and hickories were already bright and clear in the warm afternoon sun as we moved under the tall bluffs on the east bank between the mouth of the Big Muddy and the junction with the Illinois.

"Your father was like the Missouri," Nick began, "wild, unpredictable, untamed. But his wildness was not malicious, simply the result of inexhaustible energy. Even when he did a wrong thing, it was, as Father Meurin said, an *unwise*, not an *unkind* thing. Fury against the British drove him relentlessly on."

The canoe moved by the quiet waters of the Illinois. "And you, my nephew," Nick continued, "are like the peaceful Illinois, rarely roaring over its banks, serving the lands it drains, serene, quiet, unspectacular; but underneath a strong current flows. You will do less violently what your father gave his life to do. He held his mind on the obstacles as he saw them — namely, the British. You will keep your eye on the goal to be accomplished — one free land along the wide river."

At the moment, I did not think of the things Nick said about my father or myself. I thought of Uncle Nick; and thought in my uncle's terms. That lovable man was like the mighty Mississippi, always conscious where he was going, pushing his relentless way, gathering all to himself in his great capacity for acceptance. Nick kept his spirit on the straight path as relentlessly as the wide river rolled on to the gulf.

During the next days, the oaks had begun to turn, the air seemed clearer, the land had a rich appearance, and the bluffs on either side of the river rose a little higher to perhaps three of four hundred feet. On top of the bluffs I knew that the fertile uplands reached to both horizons. The river swung back and forth across the four-mile-wide bottomland, so that in the late afternoon the sun came first over my left shoulder and then my right shoulder in a continuous reversal.

On the sixth day, Nick paddled in the bow, both to give me experience and provide variety. As I watched his thick arms send the canoe rapidly forward, I realized suddenly that I would never be such a strong man. When I was younger and growing tall, people had often remarked: "You'll be a big man like your father." I had hoped for great physical strength such as my father and Uncle Nick possessed. Gradually, however, I had reconciled myself to the fact that I would never fill out through the chest as they had, but remain lean; that physically I would not be a giant but an average man; that I would not have strong muscles, but lithe, usable, and, I hoped, tough and tireless ones. I thanked *le bon Dieu* for that.

Ever since I could remember, boys my age would challenge me in short races or long races, in swimming across the slough, in throwing rocks out into the Mississippi. A group of us would be walking along, anticipating a swim in the Mississippi. Someone would shout: "I can beat the rest of you to that cottonwood," and we would take off. I would finish about fourth in a group of ten or twelve. It would be the same in a short run or a long run. In a swimming race, too, I would always finish just behind the leaders. Or when we tried to see who could throw a rock the farthest into the river from the top of the bluff. Two of the boys got into a fight over who threw the farthest. I wasn't in the fight, because my rock fell far short. There was one thing I did before any of the others, and I kept my championship through several summers. I was the first to skip rocks on the water of the slough and land them on the other side. It had been a great feat when I first did it. For an entire summer no one else succeeded. Uncle Nick had taught me the trick.

"Winning means something," he had said, "but not everything." So I grew up, trying to win at everything, but acknowledging sometimes reluctantly that others were stronger and faster than I was. One other thing he had insisted upon. At first, I tried too many things, with a new idea every day. I also finished too few. Nick wanted me to carry every project through to the end.

Had he not taught me this, I might have stopped my English study once my father had gone. I kept reading Shakespeare and talking simple sentences to the little girls. Eileen really couldn't be bothered until she met O'Neill. It was a game with Bernadette.

As my thoughts wandered on, the current drove a little stronger against our canoe, and I became aware of the Mississippi again. The wide river always made me think. Especially when I was with Uncle Nick. On the few occasions I had been in a canoe with Artime, talk and laughter never stopped. Nick was more reflective. His steady stroking seemed to blend with the waters, so that we were a part of it, even when going against the current.

Late one evening we came to a place where high bluffs on both sides seemed to almost touch one another. As we drove through this gap, a new stream came in from the east, its waters darkened by tamarack bark. This was the Wisconsin. Countless French and Indians had moved down it through the years. Here, the legends told, Father Marquette and Louis Joliet had entered the Father of Waters one hundred years before.

A short distance above this junction, a large tree-filled island divided the river into a wide west channel that ran under beautiful bluffs and a narrow east branch that looped like a bow in the middle of a flat valley. At the easternmost point of this bow, surrounded by rich farm land, stood Prairie du Chien.

Had it been built in one of the narrow *coulees* on the west bank, I thought, it would have seemed a gem. Actually, it stood in a more practical but less beautiful position. Like a comely lady with ungainly ankles, Prairie du Chien had one unpleasant aspect. All along the waterfront stretched the run-down shacks of fishermen and traders. Even though the fall woods were dressed like Sioux braves in war-paint and feathers, the prospect was not appealing as Nick and I beached our canoes in Prairie du Chien.

"*Bienvenu*! Prairie du Chien, our town, beautiful, she is," said one of the traders.

"*Merci, mon ami*," I said in surprise. I had never before met a trader who seemed to care what his village or anything else looked like.

"Ah! Yes!" the trader came back, sensing our lack of appreciation. "You saw the town coming up the river. The island out there spoils the view. If you wish to see Prairie du Chien at its best, walk out to the ridge east of town, and look down upon our city. Beautiful, you will then see it is. But be careful. There is an epidemic here."

"Maybe he's right," Nick said, ignoring the warning and thinking only of the beauty of the place. "Prairie du Rocher does not look its best from the floor of the valley. Every time we climb the bluff, I fall in love with the place all over again. It would probably be the same with Prairie du Chien."

Our seemingly casual visit to the town soon revealed what we had come to find out. The British fur traders were working in the lake country above the upper reaches of the Mississippi. If we went to the Sioux villages along the Minnesota River several hundred miles above Prairie du Chien and to the west, we would not meet rivalry or opposition.

Nick and I paid little attention at first to the epidemic that had struck the town several weeks before. We had never been sick, in spite of many epidemics. We had heard that it did not lead to death, but to a long period of weakness. That's for someone else, I thought. I was wrong.

The next day an intense fever gripped me and held on for two days. I lay in a makeshift bunk-room next to a dank warehouse. Used for storing peltries, it stood down near the river.

On the second day, a young woman of the town came in. "I'm Rosellen Rien," she said.

"I'm Hugh Roe O'Rome," I responded mechanically. The illness left me dazed.

She felt my brow. "The fever will probably leave in another twenty-four hours," she said brightly. "I've brought you a little broth."

"Thank you," I said. I took the warm bowl. When I had finished it, I felt better, but drowsier.

"Is there anything else I could do?"

"Yes," I said dreamily. "You could just stand there and let me look at your bright face for a few minutes."

She blushed, smiled shyly — and left.

Two days later she came again. The fever had subsided, but my strength had also ebbed. I noticed that my vague, initial impression was correct. She was an attractive young woman, about my own age, tall, well-formed, with brown hair and pleasant eyes.

"How's my favorite patient today?" she asked.

"If you're talking about me, I'm fine," I said. "Tired but fine. How is my favorite nurse?"

"Tired, too, but not fine. Right now I'm discouraged. More people are getting sick every day. You're the only one who has an appreciative word."

She did not feel my brow, but stood looking at me. The faint smell of lilacs overcame the rank odors of the warehouse.

"Could you stay for a few minutes?" I said.

She sat down on a rough bench and began to talk. I said little in return, and was hardly conscious of what we talked about. Suddenly two hours had gone by, and she had to leave.

Abruptly I realized once again that I was in a dank, dark room!

When Nick came that evening, I urged him to push on to the Sioux country and pick me up on the way back.

"I will," Nick responded, "if I can find some family to take care of you until I return."

The next morning Nick reported that an old couple, the Cardinals, were happy to make a little extra money by providing food and lodging for the sick voyageur. He took me to their home and moved north.

Slow days trudged on. I woke in the morning. I had my breakfast. Too tired to do anything, I lay down and fell asleep until it was time to eat again. I went back to bed until supper and still had no trouble sleeping at night.

A week went by. I began to wonder whether I would ever get my strength back. Depression gripped me. I tried to counteract my feeling of hopelessness by keeping busy. I could do little. I tried to chop kindling for the coming winter; but I lacked the strength. I went out to gather hickory nuts but scarcely had energy even for that.

Rosellen came by briefly one afternoon. "I see that you are getting along much better," she began with a smile.

"Yes, thank you," I responded.

"You're in good hands now," she said. "I wish I could stay, but there are so many other patients to help."

I wished she could stay, too. I consoled myself by casually asking Mrs. Cardinal about her.

Mrs. Cardinal's answer was matter-of-fact. "Rosellen's father was a Scotch trader from Mackinac who died on an expedition. When she was fifteen she married a voyageur named Rien."

What little spirit I had left almost died at that moment.

"Rien is always on the waterways, rarely home," Mrs. Cardinal went on. "They have no children. She has been wearing herself out lately taking care of the sick."

A few days after that, Nick and his party returned from the North. Trade with the Sioux had been good. I was still too weak for normal travel. I couldn't bear my share with the paddle and other chores, but the brief though brilliant fall along the Wisconsin had come and gone, like a tanager winging its way south. The cold wind and gray damp skies of November were close at hand.

Nick simply said, "We'll have to get you out of here."

I said goodbye to the Cardinals, and left a note, thanking Rosellen for her kindness.

The return journey was not easy. Most of the way downstream, I lay full length on a pack of pelts in the middle of a large pirogue. Nick tied our little canoe, now filled with furs, to the rear. He did the work of two men to make up for my inability to bear my share of duties. We stayed well ahead of threatening weather, but the nights grew steadily colder.

As we approached Saint Louis, the moon stood high over the wide river, a huge coin of Spanish silver, lucent and tranquil. The fatigue of the long voyage on the Mississippi fell from me like the sloughed-off skin of a water snake. I thought I would never want to travel again — a thought that did not last long.

One day in early spring, 1772, a group of traders who had come down from Michilimackimac brought a letter from Prairie du Chien. I was surprised at receiving it. The message was in English.

I opened and read:

Dear Mr. O'Rome,

Mrs. Cardinal gave me your kind message of gratitude for the little help I was able to give you while you were in Prairie du Chien. It was sad to think that your short visit with us had to be made so difficult by your illness.

Perhaps I am selfish for saying this, but had you not been ill, I probably would not have had the pleasure of meeting you. God was good to me, and I am happy that I had this opportunity to meet you.

> *Your humble servant,*
> *Rosellen Rien*

I was baffled. I had done nothing but listen patiently to the young woman. I had been, in fact, too stupefied to say much I could remember in return, or even to remember what she said. She, not I, had been the kind and thoughtful one.

I remembered that Mrs. Cardinal had spoken of Rosellen as Mrs. Rien. Rosellen had never mentioned her husband. There was no future in intruding into another's family. Then I thought: *Her husband probably doesn't understand English anyway, and my letter will only be an acknowledgment.* So I took pen and paper and wrote:

Dear Mrs. Rien:

It was kind of Mrs. Cardinal to extend to you my gratitude for your kindness when I was in Prairie du Chien.

I deeply appreciate your letter and will try to be in some small way what you mistakenly think I am.

My best wishes for a Happy Easter.

> *Your humble servant,*
> *Hugh Roe O'Rome*

I presumed that this letter would conclude the correspondence. I was wrong. A second letter came with the fall flotilla. I went to the small room that Nick and I had rented the previous summer in the stone house next to Laclede's headquarters. I read Rosellen's letter.

Dear Mr. O'Rome,

Your nice letter at Easter time was most welcome. It made the day a more pleasant one. I have thought of you many times and hope you are feeling well again.

It is so nice to have known someone like you and thus be able to drum up strength from the fact of knowing there really are people like yourself. You live in the wild world of the frontier, and yet seem utterly untouched by its evil and brutality.

I must go now to help Mrs. Cardinal who is sick. We have had severe weather, and there are almost as many ill now as there were during the days of your convalescence.

I leave you now with my very best wishes. Say a little prayer for

Rosellen Rein

I sat down immediately and penned an answer. Traders were moving north, and there could be no delay.

Dear Rosellen,

Your letter arrived in St. Louis today. It helped make the day an enjoyable one. Since traders are moving north this evening, and I myself will set off on an expedition up the Osage tomorrow morning, I had better write immediately. We will winter among the Indians.

You were so kind to me, a sick stranger, that I hesitate to suggest that you do not overwork yourself in helping the others in the epidemic. But I must say so. Do not overtax your strength.

I hope Mrs. Cardinal is feeling better by this time. And, by the way, please give her and Mr. Cardinal my good wishes. I remember them gratefully.

With all good wishes, I am,

Your humble servant,
Hugh Roe O'Rome

The trip among the Osages proved noteworthy for only one reason. It was Michel's second and last. He had gone earlier in the year with a group of men he had not previously known. On this journey, he joined friends, and soon-to-be relatives. He shared a canoe with Artime. Even that jovial companion did not make a riverman out of him.

"I'm a bottom-land farmer, I guess," he said one night as we sat around a camp fire. "That's all there is to it."

Nick looked at the short, thick-set, energetic young fellow. "Each man must do what he's made to do," Nick said. "You gave the river a try. It's not your line. You can farm the old Soumande homestead, and any acres that your father gives you."

"Thank you, Uncle Nick," he said.

"When's the wedding going to be?" I asked.

"In late October," Michel answered, "if Father Meurin's willing.

Bernadette's sewing a new wedding dress because her mother's won't fit her."

"If it fit Eileen, it certainly wouldn't fit Bernadette," I said. "One's a blond willow. The other a dark maple."

"Maples are my type," Michel said. He walked to the river edge.

"A mere liking to farm is not enough to make a good habitant," Nick said. "Michel's got more than that."

We leaned back against a large driftwood log and watched the smoldering embers of our fire. Darkness came slowly.

"Sure, a man has to like to farm," Nick went on. "But there's more. He's got to like a steady, day-to-day unchanging life. All life is dull. Some tasks, like ours, give us a change of pace and scenery."

"Maybe that's why men like to go to war," I said. "It puts a little variety into their lives."

"War's like our work. Travel and dull waiting. Then a burst of excitement. Then travel and tedium again. The habitant never has the burst of excitement."

He threw a few twigs on the fire, then went on: "A habitant has to be able to put up with the routines of a little village. He lives so close to a group of people, he has to get along with all of them. Above all, he has to be a one-woman man. I don't know whether some voyageurs take Indian girls because they can't live without their wives, or whether they get away from their wives to take Indian girls."

"Uncle Nick, they seem to live in two totally separated worlds. They have one woman in one place, another in the Indian village. Their entire lives differ in each locality."

"Your father was a notable exception," Nick went on. "He hated the humdrum life of the farm. He needed excitement and action. Though he might have denied this, I think he would have been fighting all his life, even if there were no British."

"That's probably true." I smiled.

"Your father never looked at any other woman than your mother. You remember what Pontiac said of him! I recall when I was a boy. Your father asked *Grandpere* if he could marry Rose. *Grandpere* asked if Brendan could stay still on a farm. Your father answered that he would try. *Grandpere* was not convinced, and asked several other questions. Finally your father blurted out, 'I have never touched another woman, and I never will. It's Anne Soumande for me — or nobody!' That convinced *Grandpere*."

"Michel seems to have that quality my father had," I said, "and the others, too, needed to be a habitant."

"He's a good fellow, stubby and steady," Nick said. "Nothing will down him. His father was a good farmer and so was his *grandpere*. He had a little taste of the river and that was enough."

"He and Bernadette will make a fine team," I had to admit. "This time Father Meurin will probably say yes."

"Talking about Father Meurin," Artime broke in, "you sound more like him every day, Nick."

"That could be a great compliment," I said, "or simply an indication that Artime has not heard Father Meurin give a sermon in a long time."

Nick looked thoughtfully from me to Artime, but said nothing.

Father Meurin set October eleventh, a Saturday, as the date for Michel and Bernadette's wedding. By that time I had become accustomed to giving away brides. There was one sad note. Our *grandmere* was too sick to attend the wedding. She died a few weeks later.

When I returned from Prairie du Rocher, after *Grandmere* Soumande's funeral, another letter from the North awaited me.

Dear Hugh Roe,

Your letter arrived yesterday — the most pleasant surprise I've had in such a long time. I really was delighted.

Life in Prairie du Chien is dull, while you go off among the wild tribes of the Missouri, undaunted by the fact that those Indians would just as soon scalp you as talk to you. It leaves me worried. I pray everyday to le bon Dieu — *how I love that French expression — that He keep you in His loving care.*

I do hope you will be in St. Louis for the Christmas holidays. I know how enjoyable Christmas can be in a French village. What a contrast with the drab season I knew as a little girl in Scotland.

I fear that my prayers mean little. But I shall be asking that your New Year be filled with peace, good health, and much happiness.

> *Christmas joy to you,*
> *Rosellen*

Christmas was joyful. Rosellen's good wishes helped to make it so. It made up for the things I missed from my boyhood in Prairie du Rocher, especially the *Revillon*, the gathering of relatives.

Was Rosellen coming to mean that much to me?

I reread her letter many times. Especially where she attributed bravery to me! I had never thought of going out among the Indians as a particularly brave action. To the French, trading with Indians was like visiting brothers.

Rosellen was a Scot. She probably shared the British attitude toward the Indians. At least she prayed to *le bon Dieu* for me. That showed good French influence.

On reflection, I realized that Rosellen was coming to mean much to me. Yet she was someone else's wife. I had to talk the entire matter over with someone. I thought of talking to Uncle Nick. But this was different. The best one would be Father Gibault.

I knew that Nick planned to ride down to the Old Mines country on business in early spring. We could circle into Ste. Genevieve. I heard that Father Gibault planned to remain in the old settlement until summer.

Father Gibault and five little boys were having target practice with bows and arrows when Nick and I rode into the tranquil town of Ste. Genevieve.

"The Ojibways are beating the Chippewas," the priest said, pointing to the smallest boys and himself.

"We made these bows out of willow. Later on, when the boys get older, we'll try ash. And when they get real good, we'll use the *bois d'arc*, the Osage Orange."

Then turning to the boys, he said, "Keep practicing, boys. *Le Pere* has business."

He dismissed them and turned to us. "When I'm on the east side of the river, I don't play with the youngsters any more. Your old friend Father Meurin wrote to the bishop that I play games with the young men, attend wedding festivities, lack taste for study, and drink with the best of them."

"That certainly covers a lot of territory," I said.

"With only two priests in a country four times as big as France, Father Meurin shouldn't waste time in such nonsense!"

"The good man is getting old," I remarked. "After all, here it is the spring of 1774. I thought he was old when I first served his Mass at the age of six back in 1755."

"Oh, I forgive him, of course. But that remark about drinking with the best of them! You know how some of those *voyageurs* can pour it down. They're out of my class."

I knew that Father Gibault liked a glass of wine. I also knew he set reasonable limits and rarely overstepped them. As a young man, he had been proud of his wrestling skill. No one his own size could throw him. After all, few voyageurs became priests.

"What brings you two to the Quebec of the West?" Father Gibault asked. "I'm sure it's good to get into a city once in a while."

"Be careful, Father," Nick came back. "Ste. Genevieve won't be any bigger two centuries from now. Saint Louis will grow. Trading and location will determine that."

"Here we have people with deep roots," Father Gibault answered. "You're floating logs up there, trappers and traders who never stay put." Then going back to his original subject, the priest asked again, "What brings you to Ste. Genevieve?"

"I have something to talk to you about, Father," I remarked.

Nick rode on down the street as I continued: "A girl up North." I paused, reflecting, "We're always told that all cases are much alike. I'll let you judge that. My lady love is a phantom. I met her when I was sick in Prairie du Chien, and she took care of me. Now she writes me as regularly as mail comes down the river. I'm surprised how often it does."

"Mail gets through on the river more surely than anyone would expect," Father Gibault said. "I get letters regularly from my Bishop in Canada. He finds me a constant source of worry."

We sat down under an elm whose lace-like branches almost reached the ground and shaded us from the warming sun.

"I wrote several noncommittal letters back to the girl," I continued.

"Are you sure they were noncommittal?" Father Gibault asked. He gestured with his left hand. "Maybe they seemed so to you — but perhaps not to her. Go on."

"I have a general idea that Rosellen Rien is a friendly, attractive young woman," I said. "But really I don't have a clear picture as to what she looks like, except that she's tall, and slender, with light brown hair. I was so sick in Prairie du Chien I hardly knew what was going on. I clearly remember hearing the lady at whose house I was staying, say that Rosellen was born in Scotland and came into the church just before her wedding. About her husband — he wasn't around while I was in Prairie du Chien. She never mentions him in her letters." I stopped abruptly.

"Now you want to know whether you can continue to write friendly letters to this lovely lady," Father Gibault said. He flipped through the pages of his breviary.

"That might be a dangerous thing," the priest suggested, "or it might not be at all. It depends on lots of things. On what kind of fellow her husband is. He probably doesn't understand English and might care less. Or he might care a lot, precisely because he doesn't understand English. After all, you and she may be the only people in the whole Upper Louisiana who correspond in English.

"From what you say, this girl gets a certain amount of encouragement from your messages. You might be a daydream to her just as she is a phantom to you. Someone far off, who can't hurt the domestic scene, but can lift her off and dreaming, out of the humdrum events of every day."

"Her letters break the monotony of my life," I broke in, "just like an occasional rapids on an otherwise placid stream."

"Life is dull enough," Father Gibault said, "without closing off every path that might possibly lead to dangerous ground. You may write — but be careful. Remember: You can say things in one mood. A girl snow-bound a thousand miles north can read something deeper. Courtesy? Yes. Even chivalry — why be French if you can't be chivalrous? But affection? Never! Respect her marriage promises. If the slightest suggestion comes up that her husband resents this long distance friendship, cut it cleanly and immediately."

"I'll do that, Father," I stated without hesitation.

"May I say, young man," Father Gibault remarked, "that in all my years in the priesthood this has been about the most unusual, but at the same time most uncomplicated man-woman affair that has come to my attention. The annals of Mother Church record no instance of a child conceived by parents who never come closer than six hundred miles from each other. At least we don't have that worry." He paused, then with a smirk, concluded: "Her husband might someday decide to kill you. But that happens often on the frontier."

Following Father Gibault's advice, I wrote an informative but emotionally noncommittal letter.

Rosellen's response definitely was not. She began:

I was thrilled to get your letter. It made my whole life more pleasant. I keep comparing you with other people I know and have decided you are at the top.

She mustn't know many people, I said to myself, but still felt a glow at her words.

Our meeting was rather brief; yet through letters, you know more about me than the people I live with. It has been so nice to have someone like you with whom to share all my thoughts.

My husband and I are so terribly different. On the rare occasions when he's home from trading expeditions — and he has not been home now for over two years — he shows no interest in anything I do. He says that somebody else should take care of the sick. Most women have their own children or relatives to tend, and I have no one.

If I ask about his trading experiences, he answers bluntly, 'You take care of the house and I'll take care of the trading.' He says that I'm as 'cold as a pickerel and as unsentimental as a Scottish church meeting' — whatever that means.

How wrong he is! And how afraid I am that sometime I will lose my head. I so crave affection that it would be easy to fall down. Frankly, it is a good thing you are not close at hand now. I should be thankful, but it is hard to say so.

Having your friendship has been a great incentive for me. Take care, and for what it's worth, I send my love, Rosellen.

It was the first time in my life any girl had told me outright that she loved me.

For that reason I could not resist answering the same day. My message was warmer than previous letters. I remembered my promise to Father Gibault, however, and kept the wording vague.

I marvelled at many things about the wilderness, but nothing so much as the ease of mail moving along the waterways. I remembered that Father Gibault constantly received "letters of paternal guidance and solicitude," as he called them, from the Bishop in Canada.

Even at that, Rosellen's answer came far sooner than I had expected.

Dear Hugh Roe,

I'm feeling elated because your letter came today. So I must write to you before the enthusiasm subsides. I can think of two million things to talk about. I know you haven't time to read that much nonsense. So suppose I will discuss the more important items.

I have thought of you hundreds of times each day. You are wonderful, and I remain bewildered as to why, out of all the people in the world, I should be the lucky one to have your friendship. I know I don't deserve it, but I am happy to have it. You make life much easier.

My heart skips a beat, or does two in one (I haven't analyzed which) when I see a letter coming from Saint Louis.

With all my love,
Rosellen

I was not sure of myself then. Too few people in the world had time for kind words. This girl gave me more than I deserved — or could safely accept. I wished Father Gibault was at hand, but the priest had gone to Quebec to visit the Bishop. So I plunged intensely into my work with the fur company and tried to put Rosellen out of my mind. I did not succeed.

Father Gibault stopped at Saint Louis coming down the river in the fall of 1775. He'd been up to visit his Bishop in Canada. Normally talkative, he spoke endlessly now.

"The Bishop promised to send me several helpers a few years ago," Father Gibault began. "He hasn't anybody to send. Obviously nobody is coming. At the same time, he doesn't want to take me away. So he criticizes me a lot but leaves me here.

"He complained that I brought my mother and sister out here. Everybody here thinks it was a good idea. In fact, one of my parishioners thought it was a wonderful idea to bring my sister out. He's my brother-in-law now. Some other of my relatives have moved here.

"The Bishop was either telling me how badly I did my job or how tense the political situation was getting since the Quebec Act of last year. So I got him to talk on the British. Since Britain had defeated France in India and America, the Bishop said that the sun never set on the British Empire.

"I told him: 'That's right. God can't trust the British in the dark!' The Bishop didn't even smile," Father Gibault said in disgust. "The Bishop says I'm too giddy, but doesn't even laugh at my best jokes! What do you think of that?"

Without waiting for any comment from me, he went on: "The Bishop thinks the English on the Atlantic seacoast are going to revolt. I told him I thought the English were revolting all the time. Again no laugh from His Lordship. That's the British title for Bishop. The Virginians want the Canadians to revolt too. But in the meantime, other colonists say the opposite. One of the reasons they're revolting is that the King gave freedom of religion to the Canadians."

Father Gibault paused, but only to ponder his words. "As I see it," he went on, "the problem lies with the *Bostonnais*, those New Englanders. They're a bunch of Puritans and they're bitter against us Catholics. The Long Knives in Virginia don't care so much about the religious question. They want Canada in the revolt, too, but Bishop Briand is not going to allow it. I think he's going to excommunicate everybody who joins the American cause." He finally stopped.

"The Long Knives and the *Bostonnais* don't seem united," I said. "Having the same enemy sometimes makes strange friends. As for yourself, what do you plan to do?"

"Things can look a lot different way out here a thousand miles from Quebec. We shall see when the time comes."

"Do you think the colonies can beat Britain without Canadian help?"

"With Canada, it would be much easier," Father Gibault came back. "Then all the colonies would be against England and the British wouldn't have a foothold anywhere. By granting religious freedom and winning the Bishop's support, they have a good chance of holding Canada."

"By themselves, I don't know what the English colonies can do," the priest went on. "One possibility you always have to keep in mind: England can get involved in wider troubles. Suppose France and Spain should decide to fight England in revenge for those last defeats. Suppose France should declare war on the side of the colonies. How do you think our people would feel then? Do you think they would want to fight for Britain?"

Again he did not wait for an answer, but plunged on. "Sure I got my passport from Brigadier General Guy Carleton, the Lieutenant Governor and Commander-in-Chief of the Province of Quebec. So I recognized that he was the *de facto* commander up there. I never lost my allegiance to the King of France. How can the King of France suddenly make me a British subject? Ridiculous!

"I hardly got down here when Bishop Briand complained that I had a wedding Mass for a Frenchman and an Indian girl. British law forbids it. Well, I thought Catholics had a right to marry without having the permission of the British King. Who cares what Britain says? I certainly don't. I'm taking no oaths of loyalty to Great Britain."

"You and my father would have really hit it off," I said. "He hated Britain with a passion. He spent most of his life fighting Britain."

"Good for him," the priest said. "From what I have heard, he and I would have paddled a canoe well together. But I'm glad to have you as a friend. You look at things differently than others around here. I don't mention these matters to anyone else. And I know you don't tell them to others."

He stopped, then turned abruptly to the matter I really wanted to talk about. "Has the little lady up in Prairie du Chien gotten tired of writing?"

"No, she still writes regularly. In fact, each letter gets more affectionate."

"Do yours stay neutral?"

"At least I'm trying."

"In this matter, don't try. Do!"

If my love for Rosellen had been a confusing, seemingly dead-end canyon, it was nothing compared to the next one.

The people of Saint Louis celebrated the *Revillon* after midnight Mass on Christmas exactly as they had done in the Illinois settlements. *LaGuianne* on New Year's had developed slight variations. Instead of simply accepting a glass of wine at the homes they visited, the singers collected sugar, coffee, lard, flour, maple syrup, eggs, and poultry, for a grand ball to be celebrated on the Feast of the Epiphany, January the sixth. Nick and I were on hand for that celebration.

On the afternoon of the day, the ladies brought to the ballroom all the provisions gathered during *LaGuianne*. On this particular year it was at the new Martigny home, just south of Laclede's office. The girls of the town, under the careful supervision of a few matrons, made mounds of cookies. They baked a cake and hid four small vegetables in it.

The residence was spacious; yet by the time Nick and I arrived, even the veranda overflowed with guests. Fortunately, the evening was mild. All the men of the village and of the neighboring hamlets were there; some had come from as far away as Ste. Genevieve. Many voyageurs came, too, men who would have a short taste of the civilized life and then push back into the wilderness; men who would go for months without a glimpse of a bosom pushing against a tight blouse. This was the frontier where men always greatly outnumbered women. The night was a time to forget the loneliness of the plains and the mountains.

The clothing worn by both men and women far surpassed anything one might have expected in a frontier settlement. The reason was not simply that we were either rich or more vain than other people. It stemmed from two facts. The French government had forbidden weaving so that we had to purchase our cloth from the merchants who brought it up the river from the sea. I remembered that Father Meurin had told us in our history lesson that the French minister had introduced the silk industry into France in the days of King Henry IV over a hundred years before. In turn, we had grown so much wheat in the bottom lands along the Mississippi to ship south with our furs and peltries, the Illinois Country could always purchase fine cloth. With silks and satins to start with, the ladies of the villages showed their skill with the needle. The people of Cahokia preferred blue clothes. The other villages liked all colors, especially the bright ones.

Most of the women wore ankle length dresses of satin or taffeta and embroidered slippers with silver buckles, while the men wore silk breeches — most of them a bright red — fine linen shirts, silk stockings, soft-soled leather shoes, and dress coats of wool. Those older voyageurs who came to smoke and chat on the porch rather than to take part in the dance dressed in their regular costumes: shirts of wool, knee-length breeches, long wool stockings, moccasins, and brightly colored, tassled wool caps, long enough to pull down over their ears in severe weather.

The program began with the *minuet de la court*. Only the older married people could dance this formal opening number. Then the rest of us would have our chance.

I walked from the crowded porch to the equally filled hall. I had hardly entered the room when a beautiful girl walked towards me. Her hair was as dark as a raven's wing, her form perfect, her features of incredible beauty. I had never before seen anyone so lovely. She came towards me with a smile, "Hugh Roe, why have you waited so long to ask me to dance with you?"

"Well," I stammered, as she took me in her arms.

"You are one of the sweetest dancers," she said. "Yet you always avoid me. Is that nice?"

"No. It's nicer this way," I stammered.

"The last time I saw you at a dance," she said, "you wouldn't even look at me."

Where? When? Who was she? I had been to so few dances in my life. *How could I have missed this girl?*

She went right on as we whirled around the floor. "You wouldn't dance with anybody but my little cousin Therese Brunet at the Valle party in Ste. Genevieve. Of course, I was only eleven then, and I've grown a little in the meantime."

"You certainly have," I said, uttering my first coherent sentence. "You certainly have." I recalled the party and having danced with only one girl who did bear a slight resemblance to this one.

"My little cousin really loved you. But she let you get away. Had it been Marie Colette Brunet, you would never have gotten away." She drew herself a little closer to me.

The music stopped. We walked to the edge of the room. She still held my arm.

I had never before known the thrill of walking across a room with the most beautiful girl in the place. We basked in the envious gazes of everyone.

The music began again. I swung her to the far corner of the room. I tried to assay my wonderment. I had never met so lovely a girl. I was flattered by her friendliness. *Wasn't she perhaps too friendly?* I was glad when she resumed her conversation.

"Yes, Hugh Roe. Had I been Therese, I'd have never let you get away. She married a farm boy from Kaskaskia. Her folks just pushed her into it. She's making out all right. I'm happy. I wouldn't want you for a *cousin.*"

"O, that's nice of you to say that," I said warily. "I'd probably make a fine *brother.* An older brother to keep an eye on you."

"That's interesting. A lot of boys seem to keep their eyes on me." She laughed. "Just look around this room. The boys are all envious of you. And the girls everywhere look at me with eyes as green as maple leaves. People say Marie Colette is the prettiest girl in Spanish Illinois. While I don't believe in flattery unless it's true, I'll say that you are one of the best looking fellows in this whole area. Not the dashing Spanish officer type, like the captain I met at the last dance in Ste. Genevieve. A girl can't trust his type. He honey-talks me. If I wasn't there, he would be honey-talking someone else. You're my type — the steady, dependable, brotherly type. Though I don't exactly want you for a *brother.*"

We danced several more numbers. No other man came up to ask her. For my part I did not want to dance with anyone else. Sure, Marie Colette was over-friendly. But how often did a man float around a dance floor with the world's most beautiful girl half-limp in his arms?

I knew that I wasn't close to being the best looking fellow in the

Illinois country, but I wasn't the worst looking fellow either. I was probably a bit above average, as *Grandmere* used to say, with a much better than average smile.

At that moment the host announced that all should clear the center of the floor for the highlight of the ball — the cutting of the cake. Four servants carried the entire table, with the cake on top, into the middle of the room. The girls lined up to receive their slice.

"Aren't you going to get in line?" I asked.

"Why should I take a chance? The winners will get to dance with the boy of their choice. I have mine already." She pressed my hand.

The ceremony of the choosing of the queens began. Each girl received a slice of cake. Those unlucky ones who did not find a token in their slice tried to hide their disappointment as they walked to the side of the room. Then a shout went up. A blond girl had found a token and became the first queen. In the back of my mind, I automatically reflected that I did not particularly care for blondes. Brunettes had a warmth that appealed to me. I looked at Marie Colette. She edged up to me.

I leaned over to kiss her. She turned her face. "Not here," she said, but still held my hand. She led me to the rear *galerie*, now vacant, since all the guests had gone inside to witness the cutting of the cake.

I put my arm around her waist to draw her to me. Suddenly she broke from my grasp and ran down the steps toward a patch of lilac bushes in the enclosed yard. I caught her in the protective coverage of the thicket. I took her in my arms and kissed her hungrily. As I drew her close, the full length of her body pressed against mine, calling forth an irrepressible yearning.

Suddenly I felt her whole body quiver. It was not a trembling of desire, but of fright. She pushed me back with a fierce strength. "O Hugh! Please don't!" she whispered. Fear flooded her face, clearly visible even in the pale light of the moon coming through the lilac bushes.

I dropped my arms. "We had better go back to the hall," I said, as stricken with a sense of guilt now as she was with fear.

"That would be better," she said. We walked back up the steps. She adjusted her clothing, brushed her hair back from her eyes and reentered the hall.

I leaned against the rail of the galerie and tried to calm down.

Frustration and relief fought one another. Marie Colette had knowingly led me into the privacy of the lilacs — only to freeze in fear and leave my head throbbing. Then I thought of what Pontiac had said of my father — that he never touched a woman — and I felt a deep shame.

Finally I followed Marie Colette into the *grande salle* and stood beside her. The ceremony still went on. The last two girls found their tokens. I hardly paid any attention as they walked around choosing the young men. The four queens presented bouquets to the lucky young men and proclaimed them "kings." The happy eight had the dance floor to themselves for one number. The four kings then followed the custom of discussing among themselves the time and place for the Kings' Ball they would sponsor in the near future. They announced their decision — the same house on Saturday, February the third. The crowd applauded.

Suddenly Marie Colette slipped from my side and was absorbed in the crowd. I started to follow her, then noticed that Nick and a plantation owner from Ste. Genevieve walked toward me. I recognized the man — a prosperous, stolid, middle-aged habitant, who had occasionally come to Prairie du Rocher in the pre-British days.

"You remember Benet Fontelle," Nick said. "We used to do business with him on the old homestead."

"It's good to see you, young man," Benet said. "I might say frankly you're a much more reliable person than some of those Spanish officers my wife dances with on occasions." He paused. "Marie Colette loves to dance. I'm not much on the dance floor. So I bring her to these affairs so she can enjoy herself. She gets carried away sometimes, however. I hope she was not too forward."

"Your wife — Marie Colette." I blurted out. "She's the most beautiful girl — woman, I have ever seen."

Thank you, young man, Thank you," Benet said, "We married three years after my first wife died."

Nick tried to ease my embarrassment. "Artime once said that Marie Colette was as beautiful as a picture of the Channel from the French coast."

"From any coast," I responded.

"There's an expedition going up the Arkansas River to hunt and trade," Nick said, a few weeks later.

"Good! Good! Good!" Artime came back.

"Before you say it's triple-good, Artime," I interrupted," let's hear the whole story."

"The trip will start earlier than the Missouri trading season," Nick explained. "We will see new country. The pay is good. There's nothing keeping us in Saint Louis right at this time. "Laclede plans no expedition this summer. Frankly, I don't think he's well. I say we go!"

"Fine with me," I responded. I was glad to be away and moving again. I thought I loved Rosellen — and she had a husband. I had been totally carried away by Marie Colette. She not only had a husband — Benet was right there on the veranda during the dance. I needed time to figure out what might be next.

The following morning we three pushed our canoe into the willing waters of the wide river. We visited Michel and Bernadette at Prairie du Rocher. Then we saw Father Gibault for our pre-Lenten confessions.

Afterward I spoke to the priest alone.

"Somebody ought to do something about Marie Colette Fontelle," I said.

"*Who* ought to do *what*?" Father Gibault came back.

"Somebody ought to do something," I blurted out. "After all, she's married."

"Sure she is married. Will you tell me *who* should do whatever you want done. Then when you tell me who, I want to know *what* you want done."

"O, I'm sorry, *mon pere*, let's skip it."

"I thought you liked that girl up in Prairie du Chien. She's got a husband, too."

"Yes, Rosellen's got a husband, but she doesn't go around making love to other men in public."

"Marie Colette doesn't make love. She tantalizes. When such a girl is around, the sins of desire increase; but not the sins of deed."

"This country's too small for her," I came back. "Why doesn't her husband take her to New Orleans? She needs a larger stage."

"You're right there. She's on a stage. An actress! All the Brunet girls were attractive. Marie Colette just happens to be more beautiful than all the rest. She has trouble living with that fact."

"So do the rest of us!"

"She gives men a chance to practice many virtues," Father Gibault admitted.

"She's married to the wrong fellow," I said.

"Now if you have an idea there might be a right fellow," Father Gibault came back, "you're wrong. There is simply no one for Marie Colette. Or rather she is for no one — yet. She has not grown up."

Father Gibault gestured with his index finger as he went on: "That brings me to the big problem with this province — early marriages. Marie Colette married too young. I heard that Marie Therese Bourgeois married that Chouteau fellow in New Orleans when she was fifteen. Your friend in Prairie du Chien married Rien too soon."

"One might expect girls to marry young with a woman shortage," I said. "The French King sent boatloads of casket girls over a few years back. They all had marriage proposals the day the boats landed in New Orleans."

"With our girls up here," Father Gibault came back, "it's not been the men who are the problem. It's the parents of the girls. The Brunets beat all the rest."

I agreed.

"I preach against it," Father Gibault said. "I forget to announce the banns on several Sundays so as to delay things a bit. I urge the wealthier families to send the daughters to the Ursuline convent in New Orleans. The sisters will educate them and keep them out of circulation for a few more years. Beyond that I can't do much."

Mon pere, why should these girls be tied up for life in unhappy marriages?"

"Hugh Roe, I know you're not really concerned in a personal way with Marie Colette's marriage. She's just a passing problem as far as you're concerned. It's the girl in Prairie du Chien. With some of the others, the pressures of parents may actually have kept them from a free choice. That's the bishop's task to decide — should one of them appeal to him. Rosellen freely chose to marry this Rien fellow."

"That's right," I admitted, but the marriage turned out bad."

"It turned out, you say. Isn't all life a turning out, a meeting of what we had not expected, an act of faith in the future? I had enough of the waterways when I went to the seminary. A little country parish on the St. Lawrence was my dream — where life was orderly, families solid, people devout — like a village on the Loire. My first assignment is an area three times as big as France. I'm on the go at least a third of the year. That's life.

"When a man and woman marry," the priest went on, "they make an act of faith that awes the mountains. Sickness, health — what is ahead? Only God knows. If we did not trust in *le bon Dieu*, we could not go on a day."

"But who would be hurt?" I came back. "Rien couldn't care less. There are no children. Aren't there circumstances for annuling the marriage?"

"Circumstances," the priest came back. "You talk like one of the new French philosophers. The ethics of circumstances is a big thing with them. Each situation has to be judged in itself and for itself. There must be general rules to go by. Without permanent norms of right and wrong, there could no no ordered life among peoples!"

"Cases are different," I came back.

"Yes, they are. Mrs. Rien has suffered neglect. She's lonely. Her husband doesn't seem to care. She wants you, and you want her. That's a lot different than the case where a loved wife willfully seeks another man in spite of her husband's loyalty. Nonetheless, the objective fact still holds. In marriage, people pledge themselves for life to each other.

"Hugh, I'm sorry I can't help you in the way you wish. It's a good thing you are going up the Arkansas. Maybe that's the meaning of the Marie Colette incident. It helped you make up your mind to get away."

I said sadly, "Your big brotherly friend, Father Meurin, always said: 'The test of love is time and distance.' "

"Fine, Hugh," the priest said. "We'll see how you survive the test."

The next day we went down the fast-moving waters to the rendezvous at the mouth of the Arkansas. The Arkansas Post was nothing in itself, a mere stopping point between Saint Louis and New Orleans. I had no real remembrance of the place from our short stay there, before we turned our canoes toward the barren, wind swept plains. Only one thing was to make the two years of that otherwise dull expedition a pleasant, happy remembrance. Nick and I had been able to join a small group of voyaguers who rode with Western Comanches into the mountains of Santa Fe and had spent the second winter there. It was like a different world. I took the opportunity of learning Spanish, and Uncle Nick worked on the missions with the Franciscan lay brothers. Before we left, the padre who taught me Spanish had remarked that someday Nick would come back there as a missionary. At first, I could only think of how I would miss him. The more I thought of it as we recrossed the wind-swept uplands to the Arkansas, the more I came to the conclusion that the Padre might have sensed something deep in Nick's spirit.

On our return, the Arkansas Post that had seemed so nondescript when we went through now looked like a haven — if not a heaven. We spent several days in sorting the pelts, grading them, and closing out the business details of the expedition. A flotilla was expected from the North. A day or two later one would be headed for Saint Louis. Nick, Artime, and I would go with it.

The next day the shabby post looked like heaven — at least for a few moments. I had shaved. I wore clean cotton clothes for the first time in months. The azaleas were blooming. I almost felt like saying: "Good! Good! Good!" During the last hard days of the expedition, Artime had not used the words often.

The flotilla from the North had just arrived. Soldiers and roustabouts were busy at the landing places. I walked beside a warehouse. Suddenly I looked up. Marie Colette walked towards me. She wore a sunset-colored dress that bore the fragrance of roses. Her hair looked even darker by contrast. She held out her arms.

She certainly is the most beautiful girl in the Illinois country, I thought. Or in any country for that matter.

"You haven't kissed me for two years, Hugh Roe," she said,

throwing her arms around my shoulders, and clinging as ivy to a linden tree.

I wanted nothing so much as to possess her completely, immediately, in the nearest possible place.

"Oh! Hugh Roe! Why can't we be together?"

"It's simple, Marie Colette. I don't think you fully know what together means. Further, you have a husband. One's enough for every woman. Perhaps one is too many for you."

"Benet is a good man, Hugh Roe. When my father pushed me into marriage with him, I was only sixteen. It is not Benet's fault. He is good, dependable, and dull as cotton cloth. Hugh Roe, am I a bad girl?"

"Of course not, Marie Colette, but you're not always a *wise* girl." I held her by the waist about a foot away.

"I'm running away," she said, with a semi-sad look. She motioned to the Spanish captain busy at the landing place.

"Not that one, Marie Colette. Let me take you back to Ste. Genevieve."

"I'd let you take me anywhere," she said, her face suddenly bright again. "Anywhere in the world."

"Only to your husband in Ste. Genevieve."

Her coquettishness disappeared. She went on. "You're a dear. Some lucky girl will get you someday. I'm glad for her — whoever she might be. I came too late."

"Promise me one thing, Marie Colette. Promise me. When you realize that this is all a mistake, you'll go back to Benet. You know he is an understanding man."

"I promise, Hugh Roe. I do need you for a big brother to look after me." She planted a fast kiss on my cheek and turned to the river.

Visibly shaken, I watched the south-bound flotilla move with the Mississippi current. She will be back someday, I knew, humbler, wiser. Benet will be waiting for her. A complicated world. I sat on the lowest branch of a cottonwood and watched the soothing waters. I let my thoughts ramble a long time, until the vision of Marie Colette receded beyond the boundaries of things that could be.

At length, I walked to the warehouse. A letter awaited me there. I immediately recognized Rosellen's handwriting. I put it in my pocket and went to work in the warehouse. I did not open Rosellen's letter until that evening. I read:

Dear Hugh Roe,

Ever since I received your lovely letter, I have been hoping for the time and the mood to write to you. A few days ago, Mr. Cardinal mentioned casually that you would be on the Arkansas River for two years. I have only a vague idea where the Arkansas is. Wherever it goes, my prayers go with you.

When and where this will reach you, I cannot say. I hope it finds you — and finds you well. I have so much to say, and yet fear to begin. Your friendship is so important to me. I am not accustomed to tender thoughtfulness such as yours. So I am anxious to take good care of it and pray that it may grow.

The first logical question to be answered is: why did a marriage that seems to have turned out badly, take place at all? To begin at the beginning, I was born at Inverness, the only child of Scotch parents who came to Michilimackinac shortly after the British occupation. I was twelve years old at the time. My father ran a trading post. Mother worked at the post every day, and my father, too, except for the short time he journeyed on the waterways. Naturally, I saw little of either of them. I had always had a feeling of being in the way. I still have a tendency to apologize for existing.

My father was a just man but severe. He was exactly as the English term "dour" indicates. Although for business reasons he never said it publicly, he thought the French were a lot of licentious, wine-drinkers. He never took mother to one of the dances that were occasionally held, nor did he ever allow me to go. As to the Catholic religion, he thought it the worst form of idolatry. 'Rather be a pagan savage,' he said on one occasion, 'than a French Catholic.'

As soon as I was old enough to add, I worked in the post. The Rien family lived down the street. Mrs. Rien seemed to feel a certain sympathy towards me, and I ate it up. She was especially kind to me after the death of my mother during the year of the 'great sickness.'

I was impressed at what an active fellow her youngest son was. About 17 or 18 then, he had just completed his first trading voyage on the westward-flowing rivers. By that time, my father often left me in charge of the store. Young Rien would come in. He was the first person to show any interest in me. When my father died as a result of an accident on the trapping lines, and I was completely alone, Mrs. Rien gave me a home.

I went to church with her and later was baptized. Her son, in the meantime, was busy trading farther west. He had taken up his residence in Prairie du Chien. He came back in the spring. We planned to get married shortly after Easter. Mrs. Rien did not like the idea. I was beginning to be a little skeptical before the event took place. I attempted to see Father at the mission once, but he was busy. Since I agreed to get married, pride prevented my backing out. What an example of stupidity and stubborness! When no children came, we drifted apart. He is far away most of the time on the distant river.

Why can't I get through to him that I'm not cold but hungry for affection. It is simply not knowing or understanding and maybe no desire to do either. It never seems to dawn on him how lonely I am sometimes and how difficult it may be. But at least I have you — if only to dream about.

With undying love,
Rosellen

Marie Colette stirred my desire with no possibility of fulfillment. Rosellen always seemed to leave a door open. I had time to write the longest letter of my life. Instead I wrote briefly, and to the point:

Dear Rosellen,

It was so nice to find your letter waiting for me at the Arkansas Post when I returned from the headwaters of the Arkansas and the Canadian. Frankly, I almost stayed in Santa Fe. But I love this river and still have the hope of sharing your love someday.

Right now I feel that I should end this longing by coming to Prairie du Chien, and — Rien or no Rien — taking you away with me. Maybe it is a good thing a thousand mile stretch of the Mississippi River separates us at the moment.

Always,
Hugh Roe

The next morning I tore the letter into small bits, and put it into the fire. I sat down and wrote Rosellen a long letter. I told about the wonderful country at the far reaches of the Canadian and of the glorious land of New Mexico hidden behind the mountains in the bright unending sun. This letter eventually reached her.

The delay until the northbound flotilla arrived overwhelmed me like fog in the riverbottoms. Thoughts of one girl I could not have left me lonely. Day-dreaming of two girls — neither of whom I could have — bounced me between them like driftwood in a back water. I would think of the sparkle of Marie Colette and life glowed like a glass of wine. A steady diet of wine was too much, however, even for a Frenchman. Further, I was only half-French. The letters of Rosellen brought a sense of peace and contentment. She seemed so forbearing and understanding. I knew she was kind. I had met her because she had cared for me, and others, during the epidemic. Still she was a dream. I couldn't even picture her face clearly in my mind. The more I would try to picture her, the more the image of Marie Colette would swim into my ken.

Then the flotilla arrived from New Orleans with sad news. Pierre Laclede had just died, and they buried him on the river bank.

The next day we started up-river toward a land under siege.

III

Struggle for the Mid-Continent

Artime, Nick, and I left the party of voyageurs at the mouth of the Kaskaskia River. It was early July, and the heat of the sun searched us out beneath the trees. Even the usual coolness of the forest was gone on that day. The parched grass rustled slightly under our moccasined feet. We pulled out the leather lacings of our shirts and eased our rifles across our shoulders.

The town of Kaskaskia lay before us, flattened by the heat. Except for two guards lounging in the shade at the stockade, the town seemed clean of inhabitants. No one stood by Kaskaskia's single cannon as we walked by. A few panting dogs gave the only other sign of life.

Artime broke the hot stillness: "On a day like this, no man in his right mind would walk to his front door." He mopped his neck with the edge of his shirt.

We turned into Cerre's warehouse, and met loud hellos. Father Gibault sat in the corner talking with several habitants. He rose to greet us.

"*Bon jour, mon Pere,*" we said in unison.

"So our travelers are finally back," he said pleasantly. "They return on the coolest day of the year."

We shook hands warmly. Several friends of Artime pounded his broad back.

"Big things have been happening since you have been gone," one of the Kaskaskians said, a tall fellow I had seen before, but did not know. "Commandant Rocheblave has ordered the militia to be on an alert for the Long Knives."

Artime's loud laugh filled the warehouse. "Even a bull buffalo could charge by, and those guards out there would not know it."

"Oh, the alert ended two days ago, but for five days before that — "

"*Sacre bleu*," an old villager interposed, "there was marching up and down the streets. All the habitants were called into town. Riders were sent to Prairie du Rocher and Cahokia." It was obvious to his listeners that the old man had savored the sudden commotion.

"It looks as if nothing came of it," Nick said.

"If the Long Knives have any sense at all," Artime laughed, "they won't move an inch today — wherever they are."

"True," the tall man said, and squatted in the corner. The rest sat down and lighted the pipes.

I walked over to Father Gibault. "Could I have a talk with you, *mon pere?*"

"This evening," Father Gibault suggested.

"Fine, *mon pere.*"

"My nephew," Nick said, "Artime and I will go on over to Bernadette's this evening. You can catch up with us there in the morning."

We moved about our tasks lethargically, so hot was the air. At the end of the day, the sun stood a long time in the west. The heat did not let up perceptibly when the red ball of fire fell behind the Missouri bluffs.

Artime and Nick rode off. I walked over to Father Gibault's home. The priest sat on the veranda. On a small table beside him stood a bottle of wine and two small goblets.

"Do you know what day this is?" Father Gibault asked.

I wondered. On reflection, I seemed to recall that his patron Saint Peter had a feast around that time of the year. I said confidently: "It's the *Fete de Saint Pierre!*"

"Your father would be ashamed of you," he shook his head in exaggerated disgust. "Today is the second anniversary of the Declaration of Independence from England by the Atlantic colonies."

"My father knew everything that happened against Britain since the dawn of the world."

"We should celebrate this day, my boy," the priest came back. "We'll be joining up one of these days. The Long Knives will be here sooner than anyone thinks."

"Oh, *mon pere*, you act as if you think they might come here tonight."

Father Gibault shrugged his shoulders. "I'm not the only one who said they will come. They tell me your father always predicted it. I agree with him."

"Well if both you and my father said it, who am I to raise a doubt? If they wanted to attack us, they'd come during the winter, not on the hottest day in summer!" I turned towards him. "When did they take Ft. Duquesne? In the winter!"

"That's right," he came back with insistence. "They came in the winter precisely because the French didn't expect them. So, no one expects them now. Marshal Condé always said: 'If an enemy doesn't expect you, you don't have to beat him. He beats himself.' "

"If they do come tonight," I said with a laugh, "I'll admit they're a remarkable people."

"They had a lot of courage two years ago when they broke with Britain, my boy. Let's drink a glass to that."

"All right," I said. "A toast to everyone who fights the British anywhere in the world."

"Your father would be proud of that toast."

We drank. The wine was the best I had ever tasted.

"If the Long Knives do come, *mon pere*, what will you do?"

"Support them, of course."

"Even though the bishop has other ideas?" I asked.

"The bishop does not know that the British planned to expel the Illinois French in 1770 but did not have available forces." Father Gibault twirled his wine glass in his left hand. "That puts us in a different situation from our Canadian brethren. So I always ask myself: 'What would Bishop Briand do if he were in my shoes, as Vicar General in Illinois?' " He paused, smiled impishly, and said, "I always come up with the same answer: The future lies with the Long Knives. I'll have a lot of persuading to do with the people around here, though. They don't like to budge. The budgers moved already." He laughed. "When the Long Knives come, I'm ready."

After that, we sat quietly a while. The air in the lowland between the two rivers grew more oppressive in the twilight. We knew that sleep would not come easily.

I thought about the things Father Gibault had said. If anyone were going to attack Kaskaskia, I had a hunch he would cross the Kaskaskia River to the north and move down toward the town near the junction with the Mississippi, leaving no avenue of escape by land. As I mulled over these thoughts, a group of men moved rapidly in the distance towards Commandant Rocheblave's residence. Father Gibault saw them, too, but only shrugged his shoulders. A few more minutes went by. Then suddenly loud shouts came from the edge of town to the north and across the Kaskaskia River. Then a clamor arose at Rocheblave's house.

My original unconcern gave way to fear. I realized that I had left my musket with my gear at the depot. *How careless can a man be?* I wondered. Father Gibault on his part never carried a gun even when he rode through hostile country. We had no way of defending ourselves.

"They must be Long Knives," Father Gibault said flatly.

"Why not *les sauvages*?" I asked.

"Not if there is a large force. A few renegades might occasionally cause trouble. Not a whole war party."

"I don't see why not."

"Look: the Long Knives have no Indian allies. Correct?"

"That's right, *mon pere.*"

"The tribes are friendly either to us French or to the English, depending with some on who gave the most recent presents. Correct?"

"Right again."

"If they're friendly to us, they won't attack. If they're friendly to the English, they won't attack because the town has accepted British rule, even though the British removed their troops from Fort Chartres and left us unprotected." He pursed his lips and went on, "Come to think of it, the Chickasaw and the Creek of the South used to attack the Illinois country every once in a while during the French rule — at least, that's what I heard. They haven't menaced us since the Peace of Paris."

It was a fact I had not thought of either. Nonetheless, it was true. That meant: Our visitors had to be the Long Knives.

The thought was only partially reassuring. The Canadiens and the Long Knives had shot each other on sight for most of three generations. Some of the attackers probably had lost someone dear to them during the Indian attacks on the frontier. While the Long Knives despised the Indians, they seemed to blame all their Indian troubles on us. We might not come out so well.

Father Gibault kept hopeful. "Things will work out," he said.

The next afternoon Father Gibault and I saw five of the leading men of the town walk under guard toward Rocheblave's quarters. A little later they returned. One of them stopped to tell us what had happened.

"When we walked in," he began, "the Long Knife Captain Clark and his men sat there, stripped to the waist. They looked like savages, not like an army of a civilized country. You can imagine how terrified we were. Then this Clark — he is a young man — said we were not allowed to leave town, but we could walk around the streets. He gave us a short time to choose: either to swear allegiance to the Long Knives or take our families and our possessions and cross the river to Spanish territory. *Mon pere,* he told us something else." Now excitement filled his rapid words. "I don't know whether he is telling the truth or not. He says France has made an alliance with the colonies and declared war against Britian. If that is so, we are in the war, too."

"That's the best news you've brought, *mon ami,*" Father Gibault said.

"One more thing," the man went on, "we asked Clark if we could gather all the people in the church to say our farewells — at least those who wanted to go across the river."

"I will go see Clark myself," Father Gibault said.

"Good luck, *mon pere,*" the elder of the town answered.

Father Gibault and I walked down the street to Clark's headquarters. The priest's cassock hardly impeded his quick motions. As we entered, we saw what the elders of the town had described: a motley group of men, unshaven, disheveled, unkempt, looking for all the world like a bunch of Piankeshaw Indians. The appearance of Clark gave me confidence. Even while sitting there in his disheveled uniform — he now had his coat on — he had an air of command. He held his shoulders like a king. I had heard he was a young man but had not dreamed he was so young — perhaps twenty six — three years younger than I.

I smiled at the young Virginian and said, "I presume you are Captain Clark?"

"I am," he said unhesitatingly.

"This is *Pere* Gibault, the Pastor of this village. He would like to know if the people can gather in the church to consider your words."

"Tell him what he requests is granted," Clark said and dismissed us abruptly.

"That was fast," Father Gibault said. "We'll ring the big bell and summon everybody."

"Can everybody fit in the church?" I asked.

"They all come only on Christmas and Easter. Somehow or other they manage to get inside when they do come."

"What do you plan to say to them?" I asked.

"Nothing. I'm going to let you do the talking. You know how I feel. You can be more persuasive than I. Further, how can I complain that Bishop Briand entered politics and insisted that the Canadiens support the British, if I urge my people to support the Americans? I'll let you do that."

"I'll try, *mon pere.* I don't know if I'll succeed."

"Just let Camille Couture talk himself out. The rest of his side will say nothing. Most people won't agree with him — no matter what he says — or what you say either. They will just hear what Camille says and take the other side."

We reached the belfry. Father Gibault pulled the rope, and the huge bell boomed through the bottomland — the bell with the inscription: "Cast in Paris in 1742 for the Church of the Immaculate Conception among the Kaskaskias." Those words made us feel part of France and not colonists on the edge of the world.

Father Gibault went into the church, removed the holy vessels from the tabernacle on the main altar, and placed them on a shelf in the sacristy. I opened the front door, and the habitants took their accustomed places.

Camille Couture rose. He spoke convincingly, I thought, but looked backward. I told them to look forward to the inevitable victory of the Long Knives with France and Spain in alliance. Father Gibault offered no political opinion. He simply asked us to choose. Every man in the room stood as one.

"My friends," Father Gibault said, "things are a little different than they were yesterday, as you can see. All of you are fearful. Some of you, I think, might do wrong things in your haste. Let us find out carefully first what the Long Knives will ask of us. I will go to Clark. I will ask him if he will respect our religion and protect our homes. Then we can think more calmly whether or not we will leave and go to the other side of the river."

The habitants agreed. Father Gibault, Camille Couture, four older citizens, and I went back to see Clark. I presented all of their questions at once: Would the habitants have protection? Would they be able to stay with their families? To keep their property? To practice their religion? I had tried to phrase the questions in a conciliatory way.

Clark's answer was fierce. "Do you think we are savages?" he began, rising and towering over us. "Whom do you think you are addressing? A group of Shawnee Indians? From your conversation I am not sure."

As I translated, I tried to soften the impact, but Clark's manner allowed no toning down of his message.

"Do you suppose we mean to take the bread out of your homes?" Clark went on. "We did not come here to plunder! Do you think we make war on women or children? We came here to stop the shedding of blood by the Indians. Remember they are prodded by our enemies, who are yours, too, if you would only think of it."

I noticed the change in his mood, and my translation reflected it. Clark spoke more pleasantly now. "Remember, the King of France has joined us, and this means the war will end soon and we will win.

"As for your church, we Virginians tolerate all religions. We have various religions back home, including yours. Some of your religion who live in Maryland, right next to Virginia, have signed our Declaration of Independence. We don't meddle with religious affairs." Then turning directly to Father Gibault, "If you find anyone disturbing your church, you let me know. I will see that this stops." Then, he addressed all: "You can return to your families. Tell them to conduct themselves as they have, entirely free, without danger. You people have been falsely informed, but I am willing to forget all that is past. Your friends who have been confined will be released, and guards will be withdrawn from most houses in town."

The habitants could hardly fathom all that Clark had said, even when I translated his words slowly, but their tension vanished.

"*Merci, mon capitain,*" the priest said. All the habitants joined in his thanks as we left Clark's headquarters.

Father Gibault rang the church bell again. But this time it was for a *Te Deum*, a hymn of thanksgiving.

I rode north with Captain Joseph Bowman and thirty mounted men to Prairie du Rocher. I found Nick and Artime at Michel and Bernadette's. They decided to ride north with the Long Knife Captain. Bowman was willing to have them since they, too, were friendly to his cause. When the troops approached Cahokia, I pointed out the house of the commander. Captain Bowman rode up immediately and demanded the surrender. The people asked a day to decide whether or not they would take the oath of allegiance.

In the morning one hundred habitants gathered and took the oath. That same afternoon, we were finally able to leave and reached home after two years away. So much had occurred in the past week, we had almost forgotten the earlier events.

"What happened on the other side of the river?" Auguste Chouteau asked at the waterfront.

"Many things," I replied. "Captain Clark came from Kentucky. He surprised Kaskaskia and took Rocheblave prisoner. Father Gibault then persuaded the people to join the Long Knives. There was talk before we left that Father Gibault would go to Vincennes to win over that village. It was all done peacefully. Now there is a force in Cahokia — thirty men under Captain Bowman."

"We heard something to that effect," Auguste said. "Is it true that Clark is a young man?"

"Surprisingly young," I answered. "But tall and tough. He's an impressive fellow."

"He'll have to be," Auguste said. "The tribes are gathering from the north to meet him at Cahokia."

"That's a meeting no one would want to miss," I said.

Everywhere in the city, old friends asked what had gone on in the Illinois villages. We repeated to the townsfolk what we had already told Auguste.

The river was soon filled with war canoes. The Chippewa came in one day and the Ottawa the next. Nick saw many old warriors he had fought with on the Monongahela. The Potowatomi came in — a tribe of even greater prestige than the Ottawa, now that Pontiac was dead. The Sauk and the Fox came down, the Winnebago from near Prairie du Chien, and tribes Nick and I had never met. A mighty array gathered at Cahokia — wondering, uncertain, inquisitive.

I wondered how young Clark would stand up against the tremendous pressure. After all, only his personality stood between this vast horde and his few soldiers. Unless the French aided him, the Virginians had no chance, should the Indians choose war. Few Long Knives would escape. Suddenly I remembered something Clark had said the week before in Kaskaskia. "One man with courage makes a majority."

Clark rode up with an air of confidence as if everything were in his grasp. He met first with the Spanish officials and the French on the west side of the river. Nick, Artime, and I felt important because we had already met him. He spoke frankly.

"You men have had greater success in dealing with the Indians than we have. We know it. I'm going to adopt your ways. In the past, we have broached a treaty as if we were fearful of the Indians, not as equals or even as superiors. They think our approach means weakness. This shall not be my mistake."

The next morning a large assembly gathered in council at Cahokia — tribes of all the north country on one side, the French on another, the Americans and the few French and Spanish officials in the area around Clark. Nick, Artime, and I took places with the last group.

The Indian chiefs petitioned. One of them rose and spoke: "We have taken up the bloody hatchet because we have been deceived by the British. They sent bad birds among us, flying through the land, but now we have seen our wrong ways. The Great Spirit has brought us together for good, and he is good, and we hope that we might be friends of the Long Knives and peace might take the place of the bloody belt."

As the chief said this, several of his followers threw down weapons, belts, and flags they had received from the British. The chief stomped on them; then took his place.

Another chief arose, said much the same thing, and went through an identical ceremonial. I was suprised how much of their message I understood even before the interpreter translated.

Finally Clark arose. He calmly looked over the entire group. "I will give careful thought to what you say. I will answer you tomorrow." Without further ceremony, he turned and walked disdainfully from the group. The chiefs sat in amazement.

On the following morning the entire assembly came again. This time, Clark rose first. "Men and warriors, pay attention," he began.

"You informed me yesterday that the Great Spirit has brought us together. You hoped for good, as he is good. I also have the same hope."

Clark went on to tell them of the long unsatisfactory dealings that his people had had with the British even though they were related by blood. "I was sent by the great Council Fire of the Long Knives and their friends to take control of all the towns the English possess in this country. . . .I will chase the clouds so that you may see clearly the cause of the war between the Long Knives and the English, that you may judge for yourself who is right. . . .Here is a bloody belt and a white one. Take the one you please.

"We will part this evening, and when you are ready, if the Great Spirit will bring us together again, let us prove ourselves worthy by speaking and thinking with but one heart and one tongue."

Clark stopped abruptly and turned to talk casually to those near him, as if the Indians in the council were the least of his concerns. "We will have a military ball tonight," he said. "I invite all of you."

It seemed a great stunt, dancing around gleefully with the girls from Cahokia, while a thousand Indians sat nearby, debating whether or not to split our skulls with tomahawks. I knew enough by that time not to underestimate Clark.

The Indians kindled a new fire the next morning. All the men of the village gathered, and the visitors from Saint Louis stood around the table under an oak where Clark sat. Then the spokesman of the tribes advanced to the table before Clark. He carried a belt of peace in his hand. Another followed him with a sacred pipe and a third with a fire to kindle it. They presented fire to the heavens, then to the earth, to the four winds, and then to all the spirits, invoking them to witness what was about to be concluded. Then they presented the pipe to Clark and then around to every other person.

The parley was over, and I wondered if ever again I would see such a demonstration of courage as Clark showed at this time. I contrasted the small number of Long Knives with the mass of Indians and knew it was the courage of one man, George Rogers Clark, that had saved the Long Knives from destruction.

Two months later I was in Prairie du Rocher again, visiting Michel and Bernadette. I rode the few miles into Kaskaskia to see my old priest friend.

"It was a great trip to Vincennes," Father Gibault said. "Clark gave me a proclamation to the people. He sent a troop of soldiers along and some of the townspeople here who have relatives over there. I came back in early August and things look good now. We have Vincennes in our grasp. Clark talked the Indians down at Cahokia. They really fear this man. Kaskaskia is firmly in our hands."

"That all sounds good, *mon pere*. How is the war coming out east? Did Clark have anything to say about that?"

"Things look much better. France is sending its fleet and a large army, four times as big as the army General Washington has. At least, that's what they say. The British have moved down south. They have given up their campaign in the North that has not gone well at all. So it may be sooner than we expect that we'll see some improvement in the whole picture.

"That's enough of politics," Father Gibault went on. "I forgot to tell you that Father Meurin died while you were on the Arkansas River."

"I was sorry to hear about it, *mon pere*."

"A good man," Father Gibault said. "He had courage. No one pushed him around."

With a laugh in my voice, I said, "He looked after your spiritual progress so carefully."

"Yes, indeed. He made sure Bishop Briand knew all my major failings and some minor ones, too. He did not have much else, it would seem, to write about."

With even more banter in his tone, the priest went on: "He was my favorite confessor. Now I'll have to go to New Orleans or to Canada to make my Easter duty."

"Speaking of New Orleans and people dying," I said, "did you hear that Laclede died near the Arkansas Post when we were there in June?"

"As a matter of fact," the priest said, "I heard the rumor even before you returned in early July."

"But we were the first men to come up the river!"

"Yes! Rumors have strange ways." He shrugged his shoulders. "Enough of deaths. What about life — and love! Do you still think you're in love with Amnon's wife?"

"Amnon's wife?" I came back, surprised. Speechless for the moment, I wondered how he had known of that episode. It seemed so long ago in the Missouri village. Finally I blurted out: "It was not Amnon's wife. It was her twin sister I liked."

"Her twin sister? I never knew she had one."

"It was one of those little things that blew over. I never thought to mention it to you."

"Little things that blew over?" the priest answered. "That you never mentioned to me?"

"No! I'm sure I didn't. On my first trip to the Missouri Indian village I liked one of the chief's twin daughters. Her name was Yellow Throat. She loved an Indian, Blue Cloud. Amnon wanted her. So I outbid him — but not for myself. Then Blue Cloud could take her, and we would avoid trouble. Amnon took her twin sister, Hawk's Wing, for his wife."

In amazement, the priest answered: "I usually know everything that happens everywhere, but I never heard this story before. I was not talking about these Indian girls. I was talking about Amnon Rien's wife, Rosellen, in Prairie du Chien."

"Amnon Rien? His wife Rosellen?" I was stunned. "My God! This can't be true!"

"You never did know?"

"I never dreamed he was the one," I answered mechanically.

Father Gibault spoke on. But I could not recall a single word the priest said.

How ridiculous that I had been on a expedition with Rien and never learned the man's name. The traders called him Amnon. They never used his last name. It was a French habit. Many times longstanding associates had asked me casually: "What is your Uncle Nick's last name?" Or, "What is Artime's last name?" The French referred only to commanders, like Laclede or Langlade or St. Ange, by the surnames.

I was too numb to say or think more.

Artime had agreed to lead one last expedition to the land of the Sauk Indians before settling down to the routines of a married habitant. Once upriver, I felt I could persuade Artime to push on the short distance to Prairie du Chien, or at least Nick and I could hazard the trip.

In the meantime, we agreed to help Artime and his brothers-in-law-to-be, the four Currier brothers who farmed bottom land near St. Charles, in building a home for Artime and Celeste Currier on the most impressive ridge I had seen anywhere near Saint Louis. The Curriers said little, smiled often, and worked like beavers. We soon had a house finished that could double as a home and a fortress. Then we returned to Saint Louis.

In the early fall, Artime came into the warehouse that Auguste Chouteau now controlled.

"Good morning, Artime," we said in unison.

"Good, good," he responded.

"Not a good, good, good day?" I asked.

"No! Just good, good. It's our trip to the Sauk village at the mouth of Rock River."

"What's wrong with that?" I asked. "It's nice Indian summer weather. Auguste promises good pay — if the pelts are first-rate. I'd rather be on the river than in this fragrant warehouse."

"Yes," Artime responded, his round face clouded. "But the patron wants us to take along three fellows who are going home to Prairie du Chien. One of them is our friend from the Missouri River trip, Amnon Rien."

"Amnon Rien?" I said in dismay. "Not him!"

"Sure," Artime said in a matter-of-fact tone. "I have no objections to Amnon — as long as there's a river between us — or maybe two rivers."

I tried to control my confused feelings of dismay and anger. Now I would not be able to see Rosellen — even if we reached Prairie du Chien. *Would Amnon try to patch up a union that had never really existed? How would Rosellen feel when she found him moving into her life once again? How could I control my anger on the long trip north?* I had to fight the urge to kill him. *Wouldn't the whole world—*

not just Rosellen and I — be better off without him? I walked to the far side of a pile of pelts so Artime would not see my rage and hammered my fists against the bundles.

Artime spoke on. "Things went bad for the Missouri Indians shortly after Amnon joined the tribe. Drought dried the maize fields. The animals left the region. I guess they felt about him as we did."

"Smart beasts," Nick interjected.

"Hunting was bad all along the lower Missouri," Artime continued. "The Indians blamed all their troubles on Amnon, the chief's son-in-law."

"Good for them," Nick said.

"He's been drinking," Artime said, obviously worried. "His face was always sullen and unpleasant, but there was a lynx-sharpness about his eyes. That's gone now. The Sauk never liked the Missouri Indians. The two tribes often fought. When Amnon was sub-chief, the Sauk felt his treachery many times. He would make a treaty with them, then attack a party of Sauk hunters in the area he agreed was their's. They detest him. He is using us as a shield to get through to Prairie du Chien."

As Artime talked on, I felt greater revulsion than ever. This man had married the girl I came to love and then had left her, not out of affection for another woman, but for flesh and furs. I would have smashed Amnon's face had he been standing there.

Nick broke in, "Earlier, we felt Amnon might do bad things. But at least, they would be sensible things. Now, with this drinking, he may do something that could prove dangerous to all of us."

"Artime's getting in his pirogue," Nick said. "Let's push off."

I balanced the sides of the canoe with both hands as I took my place in the front. Nick pushed away from the shore. We headed upstream for the far bank. I wore down my anger in long strokes. Neither of us said anything until we were in the shadow of the Illinois willows.

"Amnon sought himself all his life," Nick said. Now he has found himself. That's hell."

"If he lived in his hell alone," I said, "it would be all right with me. But he wants to drag Rosellen into it."

"We have trusted in *le bon Dieu* up to this time," Nick said. "Why should we quit now? It would be easy to do away with Amnon. An accident on the river? A bribe of drink and trinkets to a Sauk? No one would know. Artime might suspect, but would keep silent."

Why not? I wondered.

Nick went on, answering the question I thought but did not ask. "We would have to live with ourselves. All our lives we would know we killed Amnon. I could go far away — and never forget. You could marry Rosellen and try to ease your mind by saying you saved her from Amnon. Everytime you took her in your arms, however, you would recall that once you acted as God. Your sin would come back on you — as Amnon's evil deeds will destroy him in the end."

"Uncle Nick, you've said that before."

"My nephew, I have said it often. Remember it now. When one would do evil, he should put it out of his mind and get out of the place where he might do it. Then when he is away, he should look at that evil fully. See it in every detail. Wring out every possibility. Let the results of sin engulf his mind. Feel what it would mean to have blood on one's hands!"

"I will, Uncle Nick."

I thought back over the long years that my uncle had stayed with me, a true godfather, but more than that. In many ways he was more a father than my real father had been. *Give me patience, O God, I prayed. Let me do no evil. Let me realize, as Uncle Nick says, that evil brings its own destruction.*

Our stay in the Sauk camp began smoothly enough. Artime had many friends among the chiefs. No British traders from the north had come that far south, and the Sauk had many first-grade peltries to barter. Amnon's plans to go back to Prairie du Chien had cut off my hopes of seeing Rosellen. All I wanted now was to get back to Saint Louis as soon as possible.

On our second afternoon in the camp, Nick and I walked outside the Sauk Village toward a small stream called *La Vert*. It flowed into the Rock River a few miles above its junction with the Mississippi. We spotted Amnon, swaying a little from liquor, his face more blunt and unpleasant than before.

When he spotted us, he pointed to an elderly squaw who knelt to drink from the bank of *La Vert.* "Look at that old she-bear," he said with a sneer. To our horror, he raised his musket and fired. She sagged into the gravel at the edge of the stream, her head in the water, her feet on the bank, looking like nothing so much as a rawhide sack of corn.

Amnon stood transfixed, appalled at what he had done. Suddenly, he started for the canoes at the bank of the Mississippi. "Let's get out of here," he panted.

Nick caught him before he could run ten yards.

"We're going back to camp and see what Artime wants to do," Nick said, his arms pinioning Amnon.

We took him to Thomure's tent. "Artime, we're in trouble," Nick said. "Amnon's killed an old squaw in cold blood."

Artime blanched. "Good God!" he said. Then with an air of command I had never before witnessed, he ordered: "Get the other men, Hugh. Nick, you hold Amnon while I tie his feet so he can't run away. We'll have to act quickly. Since we brought him into this camp, he is our problem. The young warriors will want to kill us all."

When the others gathered, Artime motioned them to take seats in a circle, like tribesmen holding a council of war. He began: "Amnon deliberately killed an old squaw."

Ordinarily Artime looked paunchy. As he sat at the head of the council, however, his strong arms and barrel-chest gave him an overpowering appearance. "We are guests in the Sauk camp," he went on. "They outnumber us twenty to one. We cannot fight them. We cannot get away. They have us surrounded."

He stopped and gazed at one after another of the men before him: "We have two possibilities. The Sauk will force us to hand Amnon over to them, and they will torture him until his hair falls out; or we will punish him ourselves."

Artime looked at Amnon, aghast and trembling. He turned to the two voyageurs who had planned to go to Prairie du Chien with

Amnon, disheveled, unkempt as they always were. Ordinarily unconcerned, they now showed deep fear.

I looked at the circle of woods around us. Angry Sauk braves had quietly surrounded our bivouac. Gray clouds hovered menacingly.

Artime spoke: "We will now vote on whether we should execute this man ourselves." He turned to the two men from Prairie du Chien.

"I can not vote to shoot my companion," the one said.

"Nor will I," said the other.

Artime looked calmly at the two and then at the other man. The old man, his partner in the lead canoe, spoke first: "It is more merciful that we shoot him than let the Sauk torture him. I say: We shoot him."

"I agree," said Nick, mechanically, businesslike, unemotional. Artime looked at me. This was a moment I had never dreamed would come to be. As much as I detested him, I could not bring myself to turn Amnon over to the Sauk tortures. If Amnon did not die, however, the rest of us might not get out alive.

Oh God! Why do I have to decide this?

All things seemed to say that we had to execute Amnon. Yet all my life men would wonder what had really made me vote yes. No, it did not matter what other men thought. I did not have to live with them. I had to live only with myself. I had to answer only to myself — and to God.

Was I voting to kill a man so I would be free to marry that man's wife? What kind of man Amnon was did not enter into this issue. How he had treated Rosellen was not the consideration. The issue was simpler.

A man would die. And my vote would send him to death. What the Sauk might do to Amnon, that, too, was not the issue. Nor what the Sauk would do to the rest. It was simply: Did this man deserve to die? Had he violated the law of hospitality of the tribe? Had he betrayed the French code that saw the Indian as a brother, a fellow human being, a child of God?

An amazing quiet gripped the entire river bottom area. My words came like a musket shot. I heard them as if someone else had said them. "We must shoot him."

In their circle at the edge of the clearing, the Sauk looked even more menacing as Artime rose. He strode to the great Chief. "It is with deep sorrow that your brother Thomure must admit that one of his men has betrayed his brothers, the Sauk. That man has enjoyed their hospitality and has turned to do a terrible deed. We can only say that the evil *eau de vie* that he drank turned his mind from the straight and the right." Artime stopped to assay the warrior's reaction.

The Chief spoke bluntly: "Either you must turn this man over to your brother the Sauk, or each of you must die."

Artime pressed his chance. "It is true. This man has done a bad thing to the Sauk people. He has also done a bad thing to his own people. He has made them seem evil to their great and good friends. We French have our own customs for justice. If we follow our own way, may your brothers depart in peace?"

I breathed a prayer of hope as the Chief looked from one white man to another. He did not turn his gaze to Amnon cringing against the tree.

The Chief spoke solemnly. "My French brothers may act according to their custom. Then depart in peace."

Artime moved quickly. "Tie Amnon's wrists behind his back."

Amnon's face grew pale. He lurched against the thong that held him to the hickory tree. Then he subsided in exhaustion.

"Make your peace with *le bon Dieu*," Artime said. "You will be with Him in one minute."

Then turning to us, Artime ordered: "Take your stand at twelve paces."

We marched to the places he designated.

"Ready your muskets," Artime said.

I aimed my flintlock at Amnon's chest, then closed my eyes.

"Fire!" Artime ordered. We pulled the triggers.

The man who had made a gunny sack of an Indian woman became a dead bundle at the base of a hickory tree.

We left the Sauk village as soon as we could and turned our canoes homeward.

When we arrived in Saint Louis, a letter from Prairie du Chien awaited me. I knew that Rosellen must have written before the two men who saw her husband killed had reached their homes. She wrote:

It was so good to hear from you, after two years of silence. I had presumed all kinds of dreadful things — chiefly that you had been killed by the Indians. Certainly I should have known that men in the fur trade can be away a long time. I never lost hope. How rewarded my hope was by your last letter.

I have thought of you hundreds of times during the two years since your last letter. I prayed for you every day. I thank you for your prayers.

If I were not wearing this ring on my finger, I would wish nothing more of this world than that you would put one there. That is not God's will. So I must go on, day after single day, with my hand in His, not being able to see the way through the darkness but knowing that He is guiding me, that life is not a problem to be solved, but a mystery to be lived. I accept His loving care.

All my love,
Rosellen

How could I answer such a letter? How could I tell the woman I loved that I had participated in the execution of her husband because he had murdered an old woman wantonly.

If I went up to Prairie du Chien to ask her to marry me, those voyageurs might say that now they knew why I had voted to kill Rien when he murdered the Sauk squaw. I wanted to marry Rien's wife.

The more I thought about the matter, the more complicated it grew. I had fallen in love with a dream, a vague memory, real to me only in the steady flow of letters. Before, it had been a dream with no hope for an outcome. Now she was free, and I was free. What was the next step?

I hoped against hope that she would resolve the problem by writing first. Unfortunately winter came early. No one came down the river.

Nick and I rode out to Saint Charles for Artime's wedding. *Pere*

Bernarde de Limpach had left Saint Louis a few days before to make his missionary rounds along the Missouri River. He had the wedding ceremony in the large room of the Currier home.

Artime looked happy. He always did. Now he had added reason. Of all the girls we had ever met, Celeste seemed the perfect one for him. Actually, Artime had never seemed interested in anyone else at any time — in Prairie du Rocher, in Saint Louis, in Santa Fe, in any of the Indian villages.

As Celeste and Artime promised undying love, I wondered if I was capable of fulfilling such a pledge. *Did I really love Rosellen, or the last girl who treated me pleasantly?*

Maybe I really fitted the song the Canadiens sang as they pulled the *cordelle* along the riverbank. "None is so dear to your heart, as the girl who is now in your arms . . . ." *Did I have the stability for real, enduring love? Was I being fair to Rosellen to let her dream?*

On a clear day in February, the west wind drove all dampness out of the air. "A real New Mexico day," Nick called it.

Jeremy Maligne walked towards us on the Rue Principal. I noticed over the months that he had been slowly edging Joseph Labusciere out of the notarial work. They still kept up the rivalries they had shown as boys in St. Philippe near Fort Chartres.

"The Governor wants you at his office at ten," Jeremy said. "There's some big news in the making. Clark's coming over from Cahokia."

"Clark?" I answered. "Maybe it's some joint action against the British!"

"Could be!" Jeremy answered.

"I hope so," I answered. I thought of Rosellen in Prairie du Chien and the rumors that the British were stirring Indian attacks for the coming spring. *At least she's safe — thanks to the good God.*

I had scarcely arrived at the government house when Governor De Leyba entered the large room.

"*Buenos dias, Su Excelencia,*" I said.

"*Buenos dias, O'Romo,*" the Governor responded. "The American Colonel Clark, he will come over this morning. Some, they talk English. Some, they talk French. Some, they talk Spanish. Only you know what everyone is talking about."

"*Gracias, Su Excelencia.*"

"*O'Romo,* we fear the British will attack the Illinois country this spring." De Leyba continued in Spanish. "But there is great news for all here. King Carlos has joined France in an alliance with the Atlantic colonies. Spain has declared war. Now we can all work together."

"That *is* great news, Your Excellency," I responded.

At that moment the guard at the door announced the arrival of Colonel Clark. Several Long Knives and two Frenchmen accompanied him.

"*Buenos dias, mi Coronel,*" De Leyba said with a bow.

"*Buenos dias, Su Excelencia,*" Clark responded.

I noticed immediately the cordiality that existed between the two men.

"*O'Romo* will speak for me," the Governor said.

"You may recall we met at Kaskaskia two summers ago, Colonel," I began in English.

Clark nodded. I went on. "The governor has good news. Spain has declared war against Britain in alliance with the colonies."

"That's the most encouraging word I have had in months," Clark said "My news is not good. Spies in the north have sent word that the British General Patrick Sinclair at Michilimackinac has stirred the northern tribes for a spring raid. Especially the Sioux! He's pressuring the Sauk and Fox to join. We'll have a big battle somewhere down here."

After I had translated what Clark said, De Leyba stated: "Tell Clark I will build a tower on the ridge west of the church. We'll put the guns from Fort Chartres in it. That will scare some of the heathens. Then we'll dig a trench all along the west rim of the town and down to the riverbank on the north and south ends."

When I translated, Clark said, "That's good. We'll have to work together. Time is short."

"How much time do you think we have?" De Leyba asked.

"Till late May at the most — if the thaws come at normal times." Clark said.

"That will give me time to call in all the trappers on the Meramec and the Cuivre. Maybe I'll order Lieutenant Cartabona to come with the militia from Ste. Genevieve."

"I might have Captain Montgomery move upstream with a contingent of militia to dissuade the Sauk from aiding the northern tribes," Clark said. "But that will depend on two things: how fast the Indians get ready up north; and where the main attack will come. In the meantime, I have to make a fast trip to Kentucky."

"Whatever you plan," De Leyba promised, "count on me."

During the next weeks De Leyba amazed me. Even though he had the gout, the Lieutenant Governor got the city in action. He hobbled around from the rock pile that was becoming a tower to the interminable ditch that finally became a trench. He took up a collection from the townspeople for defense. He contributed substantially himself. He promised Montgomery a hundred men, boats, arms, artillery, ammunition, and provisions.

I always felt that Saint Louis was the most self-run village in the world. Not that I had been many places. I had never really been in any city anywhere, but I had heard men talk of New Orleans, of Quebec, of Montreal, of Havana, of Paris, of Madrid — depending on whence they came. All these cities seemed to have some head or other — whatever he might be called.

Right from the start St. Ange and Laclede had shared responsibility in Saint Louis. Each ruled his area with a light hand. The first Spanish Lieutenant Governor, Pedro Piernas had rarely flexed his muscles as an authoritarian representative of the King of Spain.

Now De Leyba was Lieutenant Governor. I liked the old man, but his illness limited his activities, and he was not popular with most of the residents of the village. With rumors of hundreds of Indians in war canoes on the river — Sioux, Winnebago, Kickapoo, Sauk, Fox, and Chippewa — De Leyba had summoned Captain Cartabona from Ste. Genevieve. The Captain now seemed to be in charge of all military matters. When De Leyba had ordered the citizens to dig a trench around the city, Auguste Chouteau had planned the rampart.

Now that Laclede was dead, Auguste seemed to have power beyond his business interests. No one man, however, really seemed in charge.

Then the people themselves decided to have a big holiday procession on the Feast of Corpus Christi, even though rumors had a thousand hostile Indians less than fifty miles away. It all sounded like the night of the big storm in Saint Louis two years before. The storm had knocked the roofs off houses. It had flooded basements and injured several citizens. The people simply got out of bed and cleaned up the mess; so that all was in shape before the Governor, utterly ignorant of the near-disaster, awakened in the morning.

That was the way with these people, stubborn, self-reliant, not easily budged, with a quiet let's-get-the-job-done frame of mind. They would probably hiss the Governor two days after he, or they, drove the Indians back north.

Could they possibly hold back the tribesmen? This procession out in the fields was really senseless. Did they want a miracle — like Saint Angela or whoever it was — driving back the Turks with a ceremonial? God could save them that way. Need they tempt Him?

The night was hot, the air damp, the twilight long. I was too tense to sleep. Nick and I walked along the *Rue Principale*. Even though I wore only a light cotton shirt with short sleeves, perspiration stood thick on my forehead.

Most men sat at their doors, their guns leaning against the door step. We carried ours. None of us could ever remember a night like this in Saint Louis.

Four men stood at the corner, talking in hushed tones. Two of them worked in the village, not on the river. The other two were farm boys from *Vide Poche*. None of them had been in danger before. The sight of my uncle seemed to reassure them.

"What's new?" Uncle Nick asked.

"Nothing sure," a villager answered. "One rumor has three men killed at Portage. Another has the Indians still above the Illinois River."

One of the farm boys broke in: "I met two men from Cahokia today. They came over to talk to the Governor. One said Clark would be back in Cahokia by tomorrow noon. The other was equally sure that the General had not yet left Kentucky."

"Believe the rumor you like," Nick said. "But don't depend on it."

"How was it on the Monongahela, Nick?" the other farm boy asked.

"The Indians were on our side then," Nick said, "and Langlade led them. I don't think he will come this time."

"Who's leading them?"

"I can't say," Nick answered. "Not Sinclair. He will stay in Mackinac and pay the Indians to attack us. I don't think he knows what he is doing — sending Sioux and Sauk on the same expedition! A man like Artime could turn the Sauk against the Sioux, and that would save us all."

"Why are they mad at us?" one of the farm boys asked. "We've always treated them fairly."

"We don't even know what they want," the other said. "Now they will try to shoot us."

"How do we know what we're supposed to do," the other blurted out, "when they attack without any warning."

"That's true," Nick said, "but it hardly matters now. What matters is what they do next."

"What do you think will happen, Nick?"

"I think they are here," he answered. "In the woods north of town. We were lucky they did not attack during the procession."

"That procession was stupid," the other townsman said.

"Not the procession," Nick countered, "but where it went — beyond the rampart. That trench is little enough — but at least it's there."

"You marched in the procession, Nick," the man remonstrated.

"I marched with one eye on the priest, the other on the woods to the north. My nephew here, he prayed. I prayed once — that the Indians would not storm out of the woods. Then I watched the woods."

"I really don't think the Indians would have attacked during the procession," I blurted out. "Maybe it's superstitious, but they respect ceremony."

"The Wisconsin Indians wouldn't attack," Nick said. "The Blackrobes have been up at Green Bay a long time. The Indians who trade there have seen the church ceremonies. But the Sauk and Sioux — who knows?" Nick shrugged. He turned west and looked up the hill. "We're walking out towards the tower. We'll see you again — after the British have gone back to their wickiups in the north."

The next day Nick and I took our places at the northwest corner of the trench. If ever I was glad he was at my side, it was at that moment. He had been in at least one battle before — on the Monongahela. I had been in none. Even though I had lived so long in the wild country, I had not even seen a man killed — until we shot Amnon.

We heard with horror that the Indians had killed men, women, and children on farms to the north of the city, out near Florissant and Spanish Lake. Such wanton killing of women and children was new to us. I wondered if Artime and Celeste had survived, alone in their castle on the summit. Could the village hold against the horde of Indians coming against us? I looked along the trench. The few men there leaned grimly against the parapet.

Suddenly a cart roared out of the woods to the north. "That's my cousin, Chancellier," a man in the trench shouted, and started out to help him. A larger man pulled him back.

We looked across the open field. The cart raced toward us. Chancellier drove, while a woman and three children huddled in the back. A second man fired from the rear, fending off the approaching redskins.

A cheer went up as the cart reached the parapet, but at that moment, the man in the rear fell dead from a head wound.

A Negro field worker loped towards the trench, an Indian close in pursuit. Nick tried to get the Indian in his gunsights, but the Negro's huge shoulders made this dangerous. The Indian was closing in. Suddenly the Negro spun with amazing agility and threw himself at the feet of the surprised Indian. Before the Sioux could recover himself, the Negro wrenched the Indian's gun from him and smashed his skull with the walnut gunstock.

Another Negro, racing toward the trench, fell wounded. He crawled for cover in a little ravine. He was too far away for anyone to go out and drag him in.

Suddenly from the woods north of us came a cry that sent a shiver through the sinews of the most hardened soldier in the trench; it was like the screech of an eagle swooping on a waterfowl; the cry of a panther crushing the neck of a fawn; the hiss of a rattlesnake striking its victim; it was all these and more; it was the cry of a human being, steeling himself to meet head-on one of his own kind; it was the war whoop of a Sioux chief launching the attack.

Suddenly whole groups of redskins poured out of the woods to the northwest, riding the high wind that brought dark clouds from the north. Hundreds drove towards the trench, braves from many up-river tribes. The attackers closed in.

"Here they come," Nick said. "You fire first. I'll cover while you reload."

Nick had been through this before. It was my first time. How good it was to have Uncle Nick beside me at that moment. My trigger finger was clammy. My mouth was parched. I dug my knees into the front wall of the trench. *Dear God*, I prayed, *let me be a man.* My whole body was tense.

"Now!" Nick said.

There in front of my musket, about thirty yards away, a thick-torsoed Sioux moved rapidly toward me. I fired. The man's chest seemed to stop before the rest of his body. His right side was a bloody pulp. He fell and did not move. I held my breath.

"Reload, now," Nick said. I followed the orders automatically. When my gun was ready again, Uncle Nick fired.

Redskins swarmed over the parapet. As a lithe Sioux began to swing his tomahawk at Nick, I fired just in time. The man fell. I swung my gun at the head of an Indian slipping up the trench from the east. He fell at my feet, blood pouring out of his mouth. Nick backed into the northwest corner of the trench and fended off two Sioux. I moved over to aid him. Suddenly the cannon in the tower boomed. The Indians leaped out of the trench and took refuge in a small ravine not far away. Nick stood guard while I reloaded.

The cannon boomed again. All along the line, the tribesmen moved back.

"They fear the cannon," Nick said. "One boom and they turn heels."

We survivors in the trench regrouped, took care of our wounded, and watched the area in front of us. Soon it became clear the Indians were retreating all along the west and north trench.

"Let's out and at them," someone shouted.

"The smarter thing — we stay here," a calmer voice said.

"A message came from De Leyba to remain in the trench until Cartabona organized a counterattack.

We defenders relaxed against the wall of the trench. *Would it only be a respite before a second raid?*

At the end of the trench, the bodies of three slain Sioux lay in a horrid cluster. They looked as if they were about to disentangle themselves. Two of the brown faces looked toward me, and the wide open eyes seemed to be watching me. My insides crawled at the sight. It seemed to me, even though it was only mid-morning, that this day had already been longer than any week I had ever known; that I was dreaming and it must have been in a dream that I had put an end to the lives of at least two of those men.

"One of those bodies could have been you," Nick said calmly, sensing my feeling, "and one might have been me."

Suddenly the mood of a moment before passed; and I felt a great relief that I was alive, that Nick was alive, and that my city was safe.

Then, with a sardonic smile, Nick asked: "By the way,. did anybody see a Britisher?"

"I didn't!" I said, trying to smile.

"Not I," a second said.

"The British will fight until the last Sioux falls," Chancellier's cousin said.

"It's a good trick, if you can get away with it," I said bitterly.

"They seem to succeed," Nick said. "This is my second fight in a war against England. In the other, we fought Scots and Long Knives."

The Indians at the edge of the woods were not regrouping. Instead they soon fled pellmell north along the river bank.

A shout went up from the line of the trench. Later that morning word came that Clark had beaten an equal number on the other side of the river.

Saint Louis had lived through its first siege.

Reports came fast now from all fronts. The attackers had killed twenty-one people, most of them habitants whose farms were far from the village, out toward St. Ferdinand de Florissant. Among them was Jean Cardinal, a relative of Rosellen's friends in Prairie du Chien. When the total count came in, seventy-one people were missing, most of these at a distance from the city.

The attack on the Cahokia side of the river had proven a fiasco also. The arrival of General Clark the day before had thrown fear into the Indians. The high wind prevented the defenders of Cahokia from hearing the heavy firing at Saint Louis. Otherwise Clark would have sent reinforcements.

"The Indians were afraid of Clark," Nick said, "and the Sauk and Fox dislike the Sioux more than they dislike us. They were tricked into the battle and wanted to get out."

"Battles will always be like this," Nick said. "Mostly confusion. You don't know what's behind it, or why it has to go on. All you can do is the job right ahead of you. Kill or be killed. It's a dreadful thought. And the fellow you kill doesn't really know why he's trying to kill you."

"Then, Uncle Nick, some men gather around a desk a thousand miles away and decide it was all a mistake. They join together for the next war against somebody else."

"Strange thoughts, my nephew, for the son of the man the Indians called 'The British-hater.'" Nick paused and changed his tone abruptly. "You did it — and that's what's most important. You stood your ground. You played the man when things were tough. Above all, you saved my life."

I began to think that this would be what men carried away from battles everywhere: not the thought that their side had beaten the enemy — or lost for that matter — but that they themselves had faced danger and had not run away. That in a moment of great fear they had played the man.

A few days later word came from Cahokia. Clark had to return to Kentucky. But he had ordered Montgomery to pursue the retreating Indians and free the captives. De Leyba would cooperate. Montgomery wanted three hundred and fifty men — Americans, Spanish, French — from both sides of the river. Many Illinois Indians had already gathered from below Kaskaskia for the campaign.

As members of the Saint Louis militia, Nick and I went to Montgomery's headquarters in Cahokia. "Could we meet the expedition at the narrows north of Saint Charles?" Nick asked. "We want to visit a friend on the way."

"My plan is to move northeast up the Illinois," Colonel Montgomery said. "Saint Charles is northwest of here. I'm sure you men know the country. Won't we be going in different directions?"

"All the rivers run confused just above Saint Louis," Nick said, pointing to a map on Montgomery's desk. "The Missouri moves north for a while; the Mississippi flows eastward; and the Illinois seems to fear making any move."

"Colonel," I broke in, pointing to a spot on the map, "our friend Artime Thomure lives here on the Mississippi. We'll go overland to Saint Charles, cross the ferry there, then ride north to Artime's home. If he and his wife are safe — as we feel sure they are — he'll ferry us across the Mississippi to this point. It's only six miles from there to the Illinois."

"It looks reasonable, men," Colonel Montgomery said. "Be there four nights from now."

"We will, thank you, Colonel," Nick said.

We left immediately. We saw little ravages of the attack in or near Saint Charles. No Indians had moved down the Missouri. They had come and gone along the Mississippi and the Illinois. We found Celeste and Artime safe and happy to see us.

We met Montgomery's men at the appointed spot and continued up the Illinois for several days. Then we moved overland to the Sauk and Fox villages. The area at the mouth of the Rock River had vivid memories for us. The Indians had fled.

Montgomery asked volunteers to raid as far as Prairie du Chien. "We'd better go," Nick said to me, "and get your future life settled."

We pushed on with a raiding party to the little village just above the point where the Wisconsin met the wide river. We sloshed along through three cold, rain-swept days — the most awful days I could ever remember — and didn't sleep through three worse nights. But the twenty-ninth of June dawned with spring-water clearness. The countryside breathed hope with fresh green foliage.

When we crossed the Wisconsin and moved into Prairie du Chien, I set out for the home of Mrs. Cardinal. I prayed that Rosellen would be there: the girl I had not seen for nine years, the girl who had indirectly professed her love so often in her letters.

I prayed to the Virgin Mother that I would not pass Rosellen on the street without recognizing her. I knew Rosellen was tall, attractive, with light brown hair, and a graceful body; but her face was not as clearly etched in my mind as her spirit. Frankly, I was not exactly sure what she looked like. I hoped that I would not mistakenly walk up to another woman and ask her, "Are you Rosellen Rien?" only to hear a disappointing and embarrassing negative.

I could excuse her for not recognizing me, unshaven, disheveled, dead tired, and dirty from the mud and grime of the campaign. I walked down the elm-lined streets. I saw no one who looked anything like my dim remembrance of Rosellen. Finally, I turned the corner. The Cardinal house stood as I remembered it. A young woman in a peach-colored dress worked among the flowers in the front yard. I quietly walked towards her. She looked up.

For a brief moment, uncertainty held her gaze. And then her eyes brightened. She smiled: "Hugh Roe."

"Rosellen?"

"It's been so long," she said, and was in my arms.

"Oh! So long, my darling," was all I could respond.

"Why did I wait?" she asked. "Once my husband died, I couldn't write to you. Before that, I was writing to a dream, to a man I knew only slightly, one who took me out of a drab existence. Now when I could have told you that I needed you, I could not bring myself to write."

"Maybe your dream is too far above reality," I mumbled. "I'm just a poor trader with little to show for a dozen years on the river."

"In all the years of our friendship," she went on, not regarding my words, "you respected the fact that I was someone else's wife. Your words were warm and kind. They made life move on. Years have gone by, but you're here now and that is all that matters!"

"Let's walk under the elms," I said, looking at the archway of branches that made the dirt road a cathedral.

We walked arm in arm. I knew that this was a day I had waited for all my life. I had so much to say. Yet I could say nothing then. I could not tell her why I had not written. But the past was past. The future would be ours together. We both had seen enough of life not to expect only springtime and rosebuds and the green promise of the soft maples. Together we could face it. Yes, together we would.

We walked on in silence. I wanted to speak, but as I began, she spoke, too, something casual to break the quiet.

I looked into her face and saw love there. Only then did I realize that her eyes were blue as the wind-swept Wisconsin sky. I prayed that I could answer her deepening love.

She tightened her clasp of my arm, and we walked on, side by side.

I pointed to a spot under the bluffs. "St. Joseph's Church at Prairie du Rocher nestles in a nook like that," I said. "My parents were married there. I was baptized there."

That is where we'll be married?" she asked.

"Would that be what you wanted?" I answered.

"I hope so, my love!"

The next morning word came that a strong British force was moving down the Wisconsin from Green Bay. Our troops had to move out immediately. We had to ride fast. No one could travel with us. As long as the war was on, I could not easily get back to Prairie du Chien. Further, until the Indian danger was over, it was not safe for Rosellen on the river.

Old Mr. Cardinal offered some hope. He wanted to visit the grave of his relative who had died in the defense of Saint Louis. If any group of voyageurs, not allied with the British, moved down the river the following spring, he would come along, and bring Rosellen with him.

Rosellen and I had waited so long! Heartbreaking as it might be, we could wait a few months more.

Three days after Nick and I reached Saint Louis, I awoke one morning to find this letter in Uncle Nick's hand:

"By the time you read this note, I will be on the way down the river with a flotilla. I thought a long while how best to say goodbye. I chose this way.

"My work as godfather is finished. If I may be allowed a word of pride, I think I've done my work well. Rosellen can look after you from here on. Of course, I was laughing when I wrote that last sentence. You've always been able to take care of yourself. I did want to see you through your first battle, as your father saw me through mine on the Monongahela. When you stood your ground during the attack on Saint Louis, I knew you had made it. You saved

my life there, too. I am grateful for that, and for countless other things, and especially your companionship.

"I'm giving you the property I own on the bluff near Sugar Loaf mound where you wanted to build your home. That's why I asked Laclede for it in the first place. You were too young to obtain a land grant at the time."

"I hope to say goodbye to Bernadette and Michel on the way downriver; and to Eileen in New Orleans. I will go on to Mexico to see if the Franciscans can use me on the Rio Grande missions. Ever since I heard Father Meurin talk of Saint Francis when I was a boy, I wanted to be like him. He never harmed bird, beast or man. We had to kill birds and animals to live; and sometimes even our fellow men. We usually called it self-defense. When we had to kill Indians who didn't even know why they were attacking Saint Louis, I said: "Enough!" Forty-four years of age might seem too old for some to begin a new life. I hope to try."

"May le bon Dieu bless you and Rosellen. Say a prayer once in a while for your,

Uncle Nick."

I cried. Tears came as they had not since my father's funeral.

Thoughts of Rosellen always looked forward with hope. Memories of Uncle Nick only took me back to what would never be again. When I did something for myself now that he had always done, I recalled the many times I had not said "thanks," the countless good deeds I had taken for granted. He had done certain tasks and I others with a kind of natural division of work. Only after he left did I realize how much I had depended on him.

After a day's work in the warehouse, we had often sat before a log fire and talked. His conversation never got dull. Whenever he repeated something, he gave it a new turn. Occasionally, a young Canadien would join us, and Nick would tell stories of the fur trade in the old days. Even these stories I heard so often had a fresh ring. Suddenly it struck me how often Uncle Nick told of our winter in New Mexico; and of the work that he did on the missions with the other friars while I studied Spanish under the direction of the Father Guardian.

Now evenings were blank. I boarded with a new family — a recent arrival from Cahokia who farmed his strips west of town and

had lots of children. He had an extra room and needed the money —
but he complained a lot and usually went out for a glass of wine in
the evening. So I taught the two oldest boys how to read and write
and kept them busy until their father returned. Their mother and
sisters spent the whole evening washing the pots and dishes and
putting them in the cupboards. The wife said nothing in my
presence.

The late fall dragged and a long winter seemed ahead. I began to
look for things to do to fill the slack. I went down to Prairie du
Rocher for a few days, then stopped in Cahokia on my return. The
world began turning again.

Clark had come back from Kentucky with a letter from Governor
Patrick Henry, commissioning him a Brigadier General.

"Detroit is the heart that controls the life-blood of the
northwest," George Rogers Clark said as he unrolled a map and
pointed out the fortification between Lake Erie and Lake Huron on
the west bank of the connecting river. He had called a council
meeting at his headquarters in Cahokia, and we all gathered around
the table. "We must take Detroit if we are to secure the entire
region."

Like Father Gibault, I had admired Clark from the moment I met
him. Within two years, he had captured Kaskaskia, faced down the
mightiest chiefs of the upriver tribes, marched through the winter
swamps to take Vincennes, and defended Cahokia against five hundred warriors.

"With Vincennes in our grasp," Clark said, "thanks to our good
friend Father Gibault, our right flank is covered. I have talked to the
new Spanish Lieutenant-Governor across the river in Saint Louis
about an expedition to secure Saint Joseph near the tip of Lake
Michigan. I hope the new Lieutenant-Governor is as easy to work
with as De Leyba was."

"Governor Cruzat had an earlier term," I said. "The Saint Louis
people like him."

"They didn't give Governor De Leyba the thanks he deserved," Clark said. "I could never understand why they did not like him."

"They claimed he lacked tact," I came back, "and that he drank too much. What really irked them was that he enforced the trade regulations and the tariffs. Cruzat had quietly, and perhaps wisely, ignored the regulations. The King of Spain, however, seemed to think De Leyba did a good job. He honored him. Unfortunately, news of the honor came only after he died a month after the attack."

"May we offer *you* our congratulations, General," Father Gibault broke in. "We were happy to know that Governor Jefferson approved your work. We doubt there are many twenty-eight-year-old generals in the entire world."

"Thank you, *Pere* Gibault," Clark came back. "Excuse me for not mentioning it earlier, but last year Governor Henry expressed his appreciation of your work for the colonial cause.

"Speaking of the Governor," Clark went on, "Virginia promises to send five hundred troops. Colonel Bowman will bring three hundred from Kentucky. With the support of the people in Illinois and of the Spanish governor, we will win the whole Northwest."

"Count on us for what support you need, General," the priest assured him. "Be it supplies or manpower."

"You're the one man I can always count on," the young general acknowledged.

When the meeting was over, Father Gibault and I walked to the home where we were staying. The priest thought out loud: "General Clark deals in objective realities. But the subjective human factors block him, like the colonial colonel in Pittsburg who seems more concerned about getting his share of the credit than in beating the British."

"I heard that Governor Jefferson made Clark a General mainly to counter that man's manoeuvers," I said. We walked along in silence. I knew that the current of the future flowed with men like George Rogers Clark. The wide river might stem Clark's westward advance for a time. Eventually, he or someone like him, would throw his men across the river and on to the Shining Mountains. The wide river was meant to unite, not divide the land. Some day it would do so. We would have to take lesser steps before the big ones, with Clark directing those steps.

"Men like Clark were made for great things, my son," Father

Gibault said at length. "Just think. He is two years younger than you, fifteen years younger than I am. Already a land as big as France depends on his courage. You and I were made to give him the help he needs."

I was happy to do what Clark asked me to do. I never doubted that I could do whatever I set out to do. I had crossed the plains through the *Comancheria*, fought the rapids on the Current River, survived a sub-zero blizzard in the mountains on a hunting trip during that New Mexican winter. In dealings with other men, however, I felt that every man was made for a particular work, and that he ought not to waste time fighting for a job another man was doing well enough. I knew what I could do. I knew what others could do. I expected them to ask me to do what I could do better than they. I gladly supported those who could do a task better than I.

Father Gibault went on: "George Rogers Clark reached out for glory too soon. An older man would know how to live with the mediocrity of others. He does not. He is like a catamount who can conquer any visible foe before him but is trapped by unseen forces. Virginia will not be able to spare five hundred troops. Even if she were able, the troops would never get this far. Whether Bowman will come from Kentucky, I do not know." The priest shrugged his shoulders.

"The General is right when he says that we must take Detroit," I came back. "It is a big task."

"Do you think the Spanish Governor will march against Saint Joseph?" the priest asked.

"Yes, I do, *mon pere*. He knows that General Sinclair at Mackinac loaded the Sioux chiefs with presents. In turn, the chiefs pledged to send one thousand warriors against Saint Louis in the summer. We must strike first, destroy their supplies, and show strength to deter them. When the troops go, I will go with them."

"The habitants have been saying," Father Gibault said, "that the Spanish want to take the whole Northwest for themselves. And that's why the Governor agreed to this plan."

"You know they are wrong," I said flatly. "Spain has over-extended itself already. She has enough trouble holding Louisiana. The Governor merely hopes to forestall another attack on Saint Louis."

"I believe you're right," Father Gibault said. "France's day on this continent is over. That's why I joined Clark. Spain is near the end of her great day, too. People will someday look back and wonder how the Spanish Empire could have lasted so long, how a little country did so many tremendous things!"

"England is going down before her own colonies," Father Gibault went on. "Strangely, I think she has played her hand well in Canada. Wouldn't it be amazing if in the future the only British part of the continent were French Canada!"

"Bishop Briand has his part in that," I said, tentatively. "Just as his one spiritual son in the Illinois country has had his hand in the end of the British rule."

Father Gibault's face held a wry smile. He said: "I always ask myself this question: 'What would Bishop Briand do if he were here in the Illinois Country, a thousand miles from Quebec?' I always come up with the same answer. He would do what I am doing."

The late months of 1780 were irritating ones for George Rogers Clark. Only one hundred and fifty troops arrived from Virginia. Colonel Bowman attacked the Shawnee town of Chillicothe and met disaster. A few surviving Kentuckians reached Clark, more intent on seeking refuge than in starting against Detroit.

I understood how Clark felt. Never before had I known such restlessness. I hounded each contingent of Indians who came into the village, asking them about Prairie du Chien and British preparations in the North. A Canadian voyageur came in one day with a group of Fox Indians. He told that the British planned an attack on Saint Louis the following spring.

The Governor, Cruzat, reacted immediately. He set up two forts, one on the Mississippi among the Sauks and Fox and one on the Illinois. A veteran campaigner, Jean Baptiste Mailliet, commanded this latter garrison.

I talked to Clark's men as often as I got to Cahokia. What did the General think? Was he expecting the British to attack? They knew as little as I did.

Only when I stopped asking these unanswerable questions did a tightness clutch my chest, and the days seemed endless since I left Prairie du Chien. How sharply the picture of Rosellen was now etched within my brain. How vividly I still felt the full warmth of her embrace when we had said "Goodbye." With what longing her image swam before my eyes as the voyageurs sang their songs of hopeless love.

Finally I decided to write a letter. I did not stop to think that no one traveled north any longer; and that even if anyone tried to get through, the ice would soon clog the river and he would never reach his destination. When I began "Dearest Rosellen," a lightness of spirit filled me. My pen raced over the paper twice as rapidly as I had ever written before. Over and over again I sprinkled the pages with the words "Rosellen darling."

Suddenly I realized that after all our correspondence this was the first real love letter I had ever written to her. I smiled to think that I would probably never be able to send it.

One day all waiting ended. Cruzat announced that he would keep his promise to Clark and send a mid-winter force against Saint Joseph under a competent commander, the merchant Eugene Pourre. The British had stored supplies and equipment to launch a campaign the following summer against the settlements in Kentucky, Illinois, and Missouri that could destroy us all. Our preventive expedition was, without question, a daring gamble. The January thaw would last for a few days; then storms could sweep in from the northwest and bury us in a swirling blizzard of white. Cruzat knew that the Indians stayed close to their villages in winter. The hostile tribes would not have scouting parties on the waterways. Surprise would be possible. It was the tactic the British had used to win Fort Duquesne and Clark to retake Vincennes.

Actually, at the time I thought little of the stark-mad difficulties. Since then I have often felt that doing a less wise thing was preferable to doing nothing. It was certainly true that winter. I walked with brighter steps once I knew we would soon be on the way. Christmas was mere anticipation — a joyous time because we would soon be moving out.

On January second, our contingent from Saint Louis swung over to the Illinois bank to meet the men of Cahokia. I was in a canoe with a veteran voyageur from Portage des Sioux. He knew the river and had a deserved reputation as a steady hand in a crisis. But he wasn't Nick Soumande. I had missed Uncle Nick every day since he had left, but never as on the expedition into Illinois.

A dry west wind pushed us across the river to the rendezvous with the Cahokians. Our force numbered sixty-five militiamen and sixty Potawatomie Indians under Chiefs Nakawine and Sekinak. Paddling close to the east bank, we passed the conflux of the Missouri. Farther on, we spotted the strange green and yellow bird painted on the limestone bluff. Father Marquette had seen it — and every voyageur after him. We pushed our canoe into the Illinois, the seventh vessel in the long flotilla.

The first night was cold, but the second day dawned clear. I prayed that the wind would hold from the west. It did the next day, and the next. On January 12, one week after setting out, we reached the point where the river turns east. We were already halfway to our destination. We met Jean Baptiste Malliet and his twelve militiamen who garrisoned the stockade on the river. They joined us.

Winter closed in. When I awoke on the 20th of January, the river had frozen so solidly that the troops had to proceed overland. We cached our boats, left a few men to guard them, and started the long trek through the snow-bound prairies. Winter fell in fury. The wind whipped at the back of our left shoulders. Four days trudged by.

Scouts went out to contact the friendly Milwaukee Indians. Late one afternoon, as we were making camp, the scouts returned with a contingent of friendly warriors. Prospects brightened.

The next day was clear again but colder than before. The wind dropped, but so did the temperature. We passed the southern tip of Lake Michigan and turned northeastward.

Commander Pourre sent into the village a friendly and deceptively clever young Potawatomie, whom the Spaniards called "Lajes," in the hope of neutralizing the Indians near the fort with a promise of booty. Lajes returned with important information: the Indians and French residents of the neighborhood were neutral. The British officer had left for Detroit after depositing rich stores. A Canadien force carelessly guarded them.

In the cold gray pre-dawn of February 12th, the converging columns completely surrounded the fort. We attackers took our places unseen.

The men inside the walls of the fort were our fellow Frenchmen — but men who by a strange turn of fate had pledged loyalty to England. To have to fight them was not pleasant. I turned my mind from the men inside to the meaning of the stockade. It seemed a lifeless mass of logs. Yet it held supplies to bring death and destruction to countless people in Missouri, Illinois, and Kentucky during the coming spring.

I felt a stirring in the cold still air — the stirring of approaching dawn. In that ghostly light I could see the men crowded near me, and had I not seen them, I would have known they were at hand because of the odor of unwashed bodies.

The false dawn passed, and the shadows grew blacker than before. A dog barked near the fort ahead of us. Someone near me cursed, fearful that the barking might arouse the sleeping garrison. I felt like cursing, too. I was cold, hungry, and worst of all, afraid: afraid that the dog might alert the men inside the walls; afraid of what lay before us. A man near me sighed, and I realized that he was as afraid as I.

I heard the call of the cardinal, the signal that the troops on the south were in position. The same signal re-echoed from the column hidden in the woods near the north wall. Then Commander Pourre ordered Jean Baptiste Malliet with his twelve militiamen to move forward stealthily through the underbrush from the east of the fort. Hidden behind a clump of willows on a sandy hill, we watched the attackers move furtively up a small draw before fanning out. I hoped that they would get to the stockade without being seen.

Malliet's men reached the log wall. Simultaneously they boosted two men to the top. These gave the signal for the rest to follow and leaped noiselessly into the compound. I waited fearfully for a blast of gun-fire, but all men went over the wall without a sound.

I saw two men scale the opposite wall and dash north. Musket shots from Milwaukee braves concealed in the underbrush cut them down. Then the door of the stockade flew open and Malliet called out that the garrison had surrendered.

We assault troops converged from all sides toward the open gate. Pourre ordered the Indians to follow. The supplies were as plentiful as we had anticipated. Only two men had been killed — the two who unwisely had tried to flee. The commander planned to release the rest of the garrison. He distributed the captured supplies evenly among the Milwaukee Indians and the friendly tribes of the immediate region.

We stayed at the fort one day. That night gave us our last comfortable sleep for a long time.

The next morning we began the long trek back. We had come through hostile country undetected. Maybe we could get back the same way. We had taken the fort without losing a single man. We had built up tension and had no way of sloughing it off. In one way, the ease of the capture drained us more than a hard battle.

We moved warily south along the lake shore. The Milwaukee Indians accompanied us to the headwaters of the Illinois near where we had met them. They had provided scouts before, but now we had to put out our own guards.

Each night we camped in the lee of a thicket or against the bank of a stream, where we could find shelter in case a storm came before dawn. The men were tough, long accustomed to winters in the open, but the night guard was bitter. I had the midnight watch for two nights straight. Nothing moved in the land beyond the forest where we camped. Nothing moved except the Big Dipper in its slow course around the North Star. Guard duty seemed so senseless. No Indians were inclined to attack at night in the snow. But suppose we had posted no guard and, for some reason, they did attack. Few of us would have lived.

Merely to survive on guard duty was a problem in itself. On the second night, I grew so cold my ribs trembled. The only way to keep alive was to keep moving; and thus an hour watch fatigued me more than a half-day's march.

The snow caught us the fifth night after we left Saint Joseph's. It came slowly in the twilight just after we had made camp. The commander felt it would be a long and fierce storm. He ordered us to gather several days supply of wood and to eat our first warm meal of deer meat since we left the Fort. By darkness the wind had risen and the snow flew through the air in frenzy, pinning us at the foot of a ledge. I slept well that night in spite of the blizzard that howled like some giant wolf out of a prehistoric past. It still howled when I awoke in the morning.

Even when the darkness gave way to a gray dawn, the whirling snow blotted out the entire world. To venture out would be senseless. We might have walked in circles; and even if we went straight ahead, we would probably have made only a few miles with a great waste of energy. The commander wisely gave orders to stay where we were.

The day dragged on. Hour after hour. Minute after minute. Unending. I thought of Rosellen and why I had come. I lightly touched Rosellen's message through the buckskin above my heart, and life and hope seemed to come back to me. Finally night came once again. My arms twitched, my knees and thighs quivered and jerked. My eyes ached, but finally fatigue overwhelmed me.

When I awoke, the storm had ended, but the wind still blew. Before us lay an endless expanse of white, broken only by an occasional oak forest, and the row of trees that lined the river bank. We moved west along the Illinois, trudging through the deep snow. The wind cut our faces. We bowed our heads into it and pushed on. No war parties would be out looking for us now — but that was small consolation. Cold day followed cold day. We reached the place where we had cached the canoes. Ice was so thick on the river, that the hopes of a swift canoe trip downstream disappeared in the snow-filled air. The supplies, however, were still intact. The guards were happy to see us back. We re-provisioned, cached our canoes in as safe a place as we could find, and trudged painfully along the banks of the Illinois.

My feet grew steadily colder as the skin of my moccasins grew thinner. Finally the right sole wore through. I cut a piece of leather from the fringe of my jacket. This makeshift patch gave slight protection. Every step became painful.

I could not think of the ten thousand steps I would have to take, but only of the next one — then the next. This was the only way to survive; to put one foot ahead of the other on the snowy ground; to lunge ahead, stumbling occasionally, but going on, not with any conscious effort, but mechanically, step after step, without thought or plan, fearing to think lest the reality overwhelm me; relentlessly on — freezing all night, even after choosing camp with care in the partial shelter of an oak forest; rising again, not because sleep had refreshed me, but because the sun was now overhead somewhere, hidden by the grey clouds; pushing on and on through country without hill or indulation, a flat bare table almost devoid of landmarks; on and on, down the endless river.

How I kept going I couldn't understand. I thought I knew the limit of my endurance, but I learned that there is almost no limit to endurance if the determination and motive are there. One week, two weeks, time was endless. Then one evening the sky cleared and the north wind died down. The stars stood out clear in a black, cold sky. The air grew colder and colder. No sleep came that night. It was too cold.

I felt better when the order came to march early the next morning. By ten, the sun warmed the clear air. The snow began to melt. We passed the ice-line on the Illinois. The river flowed free alongside us, restoring our spirits. We might have to move our legs mechanically ten thousand times more. Yet now we knew we would make it. In early March we were home.

Shortly after I reached Saint Louis, I rode out to the property on the bluff. I looked at a sugar maple I had planted the previous fall. It looked dead. With my fingernail I scratched the end of a small twig. Under the brown bark, green life showed. I felt then that my long wait would soon be over.

When the purple martins returned from the south and the silver maples began to bud, I walked down to the river every evening. The days grew noticeably longer. The trees leafed out. April gave way to May. The aroma of peach blossoms filled the air.

No one had come down from the North. Yet rumors spread through the villages like bees in a field of clover. The attack on Saint Joseph had had its effect. The ordinarily restless tribes of the North had remained calm. Peace would soon come.

Then one evening the clouds burst into orange flame as the sun set beyond the western ridge. I looked at the entrancing sky. Then instinctively I gazed up the river. A flotilla of canoes stood on the water. In the second boat, I could make out a girl in a blue dress, with her golden hair touched by the evening light.

I ran to the bank. In a few minutes Rosellen was in my arms. "At last, my darling," was all I could say.

We had planned to be married in the little church under the bluff at Prairie du Rocher. A throng of habitants gathered for the wedding — relatives of my mother, friends from the old settlements, a few families from Saint Louis, and Artime and Celeste all the way from their beautiful home above the *Memelles*. It proved a homecoming for many people.

Michel gave away the bride. Bernadette led the singing. Father Gibault performed the ceremony. Since Saint Joseph was patron of the church, the priest said a few words about "the only man who loved Mary before she became famous." What else he said I hardly remembered, except that Saint Joseph would protect our home day after single day.

The gathering at the old Soumande homestead surpassed any celebration Prairie du Rocher had enjoyed since the French days. Old friends greeted us warmly, welcomed the bride, and then went on with their merry-making.

During the festivities, Michel and a cousin from Ste. Genevieve came up to Rosellen and me. "We're ready to take you across the river," he said. "This party can go on without you."

"At least until the wine runs out," the cousin said.

Our traveling clothes were in the *caleche* we had driven to the church. Michel had borrowed the little cart from the tavern-keeper. It was the only one in Prairie du Rocher at the time. I helped Rosellen into the vehicle. Michel and his cousin would ride their horses behind us.

Ordinarily a habitant who intended to get married built his home, with the help of friends and neighbors, before marriage; and the newly married couple usually spent their first night together in their own home. We had no home in Prairie du Rocher, nor even in Saint Louis where we intended to live; and we were going on a wedding trip to New Orleans.

For two days, until a flotilla would move downstream, we would stay at the home of Michel's cousin, and he and his family would remain in Prairie du Rocher.

We rode to a river crossing south of town, far below the place where Uncle Nick and I used to dock our canoe. We tied our horses to the lower branch of a silver maple and got in a large pirogue. In a short time we were out in the current, angling rapidly across the river. Michel and his cousin were powerful paddlers. The late afternoon breeze was cool across the waters as we approached Ste. Genevieve. I helped Rosellen to the bank.

"Our house is the little one between the Valle's and the church," Michel's cousin said.

"I remember the one, thank you," I answered.

With an impish look, Michel's cousin said: "I hope you find the bed soft and comfortable."

Before I could think of anything to say, Rosellen came back unselfconsciously: "I'm sure if it's soft, we'll find it comfortable." She smiled. "Thank you so much."

The two men laughed and pushed the canoe from the bank.

We moved slowly up the maple-lined streets, cool under the mantle of the leaves. We walked to the door of the home that would be ours for two days. I knocked. No one answered.

We entered. I latched the door from the inside. Rosellen sighed. "It's lovely here," she said.

I was going to say: "Anywhere you are is lovely." But that seemed trite.

She took off her coat and sat on the side of the bed. I kissed her. She sank back against a pillow. I leaned over, embraced her warmly, and kissed her again. When I might have ended the kiss, she slowly drew me to herself, prolonging the embrace. Her arms caressed my shoulders. Moments went by. Her whole being cried out for me to come to her. That we belonged to each other.

I drew her to me. She signed, and I felt her full bosom heave against my chest. We came together in complete embrace. The ecstasy of union flooded us both.

Time passed. We lay side by side, fulfilled, at peace.

Finally, I broke the silence: "At last we have each other."

She clasped my right hand.

"Ten years," I went on slowly, "ten years have gone by since I first met you in Prairie du Chien. I wanted you then — but found you were married. Then you wrote. I hoped — and living in hope kept me for this moment."

"I know that, my husband. During those long years, when the fact of your letters told me what you never said openly — that you cared — I often came to wish that Amnon would die somewhere on the western rivers."

I sat up and looked at her. "You wished — and I had to fight the terrible temptation to bring that wish about. Oh Rosellen! I must tell you about the terrible day — "

"In the Sauk camp on the Rock River?" she interrupted. "I heard about it, my husband."

"I knew that someday I would have to tell you," I said. "Why not now?"

"The two men from Prairie du Chien," she broke in. "They were with you in the Sauk camp. They told me that Amnon was dead. At first, they did not say how he came to die. People offered their sympathy. I accepted it, hardly knowing what to say."

She clasped my hand more tightly and went on. "Then those two men began to talk more freely in the tavern and rumors spread. When they said it was the tall one with the sandy hair who cast the deciding vote — the one whose father fought with Pontiac and hated the British. Oh Hugh — I hoped you did not — " she stopped.

"That I did not have blood on my hands," I blurted out, "and hate in my heart — "

"When the whole story came out," she said, "I knew what a dreadful moment it must have been for you — to want a man out of the way — and have to decide that he deserved to go — without letting hate move you to that decision. By the time you came to Prairie du Chien with Montgomery's troops, I understood it all."

"Thank you, my darling." I sank back on the pillow.

"I could have told you," she said, "when we walked together under the elms in Prairie du Chien. But I could not break the spell of those happy moments."

I clasped her hand more tightly.

"All that counts," she said, "is what lies ahead."

I smiled. "Uncle Nick told me that on the bluff south of here seventeen years ago."

"Maybe now you'll listen." She leaned over and kissed me.

The marriage in Prairie du Rocher had been the occasion of a grand homecoming for many. Our arrival in New Orleans provided similar opportunities for those who had gone south with De Villiers. Some lived in New Orleans, most of them out in the equally beautiful country along the Bayou Teche. Rosellen and I spent several weeks with Eileen and her husband who ran a successful business in New Orleans.

"Life should go on like this all the time," I said, "quietly, peacefully, and lovingly."

"But we're not in heaven yet, my husband, although it's the nearest thing I've seen to it."

We sat on the lower branch of a live oak and swayed in the southerly breeze that carried the scent of lilacs. A grey bird perched on the branches, not ten feet away, seemingly oblivious of us. It sat quietly a minute, colorless, undistinguished. Then to Rosellen's surprise, it let out a few notes like the sound of a kitten.

"Is that the catbird I've heard so much about?" she asked.

"The catbird? Oh no, my darling," I answered. "The catbird is to this one as the crow is to the eagle. Wait." I clapped my hand sharply.

The startled bird flew gracefully to the top of a cypress tree, its feathers a beautiful blending of grey, white, and black.

"He loves the top of anything," I said, "a tree, or house or barn. Watch now!"

The bird leaped several feet straight up in the air, like a child jumping with glee, then fell limply back to the tip of the cypress. He repeated the leap a short time later.

Tentatively, he sang the two-note call of the phoebe, then the whistle of the cardinal and the more intricate song of the oriole. Next, he burst forth in a rapture of notes: first plaintive and sad, then soaring to a frenzy of joy; and finally he gathered them all together in a burst of sound that went on and on until the whole world seemed hushed in awe.

Rosellen remained in rapture a few moments, then she said, "That is the most beautiful song I have ever heard."

"That, darling," I answered, "is the greatest creature, next to man, that *le bon Dieu* ever put on this earth. It is *le moquer*, the mockingbird."

That afternoon O'Neill suggested, "Why don't you join Eileen and me for dinner this evening at the French Market? I don't think you people have had anything to eat for four days."

Rosellen only smiled, but I answered: "I can't say that eating has been a big concern for us lately."

"I bet you people don't have a *restaurant* in Saint Louis as yet," O'Neill said.

"We don't even have an inn where a voyageur can spend the night. Visitors stay with private families, and the voyageurs bunk in one of the warehouses."

O'Neill turned to his wife. "Eileen, bunk is a good old Anglo-Saxon word that means sleep for the night. Your brother forgets that he taught you little English."

"I'm sorry," I said, turning to Eileen. "I remember when you two met. O'Neill spoke no French. You spoke little English, but you seem to have gotten along well enough."

"We compromised," O'Neill said. "I learned French."

Within an hour we four walked down Burgundy Street. Though Spanish in government, New Orleans had remained French in spirit. The hurricane of the previous year had done little damage in that section. We entered a building, unprepossessing on the outside, but containing a tropical garden with palms and flowers between the dining tables in the interior.

"I've never seen anything so lovely," Rosellen said.

"Not exactly like Chouteau's warehouse, is it?" O'Neill said.

We laughed. A waiter took us to a table among the palms.

"If you ladies don't mind a bit of politics for a moment," O'Neill said, "I have a question for my brother-in-law. How did the war go up that way?"

"Good enough," I answered. "The northern Indians attacked Saint Louis and Cahokia last year. Clark was too much for them."

"We heard about that fellow Clark," O'Neill said. "Oliver Pollock provided him with material and supplies. He's a *negociant* who moves in and out of New Orleans. I've met Pollock on several occasions."

"Father Gibault supported Clark," I said. "And he won over most of the habitants — especially when he brought news that France had entered the war."

"Governor Galvez had a hunch France and Spain would fight the British," O'Neill said. "He got ready, and once Spain declared war, moved fast."

"England had almost surrounded New Orleans," Eileen broke in.

"Yes, that's right," O'Neill said. "The British set up headquarters at Pensacola. Their captain put garrisons at Fort Charlotte, near Mobile, and at several other places in West Florida." O'Neill paused. "You don't know where those places are, but you did pass Baton Rouge on the left bank of the river as you came down. That's northwest of here. The British had forces there, too. Two years ago, Galvez started knocking over post after post. He sent fourteen hundred men against one fort. Last year he took Pensacola."

"This wild Irish husband of mine fought in all those battles," Eileen said. "If the British had captured him, they would have put him to death, because he was a deserter."

"I was not a deserter," O'Neill said with a wry smile. "I was a poor Irish boy who got lost one night and couldn't find my way back." He paused. "But why talk more about wars on a night like this! It's a night for song and laughter, and — " he smiled as the servants brought in the food — "good things to eat."

A violinist accompanied a girl who walked from table to table singing songs. When she reached O'Neill, he whispered something in her ear. Then she began a French love song.

"It's for us, darling," I said to Rosellen. "The song says that she hopes our love will go on as warm as the breeze over the gulf and as steady as the flow of the river." I found her hand under the table and clasped it tightly.

When we returned home in the fall, we found temporary quarters in the home of an older widow. One day we rented a caleche from Jeremy Maligne and drove down the *Rue d'Eglise*. We passed Joseph Labusciere's large stone house and several other houses of stone. Most of the other residences were still of frame construction. We drove out of the village southwest to Chouteau's Pond, crossed Mill Creek below the dam, and climbed the oak-covered rise to the south of the waters. A short time later we reached our property on the bluff.

"Do you like it?" I asked.

"It's perfect," Rosellen said. "I hope we can build our home here."

The maples, ashes, and hickories were sturdy young trees now. The linden and sycamore were fully grown. The row of cedars formed a wind break on the terrace to the west.

Rosellen and I stood arm in arm and looked across the Mississippi to the Illinois bluffs.

"I'll spend little time on the river now and more in the office of the fur company. There is so much correspondence — and in three languages. The little Spanish I learned gives me three right hands."

"That's right. All here know French. The officials know Spanish. I know English. But you alone know all three."

"Old Father Meurin got me off to a good start with those Latin lessons."

"Yes. And you've worked hard at it, too. You should get more pay for your work."

I laughed. "Your Scottish traits are showing up already."

Rosellen smiled, too. "Really, my husband, you are little concerned about material things — and God bless you for it. But I think if you did have a little Scottish blood in you, you'd be able to get a better price for your work, especially as interpreter."

"You're right," I said. "I'm like most of the voyaguers, unconcerned about money. I notice that the men who go on the expeditions make little. The money goes mostly to the fellows like Chouteau who stay home and organize and send out the traders. What I'm really interested in is this: that this be one free land along the wide river."

"I know that, my husband. Since that's what your concern is you can speak out on that more forcibly. Remember, your brother-in-law said that when we were in New Orleans."

"Yes, he did," I said, recalling that O'Neill had remarked how deeply I felt on issues but hesitated to speak out on them. I made up my mind that I would do so. I had spoken when Clark came to Kaskaskia — but only because Father Gibault had told me to do so. In the future, I would speak my mind.

Occasionally Artime came into the city. Sometimes he rode

directly overland from the Saint Charles ferry, accompanied by one or other of his rollicking brothers-in-law. On other occasions he took the longer way by canoe. This time he came down the river and walked into the office of the fur company.

I had not seen him for a long time. He gave me a grizzly hug, and his voice of greeting filled the room.

"It's great to see you, too, Artime," I said. "I've got two things to talk about."

"Two things? Which one first?"

"The first is the new home we plan to build. We want a stone house like yours."

"Good! Good! Good!"

"Do you still have your quarry going?"

"We quarry stone every once in a while," Artime responded. "We can make a raft of logs and float a supply down the river. How soon do you want the stones?"

"As soon as possible."

"I'll see what I can do," Artime responded. "You know how Celeste's brothers are. They roar around doing nothing for a long time, but when they begin to work, they get it done in a hurry. We'll get that stone for you."

"That's good for you, Artime. I'll arrange to have some walnut timbers cut in the *Prairie des Noyers.*"

"Now that's the first thing. You said you also wanted to talk about something else."

"I want to show you the present Rosellen and I brought you from New Orleans. I think you'll like it." I removed the covering from a large picture frame.

"Good! Good! Good!" Artime blurted out. "It's as pretty as a picture of the Channel from the French coast."

"It *is* a picture of the Channel from the French coast," I answered.

"This picture is worth one rock house on your property," Artime said. "I'll get Celeste's brothers going at the quarry before they have to plant their crops this spring. In the meantime, have the axmen cut some oak for flooring and walnut for walls and door frames. Expect us in about three weeks."

When Artime left, I immediately hired a group of men to dig the basement. The methods had not advanced far from the way we had dug the cellar for Laclede's warehouse twenty years before. They had only shovels and simple wheelbarrows to haul the dirt away. The only difference was this: they did not have the help of the Missouri squaws who joined us that first fall for several weeks.

By the time they had the basement ready, Artime and his four brothers-in-law brought the quarried stone down the river. Artime borrowed a stout cart from an old friend of fur-trading days and slowly hauled the stones to the site on the bluff. In the meantime, the Currier boys began the stone walls.

We planned a house forty feet in width, twenty feet in depth. Two small rooms on each end would open on *la grand salle* that would stretch across the center of the house from the front to the rear galeries. The house would face southeast, so as to enjoy the prevailing summer breezes and give a downriver view towards Durand's Head, a projection of bluff just north of Prairie du Rocher.

"This is the sixth house they've built," Artime said. "Their own. Then mine. Now yours. They get better each time. The first one listed a bit, like a batteau with a misplaced cargo." The brothers moved like beavers, said little, smiled often, told their own jokes with loud guffaws.

"What are they laughing about?" I asked Artime.

"Only they know. Not even their sister Celeste understands their jokes. But they can really work."

They covered the ground with a load of crushed rock several inches thick, then told Artime and me to lay the oak flooring. The timbers had already arrived from Chouteau's Mill below the pond. I remembered when Joseph Taillon had built the mill shortly after I moved up from Prairie du Rocher. Auguste Chouteau had purchased it and we called the pond behind it Chouteau's Pond.

We chose two unmilled hickory logs to stretch across the basement ceiling and support the first floor. These, in turn we supported with four large hickory trunks that the Curriers embedded in stone and lime. By the time we had the oak floor of the basement in place, the Currier brothers were ready to move beyond the ground level to the first floor.

It amazed me how fast and expertly they set their stone. I hired a farm boy from Louisbourg — we now called it Delor's Settlement, after Clement Delor who founded it — to mix and carry the mortar for the wall builders. An expert woodworker in the village had built the doors and window frames, with arangement for many small panes of glass. Rosellen remarked how attractive they looked. I had to admit that she was correct. Since I had never seen any other type, I had never alluded to the fact before this.

So fast did the stone masons work on the wall that I had to hire another farm boy to mix and carry mortar and two woodworkers to help Artime and me finish the floors and ceiling to keep pace with the Curriers. We would have plenty of time to finish the four inside rooms later.

The roof had a high pitch so that the attic was spacious. Putting in the shingles required experienced men. Two in Saint Louis specialized in that task. In an amazingly short time, the Currier brothers and we, their assorted helpers, had the exterior of the house finished.

"What do I owe them?" I asked Artime.

"My guess is that they'll accept nothing. They sold the logs of their raft they put together to haul the stone downriver for far more than they expected to get. They enjoyed the work. At home they would simply have sat around, waiting for spring. If you don't mention money, I won't and, I'll bet, they won't either."

I did not take Artime's advice. "What do I owe you?" I asked the oldest of the Currier brothers.

"Nothing," he said. "If neighbors can't help neighbors, they ain't neighbors. You helped Artime. Your wife fed us well. Good cook. We enjoyed ourselves coming to Saint Louis." Then turning to his brothers, "Didn't we?"

They all laughed, gathered their tools, and left.

In a surprisingly short time, we were able to move into our new home. We sat on the front porch looking out over the wheat fields growing golden on the Illinois prairie. A pleasant breeze came across the river. A mockingbird sang as if God had just made the world. The sunset sky was orange and blue.

"The two hard maples are doing fine," Rosellen said.

"Ten years ago, my darling, Uncle Nick and I planted four. He always said if you wanted one tree, plant two. One of the pair on the left never grew. I took out the weaker one on the right the next fall."

"My husband, the cedars behind the house will make a nice windbreak in winter. These trees add so much to our home."

"And your flower garden sets them off."

"I don't want to argue," she said with a smile. "But it's your trees that make this house a home."

"We can thank Uncle Nick for them," I said.

"When you came to Prairie du Chien, you said: 'Let's walk under the elms.' I thought that sounded romantic — but I did not know one tree from another. Only later did I find out they really were elms. And now, I know maples and ashes, and oaks and cedars, and the flowering dogwoods on the side of the bluff."

"We can thank Uncle Nick for them, too. He brought those in from the Meramec hills a year after we transplanted the cedars."

"My husband, I never really believed when you told me that the sumacs would turn bright red, and the hickories yellow, and the hard maples a brilliant orange. But I've seen the change three years now. It makes autumn so much more enjoyable when I can watch for each turning. Here we have two months of glorious spring and an equally lovely fall. Yet I never hear a single word of praise for the beautiful weather. But when it's bad, everyone complains."

I smiled. "They're not complaining, they're bragging. The damp air comes up from the Gulf of Mexico, so it's obviously more sultry in New Orleans or at the Arkansas Post. Long ago, our people decided to brag as if Saint Louis had the worst weather in the country."

"I'm never going to complain of the summer heat," she said. "But I'm going to praise Saint Louis every time the day is lovely. Maybe I can start a new trend."

"I don't think you will change these people, but you can try. Remember, we built our home where we get the best breeze in summer and are still protected from the worst winds of winter."

She leaned over and kissed me. I rose, picked her up, and carried her inside our home.

In early spring, our first child was born. We named him Brian after Rosellen's grandfather. The French pronounced it Briand, the name of the Bishop in Canada. His birthday was easy to remember because the great flood came a month later.

The April showers didn't come until the first day of May that year. Then torrential rains poured steadily for several hours. The sky did not clear. On the next day the rain came again, in a slow, steady drizzle. The sun did not come through the clouds on the third day. Rain was intermittent.

The late Minnesota thaw had already raised the Mississippi to a dangerous height. Voyageurs passed the word along the Missouri that early chinooks had melted the snow in the Rockies. Her tributaries raged across the prairie like unchallenged stallions. The local rains continued.

I could do little except work indoors and hope for a break in the relentless grey sky. The air was muggy; the usually musty warehouse reeked. Men and women became edgy. They began to hope for a single day's break to wash and dry their clammy clothes. One afternoon the rain stopped. Rosellen hung out the clothes, but the air was as damp as the clothes. Soon the rain came again and sent us scurrying out to bring in the wet clothes. We kept a fire lit to dry them at the fireplace. The rain drummed unceasingly on the roof.

I stood on the front porch and looked across the bottom land, barely visible through the mist and rain. Rosellen stood beside me. "My *grandpere* used to say," I began, "that when the rains came late in the midlands, and the Minnesota cold holds long up north, the Mississippi is too high to carry off the rising mountain waters of the Missouri. The three should be staggered. In late March the Mississippi should carry off the snows of Wisconsin and Minnesota. In April it should take the local rains so that in May it can take the rising waters of the Missouri. Now we have them all at once. The Meramec is over its banks. The Osage is at flood stage, and the Gasconade, and the Illinois."

Rosellen knew that I was simply thinking out loud. Even though the Osage and Gasconade were merely names to her, she did not ask where these rivers might be.

On the seventh straight day of rain, the Mississippi went over its banks, leaving islands of timber here and there in the bottom lands. At first the farmers of the prairie drove their stock on to these higher places and returned to their surrounded homes. A few days later all began to clear the entire valley. The people of Cahokia retreated to the bluffs of the east or came in boats to Saint Louis.

Fortunately, the local rains broke. Rescue parties went out to bring in families who were stranded by the rising waters.

I wondered about Bernadette and Michel on the old farm near Fort Chartres. I said a prayer for them but did not really worry. They were simply too resourceful to be trapped.

"Look, my husband," Rosellen said one evening. "Water all the way to the far bluffs."

I had never seen such a sight before and guessed I might never see it again. The river did not sweep from bluff to bluff in a resistless surge, but in several stretches we could see water all the way across to the bluffs of Illinois.

We heard that rising waters covered the common fields of Kaskaskia and Prairie du Rocher but that all the habitants fortunately had reached safety. *Le Grand Champ*, the great prairie of Ste. Genevieve, was a broad lake.

As soon as the flood began to subside, I went down to Ste. Genevieve to see how things were. I learned that Michel and Bernadette had been there but had gone back to their farm at the first sign of receding waters. The townsfolk did not intend to return to the great prairie. Instead, they planned to build their new village on higher land at the edge of the gradually rising bluff.

I paddled across the river and hiked to the old home *Grandpere* Soumande had built many years before. Michel, Bernadette, and the little ones were all busy in the yard and about the house.

"Come on in, Hugh Roe," Michel said. "I want to show you something." All the nieces and nephews followed.

"Look at that," Michel said, proudly, pointing to the watermark clearly visible halfway up the living room wall. He had written 1784 on it. "We simply tied the house to those two white oaks so she wouldn't float away, and we took a few weeks' vacation in the Ste. Genevieve hills."

The children laughed as if they had enjoyed the whole affair. Bouncy Bernadette gave me a warm hug.

"Water still stands in low places in the fields, but we'll get going again," Michel said. "We've already got a few vegetables in. We'll skip some basic crops but get in food for the animals.

Something of Uncle Nick was in Michel's square build and indomitable attitude, even though they were not relatives. With Bernadette, it was obviously a Soumande trait. It took more than Father Meurin's delays or the Mississippi floods to down her.

"A bottom land farmer is really a gambler at heart," Michel said. "It's either flood or drought or grasshoppers, or hail, or all combined into one. The farmer gambles that once in a while he'll come through. But it's better than trading on the river. We always have plenty to eat."

Five chubby little ones smiled in support of Michel's claim.

I left for Saint Louis feeling better than on my arrival. Their enthusiasm and resilience, however, had kept me from seeing the full picture of what the flood had done. I came to realize only later that the disaster had gouged out the best acres of the old Soumande farm. It left a huge slough of stagnant waters where the choice cornfields had been. The portion of the land that I owned, and Michel worked for me, could not be brought back to the plow. It was all Michel could do to restore his own property. I was to find that out only the following summer.

I began to spend more time in Prairie du Rocher trying to restore the farm. Long hours of hard work had just begun to turn the yield upward when I realized another problem. Trade restrictions forced many of the old habitants to the Spanish side of the river. The prosperity of an entire generation was vanishing. Even Father Gibault was on the move. Not just on ordinary mission trips back and forth across the river. He had definitely changed his parish residence, once to Vincennes, later to Cahokia.

When we next met, I asked, "How are things going, *mon pere*?"

None of the old bounce was in his manner. "Not good, my boy," he said. "Not good at all. When the state of Virginia gave up her claim to this territory in favor of all the colonies together, we were left alone. There is no real organized government. No redress. Because of Spanish regulations, we can't trade with the people on the other side of the river, or in New Orleans. So people are moving out.

Some you never thought would move, ever. More and more are going to Ste. Genevieve, or New Madrid."

"What about you, mon pere?"

"I'm beginning to think of crossing the river, too. Things are in a state of change. The colonies will finally get united and organize a stable, strong government on the Atlantic coast. Lots of people will be hurt in the meantime."

Then the old enthusiasm came back. Father Gibault talked on: "Even though I may move to the Spanish Lands to stay with my people, don't for a moment think that I fail to see that the future lies with the American colonies. We seem neglected now, my son. We cannot trade across the river. We are too remote from the seacoast, but we must be patient. Great hopes are ahead."

I had always been amazed at the bounce of the man but never more than at that moment.

"The government has set up a new law," the priest said. "It is called the Ordinance for the Northwest. Five commonwealths will grow up in the area between the Ohio, the Great Lakes, and the Mississippi. Each of these will be equal in rights with the thirteen that fought against England. Illinois will someday stand beside Virginia, free and independent."

"That is hopeful news," I said. But my voice carried little confidence. My own immediate problem — and Michel and Bernadette's — remained: restoring the old Soumande farm to full growth.

"Let that idea sink in, my son," Father Gibault resumed. "Look at it in focus. To the king of France, we were pawns to be moved about on a board of chance. The colonies on the coast were 'plantations' to the king of England, places to grow tobacco and to sell what England made. The king of Spain doesn't give a picayune about Spanish Illinois, because it has no gold or silver. But to the new government in Philadelphia we are something — maybe not now, but we will be — a sovereign people, coequal with the rest."

"You make it sound grand, *mon pere.*"

"It is grand. You'll live to see the day, Hugh Roe. I may not. But as they tell me your father used to say: Someday it will be one wide land along one wide river. *Le bon Dieu* intended the Mississippi to unite not to divide the land."

I knew that day would come. But how long would we wait?

"Are you Hugh Roe O'Rome?" a voyageur asked, as he entered the office of the fur company, in the late fall of 1792.

"Yes, I am," I said. I looked at the stockily-built stranger. His clothes showed months on the trail. His confident smile suggested a man sure of himself. I wondered if I had seen the man before — many years before, perhaps.

"Then I have a message for you," the voyageur said. "Your Uncle Nick says 'Hello.' "

"Well, 'Hello' to him," I said. "Where did you see him?"

"In Santa Fe," the man responded. "I am Pedro — excuse me, I've been living with the Spaniards for so long I forgot my own name sometimes — Pierre Vial. I just came overland from Santa Fe. Your Uncle Nick is a Franciscan friar on the missions in New Mexico."

"Great! We hoped he'd make it there," I said, "but, of course, we haven't heard from him in all these years. Thank you a thousand times over."

"Brother Nick sent a letter along, just in case I made it," Vial answered. "Actually, he had some knowledge of the rivers that helped me a lot. He was the only one who thought I could make it. When he first told me that you and he had gone from the Mississippi westward to Santa Fe, I was skeptical. But everything he said turned out to be true."

"Few people believed us when we returned, so we stopped talking about it," I said. "Lots of the traders here have explored far to the west. As you yourself know, often one or two men can get through when an expedition would be turned back by hostile tribes." When he agreed that his experience had been just that, I turned the conversation back to Uncle Nick. "How is he getting along?" I asked.

"He's doing fine," Vial responded. "Such a man would be an asset anywhere. I would like to have had him on the trip with me."

Vial reached into his supply kit and pulled out a rough-looking packet. "Here's your letter," he said. "By the way, I may retrace my steps to New Mexico next year. Want to go along?"

"Sorry, but I don't think I can. I'll give you a letter for Uncle Nick, if you don't mind."

"Not at all!"

"Thanks much," I said. "If you don't have lodging, why don't you stay with us?"

"Thanks anyway," Vial responded. "I'm taken care of. I may come out to talk more about the route you took across the plains." He walked out of the office.

I hurriedly finished what I was doing, untied my horse, and drove my *caleche* across the bridge below the dam. The high waters from recent rains made a pleasant waterfall. I hardly noticed it that day as I hurried to our home on the bluff. I did notice, however, that the sunflowers along Mill Creek above Chouteau's Pond grew more vigorously than ever. *Sunflowers certainly thrive in that area*, I thought, and pushed my horse on up the opposite bank.

The children, playing in the front yard, spotted me in the distance. There were three now — Brian and two little girls, Sheila and Angelique. Rosellen was waiting with them when I approached.

"Great news!" I said. "A letter from Uncle Nick. The man who brought it saw him in New Mexico last year."

"Uncle Nick!" Rosellen said. "I saw him only a few times in Prairie du Chien, but I feel I know him well. He must be a remarkable man."

"He is, my darling," I admitted. "Most people think only of themselves. Many will be generous with things they no longer need. Some will give of their surplus without hurt to themselves. Few people in the world have such tremendous love of others that they will sacrifice their own interests for others. Uncle Nick is such a man."

I handed the unopened letter to Rosellen. She read:

My Nephew and Godson,

My wish has come true. I am working among the Pueblo Indians in New Mexico.

When I first arrived in Mexico, the Fray Guardian said I was too old. I asked if I might prove the opposite. So he let me stay and work for a while — longer than is usual to be a postulant. I convinced him.

He thought I didn't know the language since my words of Spanish were few. Somehow or other I learned enough to get along. He wondered about a lot of things, but finally sent me to the Convento Grande *in Mexico City where I made my novitiate and took my vows. Now I am back in this wonderful land of New Mexico, where you, Hugh Roe, and I spent one winter so long ago.*

As soon as I arrived here, I knew I was home. I want all of you to know that I am well, that I feel I'm doing God's will, that I am happy and hope you are too.

Pierre Vial promises he will come back. He will. So I will expect to hear from you by return letter that he will gladly carry in his pack. I want to hear all about you and especially about Rosellen.

Your's in God's love,
Uncle Nick.

Of course, I would answer that letter. Pierre Vial would bring it through the country of the Kiowas and Comanches. He had already opened up roads from Santa Fe to San Antonio and Natchez and Saint Louis — deeds few had even thought of trying over the long years. I would tell Nick what Rosellen and I were doing. But how could I really describe Rosellen? How could I say that she was the most understanding person in the world? That to her, love was a whole-souled giving, without ifs or maybes or compromises; that a springtime warmth filled her entire being; that her first kiss had been the perfect one and all since mere copies; that her initial embrace of love had been total; that she was steadfast and untiring and loyal, like the prairies whereon she lived — without the surprises of the seashores or the majesty of the mountains; that she had brought to my life the steady glow of the summer sun, and a loyalty as sure as the cornfields stretching to the horizon — a woman out of the Old Testament who could see her children's children to the fourth generation, whose husband was blessed among men. And I was that lucky husband.

Rosellen for my wife and Uncle Nick for my godfather! Where else in the world was a man who could count himself so blessed?

A month later, I looked down the dusty *Rue Principale* to the spot where it met the road to Saint Charles. Four men rode together; three seemed accustomed to the saddle; the rotund fourth man, I thought, belonged in a rocking chair. He wore a wide-brimmed hat

that shaded his eyes. In spite of the dust, I immediately recognized
Artime Thomure.

"Artime!" I shouted and ran towards him.

"Good! Good! Good!" Artime answered. "Three of my brothers-
in-law and I are in for the meeting."

"What meeting?" I asked.

"Shhh!" one of the brothers said.

The four dismounted and gathered around me. Artime spoke
more softly now. "There's a secret meeting of the Sons of France at
the Couture's tonight."

"Who are the Sons of France?"

"Do we have to come in all the way from the *Memelles* to tell
you what's going on in Saint Louis?" one of the brothers said.

"I guess I'm not up on everything," I admitted. "What's it all
about?"

"Our future! We're Frenchmen, aren't we?"

"Well, we were Frenchmen," I said. "Some took an oath to the
Spanish king. Me? I'm just waiting!"

"The waiting's almost over," a brother said. "France has risen
with the Revolution. It's *liberté, egalité, fraternité* for all Frenchmen
everywhere. Soon for us. You come with us to the meeting tonight,
Hugh Roe."

"I'll do that, but I don't know whether I'll agree with the plans."

"Maybe we shouldn't bring him!" one of the brothers suggested.

"He comes as my friend," Artime said. "That's it."

That night, many of the men of the village met in the wide
basement of Camille Couture's residence. The host and a distinguish-
ed looking visitor sat at the far end of a rough table. A candle in the
middle of the table lighted up the faces of a few in the center. The
rest stood in darkness. The doors closed.

Camille Couture rose. "Citizens of the French Republic," he
began, "you have been declared citizens, in case you did not know,
by the Legislative Assembly of our country. We have a guest who
brings great news of French advance. For the sake of security I ask
that you do not applaud our guest. May I introduce Citizen R."

"He's a French Revolutionary General," Artime said. "He's been
lining up support in all the French villages. Even General Clark is
ready to join us against Spain."

"General Clark has more sense," I said. "He needs something to challenge him, but not that."

"Monsieurs," Citizen R. began, "I am so happy to be here. I represent the free government of the greatest country in the world. I serve, as I now speak, under the tricolor of the Revolution."

In the semi-darkness I had not noticed the small flag hanging from the rafters.

Citizen R. continued: "France spreads the principles of *liberty*, *equality*, and *fraternity* beyond her borders in Europe; she longs to bring them to her sons everywhere, especially in Louisiana, her once grand province. We urge you to be ready. France's day lies ahead."

As he sat down, Camille Couture rose. "Thank you, Citizen R.," he said. "We have been separated by law for thirty years from *la patrie*, but we love her nonetheless."

"Yes, Camille," a neighbor stated, "but we did not give France up. She gave us up."

"*Le bon Dieu* knows I have no love for Spain," a merchant broke in, "but the Spanish authorities have treated us fairly. They helped when the British sent the Indians down."

"Don't credit the Spaniards," another burst out. "We saved ourselves. Clark meant more than the Spaniards."

"Speaking of Clark," Camille Couture said, "he's ready to join us against Spain when the right time comes."

I listened to the hubbub vent itself. I thought of the November day at Fort Chartres thirty years before that wrote the death of the French Empire in the Mississippi Valley. I recalled my father, indomitable in disaster, giving the last call to the glory of France. I could keep quiet no longer. I would have begun with the words, "Men of France," as my father had done thirty years before, but that would have denied my message to come. They were not men of France. They were builders of a new world in the making.

"Men of mid-America," I said, hoping my voice would ring through the meeting hall with more calm but no less authority than my father's, years before. "We welcome the General among us. We appreciate his words. We are happy that France is free. Unfortunately, he comes too late — thirty years too late."

A hubbub arose. I stared the noisy ones down. "You know it, Camille. You know it Artime. You were both at Fort Chartres when

Commandant de Villiers said he would give up Fort Chartres without a fight, that he would haul down the lilies — also a noble flag, *Mon Generale* — from the strongest post in America, with no Englishman closer than a thousand miles. France speaks too late.

"As for Spain, some of us have pledged an oath to her king. I agree that Spain has treated us well. Her day, too, is over. The future is with the United States. There is our destiny. Camille, you heard me say that when Clark came to Kaskaskia sixteen years ago."

Nods of agreement equaled murmurs of dissent.

I went on, "Sure, Britain still bullies the United States, but not for long. The United States is rich and tough. Her cities equal what our guest has seen in Europe. Her people pile up behind the eastern mountains like waters behind a dam. Soon the waters will rise. The flood will pour into the Ohio and Mississippi Valleys. No matter who owns this land — France or Spain — it will some day soon belong to the United States. I for one will welcome that day.

"*Messieurs*, we must choose tomorrow — not yesterday!"

One day the following spring, a lean, rugged-looking man, Celtic rather than French in aspect, sloshed up to me on the *Rue d'Eglise*. He wore a white elk hunting shirt that reached almost to his knees. His cape was edged with fur and the seams of his sleeves were fringed. He carried a long flintlock and a powder horn hung over his shoulders. His moccasins were cased with mud. "I'm James MacKay," he said. "I'm looking for a man by the name of Hugh Roe O'Rome."

"I'm O'Rome," I said.

"Was your wife's name Rosellen MacKennan?"

For a moment I was almost ready to say, "No, her name was Rosellen Rien." Then I remembered, of course, that Rien wasn't her maiden name. How rarely Rosellen ever had mentioned her parent's name. I smiled and said, "Yes, my wife's name was Rosellen MacKennan."

"Her mother's name was Kate MacKay," the stranger said, "and

Kate was my older sister. So I guess you're my nephew by marriage."
A big smile came to his lean, hard face. I smiled and we shook
hands.

"My sister and her husband were traders at Michilimackinac,"
MacKay went on. "They died there.

"During my trading work on the river, I found a few bits of
information here and there about their one daughter; that she
married an Irishman and moved somewhere in the vicinity of Saint
Louis. I guess I found you."

"That's right," I said. "I'll take you right home to meet Rosellen.
Let me say, quite frankly, Mr. MacKay, you have the most wonderful
niece in the world."

"I'm sure I do," MacKay said with a wry smile.

I hitched the horse to the *caleche*, and we started out toward the
home on the hill.

"I'm planning to use this as the center of my fur trade dealings,"
MacKay said. "What do you think of the idea?"

"Unbeatable," I said. "The city of the future. All you have to do
is take a look at the map and you'll see."

"Or travel a bit," MacKay said, "and you come to the same
conclusion."

"I remember the first time Laclede spoke to us," I said. "He
showed that all the rivers of the North funneled together into the
Mississippi just above Saint Louis. The wide river itself is the canal
down which the furs can be taken to the Gulf. We're not so far north
that the place is too cold nor are we so far south that it is too warm.
Saint Louis is ideal. Laclede chose well."

"To change the topic slightly, O'Rome," MacKay went on, "have
you heard the good news?"

"That England went down in the sea, perhaps? That would be
real good news."

"Not exactly," MacKay came back, with a laugh. "We Scots
would like that, too. What I referred to is the new trade treaty
between Spain and the United States."

"Grand!" I said. "We've waited a long time."

"Spain has opened the whole river to American trade," MacKay
answered. "I spoke to a man who talked with Governor Carondelet
in New Orleans a few weeks ago. All is bustle and activity near the
Gulf. More barges move on the lower river. Trade is picking up like

grass after a rain. I predict the annual value of furs and peltries from this region will reach two hundred thousand American dollars."

As we drove on to the bluff past Sugar Loaf mound, I pondered these large figures while he admired the lovely scenery. MacKay marvelled: "This is a magnificent site you have — a little remote from the village though. Isn't there danger from Indians?"

"I've lived all my life among Indians," I answered. "I can never feel that they're other than neighbors. Except for one attack, when General Sinclair sent the Indians down here during the Colonial War, we've had no trouble whatsoever. We just don't think of it in those terms."

"What a difference between French and English," MacKay said.

"Where I was born over in Illinois," I said, "two or three Indian villages stood right in the neighborhood." I pointed across the stream and past the projecting bluff. "The Indians came to our church. They were at home in our village. There may be danger, but it just never dawns on us that it might be severe. In fact, Mr. MacKay, we think of the Indians in the vicinity as a protection from more remote hostile tribes."

"How about making that 'Uncle Jim' before we see my wonderful niece and her lovely children?"

Rosellen came to the front porch. She looked puzzled at my big smile and then at the stranger.

"Don't you recognize your Uncle, Jim MacKay?" I said.

"Mother used to talk about her little brother, Jimmy," she said.

"I'm not *little* Jimmy any more, as you can see. But I do think an uncle deserves a hug and a kiss, especially after all these years."

Rosellen threw her arms around both of us at the same time, planted a kiss on Uncle Jim's cheek and then on mine. We walked arm in arm into the house.

"Uncle Jim's going to make Saint Louis the center of his fur trading activity," I said.

"I'm going to try to persuade my newly-found nephew to be my partner in some of these operations."

"I'm sure the financial administrator of the O'Rome household would have no objections," I said, nodding toward Rosellen. "After all, she paid the debts on our home."

"Good for her," MacKay responded. "We Scots brag about two things: our happy brand of Calvinism and our ability to make money stretch a long way. Since she lost the first," he laughed, "I'm glad she kept the second." He gave her another hug and turned to me. "What do you think of the United States?"

"I don't say this publicly, at least not yet. I know, however, that the future lies with her. One day she will rule one land from the Atlantic to the Shining Mountains. Our children will live in peace — free from the fear of the British."

"Hugh Roe has wanted nothing in life so much as that," Rosellen said.

"Nothing, Uncle Jim, but your niece Rosellen."

Shortly after this fortunate meeting, I became an associate of MacKay in the fur trading business. We made a fine team. I could speak the languages and knew the people of the area. He could handle business dealings expertly.

Laclede's initial grant from the French King had given him exclusive trading privileges with the tribes on the Missouri River for a period of six years. Some years had passed, however, before other adventuresome merchants, not tied in with the Laclede group, formed companies to move into the profitable business. One of these MacKay represented. They would work among the tribes of the Upper Missouri, while the Chouteaus, Laclede's heirs, had posts among the Osages several hundred miles west of Saint Louis and south of the Missouri. During these years the Spanish Government, especially under Lieutenant Governor Zenon Trudeau, himself a native of Louisiana, left many governmental functions to the trading companies. They could make treaties with the tribes, build forts manned by soldiers supported by the government, and handle other matters normally done by civic officials.

"There's lots of talk," MacKay said one day, "of pushing on up the Missouri and reaching New Mexico and the South Sea. What do you think of that, Hugh Roe?"

"Uncle Jim, I have been to New Mexico. I know where it is. Pierre Vial's trip proved what I always said. It is above the headwaters of the Canadian. Some men have gone up the Missouri and then on up the Platte to the foothills of the Shining Mountains. This river rises in the mountains just northeast of New Mexico. It runs north along the mountains for awhile before it turns straight east to reach the Missouri.

"But the second great bend in the Missouri is far north of the

Platte. The Indians always tell of a mighty west-flowing river beyond the Shining Mountains. These mountains are high and full of beaver and other fur-bearing animals. That river beyond the mountains is not the Rio Grande that flows through New Mexico. The Rio Grande itself doesn't flow into the South Sea. It turns southeast and flows into the Gulf of Mexico."

MacKay spoke slowly, analyzing the matter as he went on: "I see two entirely different things to think about: one is trade with New Mexico — a good thing in itself. The other is the route to the South Sea beyond the headwaters of the Missouri, with lots of furs to be gathered on the way. Let them talk about New Mexico all they want. I want to push up the Missouri as far as we can, to find out whether or not we can get through the mountains to that great west-flowing river. If we don't make it, somebody else will come after us. They will make it all the way."

"My darling, it's our twentieth anniversary," I said in the spring of 1801. "Let's go down to see our old friend Father Gibault."

"Why not leave tomorrow?" she said.

"We'll go by *caleche* and leave the girls with Michel and Bernadette on the way down."

"It will be a second honeymoon, my husband."

We ferried our *caleche* across the river to Cahokia, drove along the old road on the height of land, through the town of Renault, and down the *coulee* into the bottom land just above Prairie du Rocher.

We visited Michel, Bernadette, and the children for a few days. We crossed to the west side of the river at Ste. Genevieve. I saw an entirely new town in place of the one I knew as a boy. The flood of 1784 had chased the people from the prairie into higher land. Of the old houses, only the Bolduc place still stood. It, too, occupied a new location.

We turned southward. Beyond a place called Cape Girardeau, one of the predominantly Anglo-American settlements in upper Louisiana, the hills gave way to flat endless delta land. The orioles, cardinals, and tanagers sang their hearts out; but as usual the mockingbirds outsang

them all. It reminded me of the time Nick and I had ridden down to
Ste. Genevieve to see Father Gibault years before. Now a day's ride
in the *caleche* tired me more than a day on horseback had done
then.

Flatboats filled the Mississippi below the mouth of the Ohio. So
many families were on the move. At the invitation of the Spanish
government, Americans from Kentucky and the northern bank of the
Ohio River were pouring into the rich delta lands on the Spanish side
of the Mississippi. It was evening when we arrived at New Madrid.
Something of the languor of the lands along the Gulf filled the
atmosphere, even though the town was five hundred miles above the
mouth of the Mississippi.

Father Gibault rose from his rocking chair on the porch as he saw
us driving up. "I'm a lucky man to see old friends again," he said.

We greeted him with equal warmth. The thirty-three years he had
spent on the frontier showed in his sparse graying locks. His face was
like a withered winesap, transfigured by the lucent kindness of his
eyes. Everywhere he had served, the ordinary people had loved him.
He had taught the children with equal enthusiasm whether it was a
lesson or a game. He always stayed close to his flock, attending their
festivities, even though some of them wrote to the bishop that he
stayed too long and had one extra glass of wine occasionally. He
always seemed to be in trouble with the British and the bishops.

"What brings you to New Madrid?" the priest asked. A smile
moved in his eyes through his voice wailed like wind through the
cypress swamps.

"It's our anniversary, and we came down to see you," Rosellen
answered.

"So it is. How about a glass of wine to celebrate the occasion.
Twenty years, isn't it? That was right at the end of the war. Come
in."

We entered his little home. He got out three glasses and proposed
a toast to many more anniversaries. Then he pointed to his books
scattered over the table and on the floor. "I've been listing these
books," he said. "I decided it was about time to make a will."

We could see books of biblical criticism and ecclesiastical history,
a commentary on the psalms of David, a concordance of the Bible,
sermons by great French preachers.

He picked up the book of Bourdaloue and said, "You remember

this one? I gave one of Bourdaloue's sermons word for word at Kaskaskia back in 1780, the day all those Irish children were baptized. Remember, just a short time before Saint Louis was attacked?"

"I certainly do," I came back. "Two months later I was in Prairie du Chien and proposed to Rosellen."

"Bourdaloue has nothing on that subject," he said with a grin. "Here are four Latin books — *Cicero, Ovid, Juvenal,* and the *Rudiments of Latin.*"

"I remember this one," I said, as I looked at the *Rudiments.* "Father Meurin used this as a textbook when he taught me a little Latin. If you have an extra copy, Brian could use one. He's finished three years' schooling in Montreal."

"Sure, give it to him," the priest said, handing the book to Rosellen. "Father Meurin gave it to me. I believe he thought I didn't know my Latin well enough. Maybe he was right."

"I had little time for Latin at the trading post at Mackinac," Rosellen said. "My Presbyterian father would probably have thought it a devilish papistical language."

"It's devilish, all right," Father Gibault came back. "No one understands it. Yet they still keep it."

Then with a sparkle of delight in his eyes, he asked, "Did I ever tell you about one of my illustrious predecessors at Cahokia?" Without waiting for an answer, he went on, "Instead of staying on the job in Illinois, he went back to France and became a Jansenist bishop."

Then turning to Rosellen, he explained, "A Jansenist bishop is sort of a Calvinist — Catholic. He was excommunicated — not simply by one, but by three popes. That's an achievement even for a *Frenchman!*"

"You've done well yourself," I said with a laugh, "creating problems for at least two bishops, one a Canadien the other an American. How about bringing us up-to-date about yourself, *mon pere?* How are things going here in New Madrid?"

"Fine! These people have their own way of doing things. Like pronouncing the name of the town. It may be Ma-DRID in Spain, but it's New MAD-rid here! They don't write letters to the bishop complaining about their pastor. Or maybe no one knows who our bishop is.

"This new vicar at Ste. Genevieve — he beats them all. He reported me to the Spanish governor in New Orleans for having baptized in his territory without his permission. There's work for a thousand priests here, and this fellow has time to write such rubbish to the governor.

"If I thought I had troubles with Bishop Briand and Bishop Carroll — by the way, he seemed upset when President Washington and the Congress confirmed my right to a piece of property in Cahokia — this one beats them all.

"He was made vicar general, and you'd think he was the great Jehovah and the Continental Congress all put together. He bristled when I married a couple without three publications of banns. I married the parents of these youngsters, and have known them all their lives. Next, he wanted me to go to the commandant and have him put a certain woman out of the house of one of my parishioners! Instead, I'll remember that parishioner in my will. I don't have time for rash judgments.

"This vicar general just doesn't like French people," Father Gibault went on. "You've got to be Irish or you don't have a right to the Kingdom of Heaven — even if you keep all the commandments. You'll get halfway in, since you're half Irish, Hugh Roe, but the other half of you will roast."

I laughed.

"He thinks all French priests are either lax like me," Father Gibault remarked, "or a bunch of rigid Jansenists."

"Someday," I said, "I hope we begin to take people for what they are and not for their nationality."

"Even the British?" Father Gibault responded, with a full guffaw.

"Even the British!" I said. "If I note a touch of disapproval in your laugh, I want you to know that I have never been mad at the British because they were British, but because they want the whole world for themselves. They have such a superior air about it all, as if that is what God originally intended. My father used to say that the British really believed they were doing the world a big favor by starving the Irish. Over here, they were horrified when Langlade's Indians massacred their garrison at Ticonderoga — and they were right in being horrified. Twenty years later they wanted to turn

Langlade's Indians against the Kentuckians and us. Governor Hamilton even offered to pay renegade Indians for taking white scalps."

He stopped abruptly, leaning back in his chair and began a new tack. "With so many different peoples coming to the States, maybe someday we'll all get along and get over this dislike of other nationalities. Otherwise, we'll all kill each other off."

"I have only one real worry," I said. "The Americans seem to be adopting the English attitude toward the Indians. With us, there are good and bad Indians, as there are good and bad people everywhere. The same is true with the Spanish. We've lived side by side with the Indians all our lives, but no Indians survived in the English colonies."

We three sat in silence awhile.

Then Father Gibault touched a personal note. "How are Brian and the two girls?"

"They're all fine," I said. "Brian is working on Artime's farm this summer. He'll soon return to school in Montreal. The girls are staying with Michel and Bernadette during our trip. They're learning what it's like to be Americans."

"Things got organized over there about ten years ago when St. Clair was put in charge," Father Gibault broke in. "Before that it was all confusion. The last governor before him was the worst. When they finally got rid of him at Kaskaskia, he went out and rounded up a bunch of Piankeshaw Indians to attack the town. A real idiot." He paused to get his breath.

"You remember I told you," he said. "The greatest step forward in all the world is the American First Amendment. The new government can't impose a religion; or forbid one. How old Father Meurin would have liked that. When the French government told him to get out, he said, 'Who gave you a right to say that? Render to Caesar the things that are Caesar's. Religion belongs to God.' The American government has said what all other governments refuse to say: 'We'll mind our own business.' "

Father Gibault stopped abruptly. "Why do you always get me back on politics?"

"I think you simply have a passion for good government," I came back. "That's why you supported Clark in the first place. You saw what would be best in the future. Soon you'll see organized free government on both sides of the wide river."

"I don't think I'll live quite that long," Father Gibault remarked. "You and Rosellen will, but not I."

We talked far into the languid night.

The next day I carefully inspected a tree growing alongside the church. Although it was a hard wood, its shape was conical like a pine. The leaves had five pointed lobes, like a star.

Father Gibault walked up to me. "That's one you people in Saint Louis don't have!"

"Right you are, *mon pere*. It's beautiful. What is it?"

"A sweet gum!" the priest said. "In the Tywappity Bottom — as the Kentuckians call the swamp near here — some of these trees grow to be 140 feet high. One, I've heard, is 16 feet in circumference. Quite a tree! I've never seen it. Can't get that far into the swampland."

"I've never seen a tree that big anywhere!"

"This red gum grows fast," the priest said. "The lumber's good. When fall comes, the leaves flame up like the sumacs. You ought to bring a few back and try to grow them in Saint Louis."

"That just might be possible," I said.

After several days, Rosellen and I started for home. As we drove away, I remarked, "My darling, we will probably never see Father Gibault again. He hasn't much longer to live. With all his joshing about bishops and vicar generals, he has never shown real bitterness, never lost his good humor."

Now I was not really talking to my wife, but to the whole world. "If all those charges people made against him had been true, he could never have lasted alone in this country for a third of a century. He was the one priest who stuck it out through droughts and high water, the one man who never wavered. He traveled through this wilderness thirty years unarmed. He wagered his entire future on his belief in the justice of the American cause. He did his duty as he saw it with the two hands God gave him. He's the kind of man who holds the Church, who holds the world together."

IV

One Free Land Forever

"Are we going to change our allegiance once again, Auguste?" I asked one morning in early March, 1804. I was never a close friend of Chouteau, but I always admired him.

"Right you are!" he responded with unusual enthusiasm. "We were French once. Then under the Spanish flag." He looked across the street to the Governor's office. "Soon, Hugh Roe, I'll lose my tenants over there, and we will be part of the United States."

I looked at the old house on *Rue Principale* that had been built across from the Laclede home back in 1766. A Spanish governor had sold it to Chouteau some years before, but it had remained the office of the government. It had been the place of the Queen's Ball the night I met Marie Colette.

Chouteau went on and brought my thoughts back to the present. "I received word from Kaskaskia the other day. The United States Government has sent an artillery officer by the name of Stoddard to handle the transfer." Chouteau drew an envelope from his pocket.

I read the words in large handwriting on the envelope: "From Captain Amos Stoddard, U.S.A., Village of Kaskaskia, Illinois Territory, to Auguste Chouteau, Esq., Village of Saint Louis, Upper Louisiana."

Chouteau pointed with the envelope. "This man has been authorized to act in the name of France and to accept the territory from Spain. It's a bit complicated, but our surmises were true that Napoleon had made a secret treaty with Spain to get Louisiana back."

"How soon can we expect the change to take place?" I asked.

"Perhaps this month," Chouteau responded. "Napoleon moves

fast. It seems that he had planned to rebuild France's Empire over here. He sent an expedition to the island of Santo Domingo. Yellow fever destroyed it. Napoleon never sends the Old Guard to rescue a battered brigade. So he is selling while he can sell. We'll belong to the *Bostonnais* before April comes."

Chouteau proved correct. The Spanish Governor announced the ceremonies of transfer for Friday, March the ninth.

On that morning we awoke early, ate hurriedly, and drove along the south bank of Chouteau's Pond past the dam. It was a damp, uncertain March morning with a penetrating breeze from across the river. We drove through the village on down to the waterfront. American soldiers came over from Cahokia.

"There's Captain Lewis," Brian said. "He's going up the Missouri with Captain Clark this spring."

"That must be Captain Stoddard with him," I remarked.

The American troops landed on the west bank of the river and marched to the government house. My family and the other villagers followed the troops.

Governor Delassus and his officials greeted the Americans. Then he stepped to the front of the porch to address the people of the city.

As he did so, I noticed tears in the eyes of some of the old habitants. The rule of Spain had generally been benign. The Lieutenant-Governors had actually left much administration to the directors of the fur companies. Adding Louisiana must have been a great drain on the financial resources of the little country with such an extensive empire to administer. Spain had gained so little in return for its efforts. Yet the previous thirty years had seen a little of the energy that had made Spain great two centuries before. Now its days were almost over. This first sign pointed to the Spanish empire's ultimate ending.

Yet all the dignity that made the men of Spain a power to reckon with through the centuries appeared in Delassus as he began his speech: "Inhabitants of Upper Louisiana: By the King's command, I am about to deliver up this post and its dependencies.

"The flag under which you have been protected for a period of nearly thirty-six years is to be withdrawn. From this moment on you are released from the oath of fidelity you took to support it.

"The fidelity and courage with which you have guarded and

defended it will never be forgotten. And in my character of representative, I entertain the most sincere wishes for your perfect prosperity."

Governor Delassus turned to say a few words privately to Captain Stoddard. The American officer said something in reply. At a prearranged signal from a soldier standing at the northwest gallery, the Spanish troops at the fort on the hill fired a salute. An aide of Delassus spread documents on the table. Captain Stoddard signed, followed by Governor Delassus, Captain Lewis, and two witnesses.

The flag of Spain came down slowly for the last time. In its place rose not the old Lilies of France, but the new tricolor of the Revolution.

All the spectators walked along as the American troops marched up to the fort on the slight ridge to the west. The Spanish soldiers received them under arms. The flag of Spain came down there, too. The tricolor floated that one day over the city named for the saintly King.

I understood the combined joy and tears of my neighbors that night. These were Frenchmen. They had always loved their country. Yet without their consent they had been ruled by another country — a country that had been a rival in previous centuries but more recently an ally — a country bound to them by strong religious ties.

Tomorrow they would be part of another, a newer ally, a country whose way of life was far different; a nation that guaranteed them religious freedom, but actually had little acquaintance with and oftentimes hostility for their beliefs; a nation made up of people whose ancestors they had fought for centuries. I could understand the concern of my French neighbors.

For me there was only joy. I had looked forward to such a day ever since the council at Fort Chartres forty years before. I thought how proudly my father would have walked through the streets of the little city he had never seen. And Father Gibault! But the old priest had died at New Madrid less than two years before. As to Rosellen, I knew she shared my joy.

When I returned to the center of the village, the next morning, Saturday, March the tenth, I saw a new world. The Stars and Stripes rose for the first time and, I hoped, forever, over the west bank of the wide river.

But would it be forever?

Delassus himself did not leave Saint Louis immediately. He stayed until October of the same year, closing up the affairs of the Spanish government and awaiting further orders. Good ruler that he was, he did all that he could to aid the United States officers in the discharge of their duties.

He went out of his way to promote good feelings between the two groups. He assured the Indians of the area that they could expect from their new American Father the same good treatment they had received from their French and Spanish fathers. I wondered if this assurance was not more words than reality.

During the weeks of the transfer, Brian and I were busy. We had endless little tasks since most of the new officials spoke neither French nor Spanish.

Captain Stoddard wisely followed the example of Piernas thirty years before. He changed as little as possible of the administration. He even asked Delassus for an evaluation of the leaders of the region. Delassus decided to do a thorough job and put it in writing. He employed Brian as his secretary. Brian occasionally asked my help in a concept he found difficult to turn from Spanish to English.

"I can see why Delassus was such a good governor," Brian said one day. "He knows men. I've been surprised how detailed and accurate his analysis of everyone is."

"That's one big difference between an average and an outstanding leader," I answered. "Take a man like our friend Artime. He could handle ordinary things on any expedition, but conniving people sometimes baffled him. A man like Delassus can sense motivation."

"This report has taught me two big things," Brian said. "The first is this: men who drink too much gradually lose their grip; and secondly, knowing how to write is even more important than you have insisted. Other things being equal, a leader who can't write slips behind the one who does. I can see that in every position in the region."

I had never explicitly thought of that before; but in every case I knew of, the literate man moved ahead of any but the most able who could not write.

Finally the day came when Delassus moved out. *Would Saint Louis forget him?* I wondered. Perhaps. He had been a great asset to the little city and to the new government. He left with dignity.

The Spanish sunset I had witnessed at Saint Louis was as worthy of that proud people as the sunrise over Granada three hundred and thirteen years before that I had read about in Father Meurin's history books.

Even before the official handing over of the city to the American authorities, I had felt a new spirit of vigor in the air. Meriwether Lewis and William Clark, a younger brother of George Rogers Clark, camped across the river, ready to move up the Missouri. Their bivouac was all drive and energy.

Saint Louis, in contrast, had always been an easy-going city. The men engaged in the Indian trade had prospered, but the French had a joy of life and a tendency rarely to over-exaggerate mere possession of the things of this world. After all, with twenty-nine holy days of obligation, they had plenty of occasions to celebrate. Few new settlers had come into Saint Louis after the initial influx at the time of the founding. Most of the city's growth came from the natural increase in families already there. I knew everyone in the entire village by his first name.

Now the influx came. People were on the move. Lewis and Clark started up the Missouri. The entire wide river was open to American trade.

Ever since I had entered into business association with James MacKay, my family had prospered. Now with the growth of new businesses, Brian and I worked constantly and profitably as scribes and interpreters.

One quiet evening, Rosellen and I sat on the porch and watched boats moving on the river below.

"Do you think the city will change much?" she asked.

"In some ways," I said, "but I think much of the old spirit will remain."

"I know that you looked forward to this all your life, my husband," she said. "It is definitely a gain; but there may be some losses, too, as there are in all changes of life."

"Saint Louis has always moved slowly," I said. "The new people will be wanting to speed up. They'll complain about the old ways, but few of them will want to move on. They'll explore the West but keep their homes here. People have their complaints, but the most amazing tribute to the place is that they stay here." Then turning directly to Rosellen, I said, "And you will like it more."

She looked surprised for a moment and then smiled, an understanding smile.

I knew that through the years she had been an outsider to so many in the village. Not just a person of different ancestry, but something more rare, a convert to the faith. Even though I was a puzzle to many at times, I was half-French and a Catholic by ancestry. She was totally different in outlook.

"What I found so strange in the beginning stemmed from my Scots background. In my upbringing clothes were not decorations but covering and protection. When I came to Saint Louis, I found these ladies on the fringe of civilization agog about what they heard women were wearing in New Orleans and Paris."

"It was that way from the beginning," I came back. "When the first Spanish Lieutenant-Governor Piernas arrived, the ladies gathered around his wife to find out about the latest styles."

"Then, too, many wanted to know if I had any French ancestors."

"A wandering missionary who went through here not long ago," I remarked, "made the comment that it seemed more important to some here to have a French ancestor than to be in the state of grace."

"Not everyone was pleasant to me at first," Rosellen admitted. "When I was a little girl my mother told me to go on liking people even if they did not seem to care, and someday they would change. My husband, they have changed. Now our whole world will change."

I had presumed that the new régime would never have the happy relations with the Indians that the French and Spanish had fostered. Trouble broke more quickly than I had anticipated. Hardly had Stoddard taken over when he felt compelled to execute a band of wandering Indians who had wantonly killed several settlers. At the same time, just man that he was, he knew that the Indians often had valid complaints that went unrighted. A grand jury refused to indict a white man who had killed an Indian for no apparent reason.

In the spring of 1804 a group of Osage Indians drifted towards Saint Louis in a boat belonging to one of the local fur companies. Sauk warriors ambushed them, killing some and capturing the others. Relations with the Sauk grew worse when a band of young braves attacked a white settlement on the Cuivre River, not seventy miles northwest of Saint Louis. They seemed to think this could strengthen their bargaining position with the United States, since the British had invited them to a meeting in Canada. Settlers along the Cuivre appealed to Major James Bruff to lead an attack on neighboring Sauk villages to deter the tribe. He wisely calmed the whites.

The slaves grew restless, too. The area numbered about 2,000 with well over half in the Saint Louis area. Certain whites began circulating rumors that freedom would soon come. As a New Englander, Stoddard found the slave system distasteful; but he had the immediate responsibility of maintaining order in the territory.

I felt that when the seven months of Stoddard's régime came to an end, he would feel a great relief to leave unsolvable problems to others. The Saint Louis residents, however, did appreciate all his good work. He was one of those rare men who knew men's appreciation while he worked with and for them.

During the months that Brian and I worked with Stoddard and De Lassus on the territorial transfer, I came to realize how naive had been my view of life in a Republic. The addition of the Louisiana Territory presented complicated issues earlier congresses had never faced. New rumors came in every day: that the government would close the area to future settlement; that it might move the eastern Indians to the region; that it would confirm only those Spanish grants that the earlier régime had confirmed before October 1, 1800, the date of the Treaty of San Ildefonso that had restored the area to France from Spain. Saint Louis' citizens were to send in complaints in response to these rumors too late to have any effect.

The Government divided the territory into two sections: the Territory of Orleans — the area south of the thirty-third parallel, a line about seventy miles south of the junction of the Arkansas and the Mississippi; and the Territory of Louisiana — all the rest. What worried us most was that we would be under the officials of the

Indiana Territory. The government was not joining the two territories, simply having the same officials for both, with residence in Vincennes. We had no complaints against Governor William Henry Harrison himself. But I knew Saint Louisans would look upon being ruled from Vincennes with about the same enthusiasm people in New Orleans might accept a governor in Mobile. Almost immediately a group of citizens, led by Auguste Chouteau, Bernard Pratte, and Charles Gratiot, met to discuss what lay ahead. They planned a convention for early September with representatives from all parts of Louisiana.

Brian and I did not attend these meetings for two reasons: we were busy; and we actually worked for the government during those months. That didn't keep us from discussing the matters, however.

"It seems to me," Brian said, on a summer evening as we enjoyed the cool southeasterly breeze coming across the river, after a hot and tiring day at the government offices, "it seems to me that only two things really worry these fellows."

I knew "these fellows" of whom Brian spoke were Chouteau, Gratiot, Pratte, and the rest who intended to complain to Washington.

"They don't care about being ruled from Vincennes," Brian went on. "They can get over that. What worries them are the Spanish land grants and their slaves. As to the first, I don't give a Connecticut continental in itself, but you can be sure that the men who get the big land grants will be the *ricos* who bring in slaves to work the land. They will control the Territory in the days ahead. Slavery's the real issue. I think our area should be like the Old Northwest Territory east of us. No slaves! Like Illinois, Indiana, and the new state of Ohio. A non-slave situation brings in a different kind of landowner and develops different attitudes."

I was amazed how acute Brian's judgment was and how intense his feeling on the matter. I wondered if many of the young men felt as he did. "Right from the earliest days," I answered, "many of the people of Saint Louis freed their slaves in their wills. We ought to get rid of the whole system. The government could pay the owners a fair price."

"Renault put a curse on this territory when he brought the slaves here to work in the mines," Brian said. "The sooner we end it the better."

I was amazed that Brian knew of Renault. He had been here only a short time — three generations before. "I agree. But how many others feel as we do?"

"Most of the young people. Sure, the oldsters have their worries. More than a third of the people in Saint Louis are blacks. We've taught them their religion. They go to Church on Sunday. They should belong to themselves — be free men — if President Jefferson meant what he said in the Declaration of Independence."

In spite of his confidence, Brian and I were definitely in the minority. All the long summer, groups held heated meetings. The Gratiot-Chouteau forces turned out to be moderate — so outrageous were some of their opponents. Auguste appealed to Stoddard. He showed me the intemperate statements.

"Whom are they writing this to?" I asked. "Genghis Khan, or Ivan the Terrible?"

"They want to send this to the Congress of the United States!"

Even when Stoddard proposed changes that the petitioners accepted, they still called the Act dividing Louisiana into two territories, "the dictates of a foreign government!" They protested "an entire privation of some of the dearest rights enjoyed by freemen!"

"It's all a game," Brian said. "They talk in this outlandish fashion so that Congress will forget to face the crucial issue: the recognition of slavery in our area."

The young man amazed me more every time he gave an opinion.

The two of us finally attended one of the meetings in late September when Stoddard concluded all details for an official visit by Governor Harrison scheduled for the middle of October, and our work with him was done. Auguste Chouteau hosted the meeting. He walked to the door to greet us as we entered.

"Welcome, Hugh Roe," he said with his usual urbanity.

"You remember my son, Brian," I responded. "He has been away at school in Montreal."

"I certainly do, Hugh Roe. I'm glad he's had a chance to study in Canada. Let's hope we can have our own school soon."

At that moment, a man I had never seen before entered the door.

"*Bon jour, Elige*," Auguste said effusively. "May I present my long-standing friend, Hugh Roe O'Rome, and his son Brian. *Monsieur Elige Fromentin.*"

"*Bon jour, Monsieur Fromentin,*" I said.

"O'Rome? An unusual name, is it not? Especially for this part of the world?"

"It may seem strange, Elige," Auguste came back, "but Monsieur O'Rome is one of our oldest citizens. He was born fifty miles from here. His father was a soldier in the army of *Roi Louis Quinzieme*, his mother a Canadienne. We came to Saint Louis at its founding."

Just at that moment, the press of the crowd suggested that Auguste had better get on with the proceedings. He walked to the podium while Brian and I sought seats in the rear.

"Fromentin was a priest in France until the Reign of Terror," Brian said. Again I wondered at the young man. Where had he learned this?

"He's bright and talented," Brian said, "but too slick for me. With the shortage of priests in this country, why did he become a lawyer? That's what he did in Pennsylvania before he came out here."

"Where did you learn this?" I asked.

"Rumors travel. Mostly true ones," he answered.

Just then, Auguste called the meeting to order, and asked Charles Gratiot to preside. Gratiot accepted nominations for delegates to present the petition to Congress. The first name was Auguste Chouteau, the second Eligius Fromentin. The seconds seemed prearranged.

"Are there any other nominations?" Gratiot asked. He seemed to presume, as I did, that they had already settled the issue.

To my surprise, Brian rose: "I nominate my father, Hugh Roe O'Rome. He knows both languages well. He has lived in the area all his life."

The whole meeting was tense. Silent. Then another young man arose on the far side of the room. I did not recognize him. "I second the nomination of Mr. O'Rome." Murmurs of disapproval came from every row.

I appreciated the courage of the young men. They had made their point. No one would stand with them, I knew. I asked for the floor. Gratiot recognized me.

"Gentlemen of Upper Louisiana," I began. "I appreciate the honor of this nomination. I understand your feeling of consternation that men thousands of miles away decide our destiny for us. They have not consulted us according to the ancient custom of the city of Paris that gave us a right to decide our own affairs. In the lifetime of many here, King Louis XV of France gave us to King Charles III of Spain. His successor, Charles IV, gave us to the Emperor Napoleon. He in turn sold us to the United States. Now the Congress of the Republic does not so much as ask what we might wish — in spite of its just claim to liberty of action. Nonetheless, we should welcome the opportunity of joining the United States. I have looked forward to this boon all of my adult life. Thus I must state that I believe your petition, while well-meaning in places, is intemperate and totally outrageous in others.

"Further, my conscience forbids me to recommend the continuance of slavery in this territory or the future importation of other slaves. I think it against the spirit of the Declaration of Independence and fraught with a danger that will fall not on us, but on our descendants. In view of this, I must decline this nomination."

"My father," Brian whispered, "you made me proud!"

"Not nearly" I answered, "as much as your courage made me!"

"Do you think you could spend a winter in Saint Louis with the girls while Brian and I went up the Mississippi with Lieutenant Pike?" I asked Rosellen one day in early July, 1805.

She was preparing a pie crust in the kitchen. She slowly trimmed the edges. "I spent so many lonely winters up north while you were down here" she finally answered, "a 'no' would be inconsistent."

"It won't be too much of a change for Brian" I said, "since he has spent five winters in Montreal. For me, as you know, a winter up north will be a new experience — or penance — depending on how one looks at it." I picked up an apple and began to peel it.

"I suspect my husband wants to be able to say that he's the first American who traveled the entire Mississippi from the mouth to its source — wherever that might be."

Surprised, I countered, "Strangely, I never thought of that. It will probably be true, unless one of the soldiers came by boat from the Gulf. If that should be true then several of us will tie for the title.

Both ends of the wide river! It's a great thought — and an added incentive."

"It might also be an opportunity for you to find out what's going on in Brian's mind," Rosellen said. "He certainly amazed us all last summer with his analysis of the petition to Congress."

"It made me realize how little I knew my own son." I finished my first apple, sliced it, and began a second.

"While you're getting to know Brian a little better, I believe I'll get to know our daughters a little better. Frankly, I think both of them are going to get married soon. My guess is that we'll find that out shortly after you return in the Spring."

"The girls seem to have certain young men in mind," I said. "As to Brian, when we go to a party, he dances with one girl after another. He seems to enjoy the company of all of them. Several were a little cool when their fathers complained that he wanted them to give up their slaves. The girls got over that in a hurry, however. After all, they know that whatever he's going to do, he's going to be somebody." In a more reflective mood, I went on: "He has a touch of Grandpere Soumande's strength, my father's courage, and your father's canniness — as you Scots call it."

"You're probably right," Rosellen said. "I always hoped he would be like another man I know, but no two people can be alike. Fortunately he has enough of that man's qualities to make me happy."

No answer seemed advisable, so I just kept peeling apples until we had enough for the pie. The following morning, I went to see Lieutenant Zebulon Pike. A sergeant ushered me into Pike's office. "I'm Hugh Roe O'Rome, Lieutenant," I began. "I've been on the river many years. I was born in this country. I can speak French, and Spanish, and as you notice, English. I've dealt with several northern tribes, especially the Sauk and the Sioux. I believe I can still hold my own with the younger men in most work. My son Brian is twenty-one, strong, experienced, and has lived in Canada several winters. Could you use the two of us?"

Pike looked at me with knitted brows. A thin nervous man, his left arm was always moving. This twitching put some men ill at ease, but it did not bother me. In my initial impression, Pike seemed a full head above the average man, but not quite the stature of the Clarks. "I take you to be in your mid-forties," he began. Since most people thought of me as ten years younger than I was, I did not see fit to affirm or deny. I let him talk on. "We will be gone all winter. It will be a rough trip, but I need men who know the area."

"Lieutenant, I have been on the Mississippi from Prairie du Chien to the Gulf of Mexico."

"Your pay will be about the same as that of a private in the Army. Now that's not much. The meals will be good when we find food. Of course we'll take some supplies with us when we go. We can expect many terribly cold days in the open country. Are you still interested?"

"Definitely."

"We leave from our encampment on Friday the 9th of August. Our keel boat is seventy feet long. We'll have provisions for four months. After that we'll need some good shooting and hope the game is plentiful."

I walked down to the river and looked at the keel boat. It would not be easy to take upstream. Sometimes we'd row. Sometimes we'd be poling it along the shallow waters close to the shore. Sometimes we'd pull it, as cordellers pulled the *batteau* of Laclede back in 1763 when they first came up the river. It had a square sail on the center mast. It was nice to think that we were leaving in the middle of August when the winds usually came up-river. While the boatmen generally didn't count on the sail, I felt it would help at that time of the year.

Normally the keel boats could travel between ten and fifteen miles a day upstream full of merchandise. That's what the old veteran keelers said. I guessed we'd make a little bit more on our trip.

In the meantime, the girls, Angelique and Sheila, decided that they would relieve their mother of the duties in the kitchen on the last night before our departure and fix a special chicken dinner as a going-away party for their brother and father. Angelique had her mother's skill with apple pie. Sheila roasted the chicken.

It proved a pleasant evening, cool for August, and the girls decided we'd eat on the porch. All went well.

At 4:00 on the next afternoon, Friday the 9th, 1805, the seventy foot long keel boat began its trip up the river. Pike had the sail up. The wind was at our backs. We traveled just far enough that first night to get across the river and say we were on the way. The second day we passed the mouth of the Missouri. Once again I noticed how different the Mississippi was above the confluence with the Big Muddy. The lower river absorbed some of the spirit of the Missouri; yet the Mississippi was the Father of Waters to Indian, Frenchman, Spaniard, American.

We did a little rowing in those curving parts where the river swings in and out, before it decides that it's really going in a southeasterly direction. As I rowed behind Brian I realized that a little of Uncle Nick showed in the way his shoulders were developing. Brian squared into the toughest problems in the same straightforward way.

That night as we sat around the fire after our dinner, I remarked, "I've often wondered why we didn't get out together on the river more, son."

"You've spent so much time behind that desk these past few years," Brian came back, "I began to wonder whether all those stories they tell about you and great-uncle Nick were really true."

"What stories?" I asked.

"Oh! That you and great-uncle Nick went up the Arkansas to the kingdom of New Mexico, for instance. That was the best one."

"Well, that one is true," I said. "When we came back we wanted to tell about the wonders we had seen. Unfortunately, at that very time Clark conquered Kaskaskia. Everyone wanted to know about Clark. I quit trying to tell them about New Mexico. You do remember that Pierre Vial seemed to believe that I had been there."

"Yes, he convinced me. Uncle Nick's letter confirmed his remarks. Now a far different question. Did Mother's first husband have a squaw in the village of the Missouri Indians?" I sat stunned as Brian went on. "Everyone said so." The fire had burned down to a few embers, but its smoke kept the mosquitoes at a distance.

"Amnon Rien had a wife in the Missouri village," I responded cautiously. "She was the daughter of a chief. For a while things went well with him. Then the fur-bearing animals disappeared. Rien came back."

I wondered how much more the boy had heard. Did he know that Rien had married Rosellen first, then left? Had anyone told him of the day in the Sauk camp? Had he perhaps heard the whole story? Who would have told him? Certainly not Artime. Not Rosellen. So there was no one who could have.

"In the old days," I went on, groping my way, "when a voyageur took a wife in the Indian villages, he lived in her village, or he brought her to the French village. Now things are different. The white man's squaw is a temporary wife, but there can be no such thing as a temporary wife."

"I know that, my father."

"Things have changed rapidly from the old French days," I said, "and they will change still more. Your grandfather predicted that this would someday be one land along the wide river. Now it is."

"The Spanish treated us well," Brian came back. "Even Uncle Jim became a Spanish citizen."

"Yes, the Spaniards were good rulers. They handled hard things well. We should be grateful to them. This is a new day, however, and we must welcome it." I sat quietly for a moment and then went on. "There will be many changes. The city will grow rapidly. Thousands will come. Many will move on west. The government eventually will be better. Governor Wilkinson, I don't know what to say of him." I stopped.

"I think he's too clever," Brian broke in, "too slick a person. He reminded me of that Fromentin whom we met that night at Auguste Chouteau's. I would not trust him."

"You may be correct, son. He seems up to a lot of scheming. Now if I may turn to a new subject. The biggest change will be a religious one. All of us, white and black, were Catholic in Spanish days. Not that we all fulfilled our religious duties or kept the commandments. We did, however, accept its general framework and outlook. Soon we'll have many different types of Christians and churches you know about only from history books. Before, our religion was a part of things, like the air and the trees. Now we will have to live our faith."

Brian stirred the embers with a hickory branch, but said nothing.

"The biggest change," I said, "and the saddest one, will be with the Indians. The French have lived among the Indians as brothers. The English did not. They drove the Indians out of their villages on the Atlantic coast. They have steadily pushed the tribes back. When the colonists became independent of England, they continued to mistrust the Indians. A few men like General Clark will always deal fairly. Even a good man like Stoddard had trouble controlling the newcomers who think they are better than other peoples. We will see more of them.''

The night was cool and we slept well. Each day as we moved the 130 miles to the mouth of the Des Moines, I came to appreciate a little bit more how much my relationship with Brian had been teacher to pupil rather than father to son. I had taught him to read and write both English and French, enough Spanish for ordinary conversation, and enough Latin to know the server's prayers at Mass. I had to admit that I was not as persistent at the task as old Father Meurin had been with me. The tasks we shared as the expedition pulled steadily up the river forced me to treat him as a man.

When we reached the Des Moines River, I recognized several of the Sauk Indians at our Council on August 21st. The parley was short and hopeful. We had suffered through several hot days, but we knew August would soon be over, and we moved steadily north. Ten days later we reached the area of the lead mines, still going at a steady pace. On September the 4th, we camped at Prairie du Chien, the place of such happy memories. I showed Brian where his mother had lived and where I had stayed during the time I was ill.

The days and nights were cool now, the wind at our backs, and in nineteen days we reached the Falls of Saint Anthony. Pike had sent interpreters on ahead to arrange a meeting with the Sioux. They awaited our arrival, arrayed in colorful costumes that matched the oaks and maples in their early autumn glory. It reminded me of the council that George Rogers Clark had had so many years before. The thought came to me that Pike was twenty-six years old, the same age as Clark was at the time of his meeting. For a moment I envied Brian and Pike and wondered if the world had passed me by. How silly, I realized on reflection. My life had been more full than most men I had ever known.

Pike did not have the commanding appearance of Clark. His twitching arm gave a certain unease, visible even on the countenances of the usually inscrutable Sioux. Nonetheless, he let them know that now the United States was a powerful nation. The Great White Father in Washington would hold his hand over the land. He would set up a post in that region and another at the mouth of the *St. Croix* not too far away.

The Sioux agreed to hand over about 100,000 acres. In turn Pike gave them trade goods that amounted to about $200 in American money.

"Two hundred dollars worth of junk," Brian whispered, "for land worth $200,000." Pike allowed traders to give liquor to the Indians. I thought this a mistake.

Above the mouth of the Des Moines, the river had arched to the east for a while, but now it was again moving from a little west of due north. Unfortunately, by this time the wind had changed. It was brisker, colder, hostile, threatening. All the while we passed the most beautiful part of the river I had ever seen. It was narrower, more at ease with its banks, less prone, it seemed, to veer and change its course — steady, serene. *How beautiful this must have been a month ago*, I thought. We reached a place called Little Falls.

On October 16th heavy snow fell. We set about building log cabins. Some of the hunters went out, Brian among them, and laid in a supply of game. By this time, Pike had begun to wonder whether I had evaded his question about my age. I had to do a lot of talking to persuade him to include me among the few he would choose to push farther upriver. With Brian there was no question at all. Pike finally gave in to my request when he found out I was the only one who had seen the mouth of the river at the gulf. "It's against my better judgment to take along a man thirty years older than I am," he said. "But I understand why you want to go. I admire your spunk." Then with a laugh, "Your son might have to drag you back on a sled."

"Thanks, Lieutenant," I said. "I'll make it. I survived a winter in Northern Illinois that's been worse than this so far."

"We've only seen the beginning," he said.

On December the 10th we pushed on with sleds and a pirogue beyond Little Falls to a British trading post at Red Cedar Lake.

I never thought I would ever be happy to see the flag my father had always called the *croix bâtarde*, but by that time the winds were so cold and the snow so deep even an English jail might have been a welcome refuge for a while. We celebrated Christmas there, then pushed on to a Northwest Fur Company post at Sandy Lake. We arrived on January the 8th. The British had operated this post for twelve years. They'd grown potatoes and wild rice. They purchased maple sugar from the Indians and had shot much game. Even the most violent British-haters were not at all adverse to accepting the hospitality of the Northwesterners. After some days we moved again. We reached Leech Lake, huge even for those large and endless lakes that covered the region, on February the 1st. I didn't remember one day from the next, but the business-like Lieutenant kept an exact journal. Some days he'd not get a chance to write anything down, but he'd fill in with our help at the first opportunity.

Pike thought we had reached the source of the Mississippi. Another British post welcomed us. A man by the name of Hugh McGillis was in charge. Most of the employees were Canadiens or *metifs*, half-French, half-Indian. I got along well with all of them.

"Since your name is also Hugh," Pike said on the second day, "I will give you the honor of notifying Hugh McGillis that the British flag should not fly on American soil."

"That's not too heavy a price to pay for the chance you gave me to come along, Lieutenant."

I had long before learned that the best time to do anything was the first possible time. Instead of waiting and fretting, I went right over to McGillis' headquarters.

"I'm Hugh Roe O'Rome," I said.

"Irish?" McGillis asked.

"Irish-French. What about you?"

"Scotch!"

"So is my wife," I said. "Her father was a trader at Michilimackinac."

"You chose a good wife, O'Rome. Now what can I do for you?"

"Lieutenant Pike has commissioned me to notify you that the Union Jack should not fly on American soil."

"No problem," he said, with a shrug. "Put your flag up tomorrow morning."

Surprised, I said, "Thank you, Mr. McGillis for making my task easy." As I departed, I wondered if he felt we'd be gone in a few months, so that it made no difference.

Nonetheless, it was a thrill to see the Stars and Stripes rise near the headwaters of the Mississippi.

Pike held a council with the Chippewa Indians and told them that the day of Great Britain's dominance in the area had ended. The United States had come to stay, and they'd better keep that in mind. He told them to give up their British flags and medals and, in contrast to his action among the Sioux, he suggested they abandon the use of liquor.

The canny Scots wisdom of my son began to assert itself about this time. "My father," he said, "I don't want to disappoint you, but this lake is not the headwaters of the Mississippi River. I don't think we can really say any one of these places deserves that claim. Countless little streams flow into all these lakes. Each of these little streams in turn begins with a spring. I say there are many headwaters. Even if somebody finally decides that it's this one rather than that one, I won't believe it. They're five or ten or maybe even twenty — but not only one. This lake would not be the one — even if there were only one.

"I can't deny that, Brian,"

"Now, my father, I don't say this to keep you from saying you traveled from one end of the Mississippi to the other, because really you have. Someplace around here, maybe twenty miles to the west, twenty miles to the north, twenty miles to the east, men will some day come to call the headwaters of the Mississippi. It's just like the time Lasalle went down the Mississippi to its mouth the first time. There were three different courses. They all ran into the Gulf, which one was the Mississippi at that moment? Who knows?

"So congratulations, you made it from one end to the other."

On February the 18th, in spite of the cold and the snow, we began our return journey. I often recalled the expedition to St. Joseph twenty-five years before — was that a quarter of a century before? The snow was deep. Fortunately we had gotten snow shoes from the Indians and learned the tiring ways of using them. The wind blew fiercely. The cold, bad all day, grew intense at night. We could, however, build fires and cook our ample provisions. We would make it.

On March 5, 1806, Little Falls looked as lovely as Saint Louis had on March 6, 1781. Ice still clogged the river. We waited close to a month, hunting, telling stories about French and Spanish days. Then suddenly the river opened, and we started downstream. The voyage back was swift and uneventful.

On the last night before we got home, Brian and I sat around the fire just as we had on the first night we left Saint Louis. It was obvious he wanted to talk, but there was little of the carefree manner in the way he approached the subject.

"Ever since Pierre Vial told me about Uncle Nick's work with the Franciscans in New Mexico," Brian began, "I have wanted to become a missionary and work with him among the Indians."

"Uncle Nick is a man without an equal," I said, more to be saying something than to be contributing anything to Brian's thoughts. I had told him this very thing so many times over it must have seemed like saying "Hello" or "Goodbye."

"Taos, or Acoma, or Santa Fe," he went on. "There are no places like them. You said that yourself. For a long while I thought of becoming a lawyer and then perhaps going into politics. Those manoeuverings after the purchase of Louisiana soured me totally on that. I want nothing to do with the crowd that will be running the show. They will ask too many compromises in matters I can't compromise on."

"Have you thought of moving over to Illinois, to Kaskaskia or thereabouts?"

"I might have given that some thought several years ago. Now I know what God wants me to do."

I remained silent for a long time. Finally I asked, "You have thought this over carefully?"

"Especially during my school days in Montreal. I talked to the priests there about being a missionary. Naturally they wanted me to work among the Indians in Canada. Frankly it was too cold for me up there. I could stand an occasional winter, like this one, but not every year." Then he laughed. "I told them that my grandfather would never let me live permanently under the British flag."

I smiled. "That was a clever answer. And true! Your grandfather might have come back to life and started the Pontiac War all over again."

I could not, however, get the immediate reality out of my mind. Brian's remarks about Montreal made me remember how lonesome

Rosellen had been while he was away. I asked: "Have you talked to your mother about your plans?"

"She simply said," he responded, " 'We want you to do what you think God wants you to do. We raised you to be a man. A man must make his own decisions. You must make yours.' "

How like Rosellen! I thought. Her heart would be breaking. Yet she would accept reality. With me it was different. Suddenly I began to think how little time I had spent with Brian before this winter! How many times I worked at unimportant things when we could have done hundreds of things together. Now I looked back with regret — and a little remorse. I thanked God we at least had the past winter together.

His enthusiasm broke my reverie. "I can go down the river by boat to New Orleans, then sail across the Gulf to Vera Cruz. From the coast to Mexico City — to the *Convento Grande* of the Franciscans. Then some day — New Mexico! Uncle Nick and I will have the best mission in the Kingdom."

He knew what he wanted. He had thought the matter out. My heart could ache; but I, too, had to play the man. "If God wills it, my son. You have my blessing."

I tried to feign the joy Brian showed. All I could do was pray, "Help me, dear Lord," and try to hold back the tears that wanted to come to my eyes.

Not long after we returned to a warm welcome in Saint Louis, Angelique and Sheila greeted me with plans of their own.

"I'm engaged to Lawrence Aubuchon," Angelique said.

"I'm going to marry Pierre Laramie," Sheila added.

"It looks as if everybody in this family is going to Florissant," I came back. The Aubuchons and Laramies had lived in Florissant for a full generation. "What does your mother think of this idea?"

Before Rosellen could answer, the girls replied simultaneously, "She thinks it's fine."

"Father Meurin used to say that the test of love is time and distance," I said with a cautious smile.

"We've known them for four years, ever since you took us to the St. Ferdinand Parish Festival," Angelique said.

"Florissant's way out," was Sheila's comment.

"Shouldn't your young men put on their going-to-Saint Louis suits some Sunday and ask your mother and me themselves?"

"They already asked mother," Angelique said, "and mother said that you agreed — " She stopped abruptly and looked at her mother's slight frown. Then she began again. "And mother said that you were always reasonable about things."

"I guess your mother and I will have to see Lawrence and Pierre's parents soon. Then we must get in touch with our new pastor."

The girls gave me a kiss and ran inside to talk about their plans. Rosellen and I remained on the porch.

"You had better see the pastor soon," Rosellen said. "He's a wandering Irishman like you and your father. He may not stay long."

"Even if he leaves," I said, "we won't be without priests for long. I heard that some Trappists are coming out this way. Nicholas Jarrot is willing to let them have the big mound over beyond Cahokia."

"The big mound?" Rosellen said. "I've heard people talk about it so often. Yet, I've never seen it. I've seen *Cote Brilliante*, the shining hill out near the road to Saint Charles; and *La Grange de Terre*, the 'barn of the earth' north of town, and our own Sugar Loaf Mound, of course, and several others on this side of the river. But never the *big* mound."

"Actually, I think we could see it from here on a clear day," I said, rising and looking northeast across the river. "It's close to the ridge on the far side. We probably can see it, but it blends with the bluff behind it." I was disappointed that I could not spot it clearly. "It rises in terraces and is as big on top as Laclede's original city. Not far away are smaller mounds, some of them flat on top and some like cones." Then suddenly, "Why don't we have our last family picnic over there, before the girls get married?"

"Angelique and Sheila wouldn't want to go without Lawrence and Pierre," Rosellen answered. "Why don't we just go ourselves?"

"You name the day."

"How about next Sunday?" she said.

"Pray for good weather," I responded.

"Now that family and personal plans have been settled," Rosellen said, "let's talk about the city. I think we can call it that now. Have you noticed how its grown in the few months you've been up-river?"

I looked toward Saint Louis. New houses reached along the rise towards Sugar Loaf Mound. I had already seen that business houses stretched along the original streets where once two homes filled an entire block. So many people gave different estimates of the number of houses in the village I decided to count them myself. There were over two hundred. The streets were still unpaved. They had always been dusty in summer, muddy in winter. Frederick Bates was acting governor, Silas Bent judge, and Edward Hempstead attorney for the Territory.

Two vigorous Irishmen came, John Mullanphy and Joseph Charless. Mullanphy stayed a short time, then moved south so he could send his many daughters to the Ursuline school in New Orleans. I felt he would be back. Charless began a newspaper, the *Missouri Gazette.*

When I felt that Charless had enough time to get his newspaper organized, I walked into his office. Two men were in the shop. I looked at the taller of the two. "Are you Mr. Charless?"

"Yes, I am. A subscriber to our newspaper, I hope? Or maybe even an advertiser? You've got that prosperous look so many Saint Louisans have."

"Thank you, Mr. Charless. I'm Hugh Roe O'Rome. My father used to say that back in the native land you two shared, the people near Blarney Castle had a special expression for that particular approach."

He reached over the counter to shake my hand. "I never found it hurtful to say nice things, Mr. O'Rome."

"Right you are, Mr. Charless. Put me down as a permanent subscriber. You're a courageous man to start a newspaper in a town that claims to be bilingual, but is still strongly French-speaking."

"Mr. O'Rome, I had the opportunity of working under Matthew Carey, one of the best newspapermen in the country today. I've had to face challenges all my life. Back in 1795 'perfidious Albion' — to use Napoleon's term — threw me out of Ireland. I had to flee to France. Then to this country. I had to start over in each place. I think this will be my final stopping place. By the way, how did *you* get here?"

"An angel brought me, as the French say. I was born in Illinois a few miles south of here. I came over with the original group when Laclede founded the city."

"But your name is not French."

"My father escaped from Ireland to fight in the army of King Louis. My mother was a native of the Illinois village of Prairie du Rocher — as are so many people here — of Canadian ancestry."

"Interesting, O'Rome. To change the subject dramatically, may I ask what you think of this ad?" He showed me an advertisement for beverage called beer. "I have never tried it myself."

"I heard some of the old French residents talking about it the other day," I said. "They like cognac and brandies and good Bourdeaux wine. With the new Embargo Act President Jefferson wants, I think they'll have to make their own drinks. These new arrivals from Kentucky and Tennessee drink whiskey. The New Englanders fulminate against all drinking. About this beer? I can't say."

"Maybe the beer people will have to bring their customers with them."

I laughed. "Perhaps they will. Who knows?"

"Here's a speech you will like," Joseph Charless said one day in early January, 1812. I took off my heavy coat and sat down in the warm print shop.

"Read it, please, Joseph," I said. "I hope the government has decided to stop the British once and for all."

"At least Congressman Richard Johnson of Kentucky wants it to do so," Charless came back. "Listen to what he said in Congress last month: 'For the first time since my entrance into this body, there now seems to be but one opinion with a great majority — that war with Great Britain is inevitable. . . . Considering her deadly enmity, I shall never die contented until I see her expulsion from North America.' "

"Good for Johnson," I said. "If it wasn't for those young congressmen from Kentucky, Britain would strangle us."

"She's done what she pleased too long," Charless answered. "She captured our seamen. She has stolen our merchandise. Driven our ships off the high seas. Stirred the Indians of Canada against us."

"We've been willing to lean over backwards far too long," I came back. "When I went up the Mississippi with Pike six years ago, the British hoisted the Union Jack wherever they wanted. Great Britain will try to make the whole world her backyard. We've got to finish what George Washington began."

"Richard Johnson called our fight 'a second revolution, as important as the first,' " Charless responded. "Britain is locked in her struggle with Napoleon. That gives us our chance. Bullies stop only when they meet a stronger jaw. Hugh Roe, I'm not sure we in the West are ready for this war. But there is no alternative."

War came that summer. I attended a meeting of the townsmen to elect a Committee of Public Safety. We chose some French-speaking and some Anglo-Americans. The citizens were obviously worried in a way that they had not been even back in 1780. Fewer than 250 regular soldiers defended the trans-Mississippi. Reports came that the Winnebago, Kickapoo, Potawatomi, Shawnee, and Miami Indians had met in the Sauk villages along the Rock River and declared war against the United States. *They used to go on the warpath*, I thought. *Now they declare war.*

The British took key posts on the upper Mississippi and Major General Hull failed in his invasion of Canada. The local committee got so worried they suggested to Governor Benjamin Howard, who spent most of his time in his Kentucky home, leaving the actual day-to-day management to Bates, to induce the Osage to declare war on all tribes hostile to the United States.

Charless commented, "I hope our Indians can beat their Indians."

Even when good news came, bad news accompanied it. The Americans under my old commander, Zebulon Pike, now a Brigadier General, took York, a principal city in upper Canada on the north coast of Lake Ontario. Unfortunately Pike had died in an accidental explosion after his troops had captured the city. When Charless showed me the dispatches, tears came to my eyes.

"My father would say that fighting the British is the best way to die. But I wish we could live, live on our own free ground, without Britain's hounding us forever."

"That's what the war's for, Hugh Roe. We've said that over and over again: to make the British realize they can't have the world."

"I believe she'll make one more try."

In the spring of 1814, Rosellen and I received a letter that had been long on its way from the villa of San Antonio de Bexar in the province of Coahuila, Mexico. The handwriting was familiar. The language was English. I opened the envelope. "Do you want to read it, Rosellen?"

She eagerly grasped the letter and began to read in a soft voice:

Dear Father and Mother,

In my last letter I told you of my ordination at the Convento Grande *in Mexico. It is hard to describe my feelings at that time. I can only say that my life has been marked by a joy which comes from the knowledge that I can spread God's love to the world.*

At the time of my last letter, my first assignment was still uncertain. You knew, of course, that I had hoped to go to New Mexico to work with Uncle Nick.

You often told me marvelous things about him. I can assure you that within the Franciscan Order, I have heard even more amazing stories, all describing the same whole-souled, lovable man that you knew. He is with God.

Once he had gone, New Mexico had less pull for me. One thing is clear from the years of my study and meditation: souls are where one finds them. No matter where a priest may be sent, there are souls to be saved.

I liked San Antonio de Bexar immediately on arrival. We have no high mountains here, as in the kingdom of New Mexico, but also no desert. This is high, open country, fine for cattle raising. It rains enough to grow what the people need to eat. The missions were suppressed by the government last year; so we no longer have the organized Indian communities we had before. The Indians live nearby. They are peaceable and willing to listen to our message.

San Jose mission is a village in itself, about eighty acres in extent. The church is huge, its walls so thick that on the hottest day I feel cool reading my psalms in the santuario. *How I wish you could see it!*

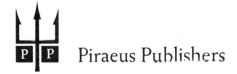

Piraeus Publishers

This book is being sent with the compliments of
Mrs. Mercedes Swanson.

National Sales Office: 2213 First Capitol Drive, St. Charles, Missouri 63301 (314) 723-1400

I travel to several other mission churches not too far away. They are not big like San Jose, or Concepcion, north of here, or San Antonio de Valero, the old one we call the Alamo, along the river in the heart of San Antonio. But they are my churches, and the people feel they own me, even though I have been here such a short time.

Give my love to everyone, and pray for your son

Brian — Fray Ramon, O.F.M.

Rosellen and I sat quietly, arm in arm, on the front porch overlooking the wide river. "He sounds so bright," I finally said. "He so loved Santa Fe I thought surely he would be sent there."

"This is closer," Rosellen came back, a tone of anticipation marking her words. "Travel to San Antonio is not impossible. We can go by boat to Natchitoches. Then overland."

"It is a difficult trip," I said.

"We can make it," she insisted.

As our son had written, the mission of San Jose was a beautiful and formidable building, at once a fortress and a church, a real sanctuary in every sense. It was even more impressive than the cathedral we had seen in New Orleans on our honeymoon. While the air did not have the vigor of the pine hills of Santa Fe, I immediately felt the same sense of peace pervading it.

Brian seemed a bit taller now. He stood broad and rugged with the look of a man who could take the wild winds of the plains and could plant his feet wide apart against drought and destruction and discouragement.

The warm San Antonio sun beat down outside. Inside, the church was cool as the altar boys lit the candles for the Mass our son would offer. Time stood still. There were some moments of Calvary, some intimacy of the upper room where Christ took bread and blessed and gave it to his disciples, some moments, too, of that peace most people find only in eternity.

We received from the hands of our son the Body of the Lord who made us, and the heavens, and the earth; and then we walked back to our pew and knelt down in love-filled adoration. Brian turned and blessed us. Mass was over.

Afterward we drove in a little carriage to his mission in the chapparal. In contrast to the mighty *santuarios* of Concepcion and San Jose, San Francisco de la Espada was a small stone church with a belfry for three bells. Set in the midst of a thick growth of young oaks, off on a side road away from the *Camino Real,* it was utterly unimpressive. But as Brian spoke of it, it became a cathedral: St. Peter's of Rome, St. Mark's of Venice, St. Louis of New Orleans. After all, when he uttered the sacred words, Christ came down in this modest building no less than in the wonders of the world.

The little children shouted: "Padre Ramon! Padre Ramon!" They came up and kissed his hand over and over again.

"This is my father and my mother."

"Your father and your mother, no!" they answered incredulously, as if a priest should not have earthly parents, but have come down from heaven on the wings of angels, or sprung like a bluebonnet out of the Texas soil. They smiled. Life was good.

"All that has gone before, my husband," Rosellen said, "all the sacrifice and lonely years — all is nothing now. God has been good."

The sun went down early in the southwestern sky by the time we reached Nacogdoches and started for the Red River. We decided to spend the winter in New Orleans and return with the coming of spring. The visit was like another honeymoon. We sat in the plaza across from the cathedral of St. Louis the King. We walked along the Bayou St. Jean out toward Lake Ponchartrain. We visited countless relatives.

The fan shape of the live oaks of Louisiana was beyond loveliness. The Spanish moss clinging to so many branches gave an added fullness to the rich foliage that stayed green during the short winter.

We enjoyed them equally when the early morning fog from the river filtered through the branches, or when the bright sun of midday could scarcely penetrate the thick growth of leaves, or when the full moon of night sent varied shadows as the Spanish moss waved in the gentle breeze. We sat on the lower branches that stretched their long serpentine arms a few feet above the ground. This was fulfillment.

We hardly gave a thought that a war still went on. The struggle begun so vigorously in 1812 by the Warhawks of the West, Henry Clay and his young associates in Congress, had almost run its course. But not quite!

We heard that the European powers had beaten Napoleon at Leipzig in central Germany, and that Wellington had pushed the French out of Spain and crossed the Pyrennes. Now England was going to make another effort to control the Mississippi. She had sent Wellington's veterans across the sea, under the command of his brother-in-law, Sir Edward Pakenham, who had fought with him in Spain. Rumors had the British fleet in the Gulf of Mexico. Soon the men who had fought Napoleon's forces were moving up the Mississippi.

What did we have to meet this formidable force? We had Andrew Jackson. He had beaten the Creeks, the powerful British allies among the southeastern Indians. So angered was he when he heard the news that the British had burned the city of Washington, that he crossed into Spanish territory without authorization from the Secretary of War, to drive out of Pensacola the British who were using it as a base of operations. In early December, 1814, he had moved to New Orleans, wisely judging that the British would make their crucial campaign in that area. Shortly after his arrival, word came that the British were near at hand. Jackson called in his cavalry from Baton Rouge and urged his artillery to move as fast as it could. He accepted Governor Claiborne's offer of the state troops and all volunteer citizens who could shoulder arms. He welcomed the help of Jean Lafitte and the countless buccaneers he could rally to the American cause.

I had felt uneasy when news came that Pakenham's troops were moving toward New Orleans. Then the lean, rugged, red-haired Jackson rode into town, erect, defiant, with the look of an eagle and the flair of a lion, riding as if he would drive his own sabre into every Britisher. A man of destiny had come.

I knew that the full cycle had run its course. The war was at our door. The final test lay just ahead. The decision the good God wrote in land and water so long ago would finally be clear forever.

Rosellen and I sat together one last time in the *Place d'Armes* across from the Cathedral. "It seems that the British will always be over my shoulder," I said. "Just a few steps behind. My father hated them with an intense passion. I see them differently, without passionate hatred, rather with a calm reasoned dislike of the hypocrisies of an otherwise great people. Why must they try to take over everything worthwhile that others have?"

Rosellen sensed that I was in reality thinking out loud. She said nothing.

"When Napoleon sold us Louisiana," I went on, "he is supposed to have said that now he had given England a counterbalance in the world. As yet we are not that. Someday, we will not only counterbalance her. She will have to come pleading for us to bail her out of troubles."

Then I smiled and spoke directly to Rosellen, "But they gave me *you*, my darling, and so I can forgive them for lots of things. Had they not taken Canada, you would never have come to Michili-mackinac. Had they not chased my father out of Ireland, I would not have this wonderful land to live in." I grinned. "When the British do good, it's always an accident. Not their intention!"

"God be with you, my husband," Rosellen said. "You have to join Jackson, as your father had to fight when he went to the Forks of the Ohio." She spoke as lightheartedly as a young girl sending her sweetheart off to his first battle. "I will pray over at the convent of the Ursulines. It seems more fitting to be praying in the quiet seclusion of the little chapel of our Lady than in the vast cathedral."

I prayed, too, as I trudged out to battle. The years had taken the suppleness out of my step. But I pushed on. I felt that this would close several doors: the long war between Britain and America, and my own personal hope for a united land.

We volunteers moved east of the city marching behind the regulars into the flat country to the left of the river and took positions behind bales of cotton. Dominique Youx, Lafitte's cannoneer, filled his weapons with steel right up to their muzzles. Jackson's regulars, the riflemen of Kentucky and Tennessee, and the men of Louisiana awaited the veterans of Wellington's campaigns. We slept little all night.

I had fought in two battles before. All that I had seen previously was as nothing compared to what the lifting fog revealed. This was pageantry, not war — majestic, but terrible. The British fighting men lined up in overwhelming numbers for an eighth of a mile. Their crossed white baldrics made a perfect target against red uniforms. They marched shoulder to shoulder. Flags waved in the bayou breeze. Officers brandished their swords, as if they were parading before the King at Windsor Castle rather than marching against a makeshift defense beside the Mississippi.

I recalled what my Uncle Nick had said of the British at Monongahela, a lifetime ago. They never seemed to learn. Yet this was their plan: to overawe by brilliant display.

I looked over my shoulder. Jackson sat calmly on his horse, unmoved by the amazing spectacle.

The riflemen and cannoneers watched in awe. I waited tensely behind the breastworks of cotton bales, wondering if perhaps the enemy might be too many. I leaned against the parapet and sighted my gun at the end man of the first column. When it seemed as if I could reach out and touch the front of the British line, I heard the command: "Fire!"

A tornado swept the British to the ground. No human beings could have survived that devastating blast. Yet, to my amazement, the remnants of Redcoats reformed and, with reinforcements crossing over from the river bank, came on once again. A second volley shattered their ranks. The bastard cross of Britain, ripped and slashed to bits, went down for the last time in the mud of the delta. The groans of the dying sounded the death-knell of English hopes in mid-America.

Then with the tension of battle over, I sagged against the bales of cotton. The smoke of an hundred guns clung low over the battlefield. I felt a warm dampness low on my left shoulder, where a bullet had hit me. I looked down. From a small hole in my shirt the blood spurted, spreading the red stain over the plaid cloth. The taste of fear filled my mouth.

Memories flooded my mind: Uncle Nick's stories of the Battle on the Monongahela; my father's tales of Pontiac's War; my own first battle in defense of Saint Louis; the fear I had felt on that occasion, quite unlike the fear that gripped me now.

I thought of Rosellen; of Brian and the girls.

I smiled a wan smile; for I knew that even if death came, the wide river would flow free forever.

Acknowledgments

I wish to express my deep appreciation to novelists Tere Rios Versace, Patricia McGerr, August Derleth, William E. Barrett, and James Horan; to poet Sara Lindsay Rath; to consultants Frank McKenna, Joseph P. Donnelly, S.J., John Martin Scott, S.J., Claude Heithaus, S.J., John Francis Bannon, S.J., Harry Cargas, and Professor John Francis McDermott; to Bonnie Vaux, Sheila Harris, Claudia de Gruy, and Susan Medgyesi-Mitschang; and to Miss Phyllis Casey of the Carpentier Branch of the Saint Louis Public Library. I am also grateful to Linus J. Thro, S.J., former Provincial of the Missouri Jesuits, and to His Eminence, the late Joseph Cardinal Ritter, who approved this commemorative volume of the Bicentennial.